Praise for Lindsay Gibson

"Gibson's romance is as bright and sparkling as the ruby ring at the center of the painting ... A charming romance that's as warm and cozy as hot chocolate on a winter's day." —*Kirkus Reviews* on *The Christmas Promise*

"Lindsay writes the type of stories that will stay with you and have you reaching for your loved ones." —*USA Today Bestselling Author Jenny Hale*

"This new author is automatically a favorite." —*Page-Turners Reviews*

"...an engaging story and a sweet romance with a dollop of mystery." —*Book Banter Café* on *The Christmas Promise*

"A truly lovely story that gently unfolds..."—*Splashes into Books* on *The Christmas Promise*

Included in "That Artsy Reader Girl's 2023 Christmas Romances"—*thatartsyreadergirl.com*

Included in "Over 50 Must Read Kindle Unlimited Christmas Romance Books"—*everydayeyecandy.com*

"A delightful romance with dreams at the heart," set in a "glorious setting with family dramas."—*Splashes into Books* on *Fly Away Summer*

Where It All Began

Where It
All Began

LINDSAY GIBSON

HARPETH ROAD
PRESS®
Nashville

HARPETH ROAD PRESS

Published by Harpeth Road Press (USA)
P.O. Box 158184
Nashville, TN 37215

Paperback: 978-1-963483-25-3
eBook: 978-1-963483-24-6
Library of Congress Control Number: 2025936267

Where It All Began: A Wonderfully Captivating, Heartwarming Romance

Cover Design by Kristen Ingebretson
Cover Images © Shutterstock

Harpeth Road Press, May 2025

My beloved Jason,
To the memories that have shaped our path, our bond that
weaves it all together, and the moment that set our love in
motion—never letting me forget . . . where it all began for us.

PROLOGUE
MAY 2017, PROM NIGHT

Willow

"I've never worn this much makeup in my life." Willow Anderson turned from the full-length mirror in her bedroom. "Are you sure it's not too much?" she asked her older sister, Whitney, who walked over to stand next to her.

"If you think it's too much, just wipe the lipstick off." Whitney touched the end of one of her wavy locks. "Your hair came out perfect. I've always been so jealous of your curls and this color." Her sister had straight, brown hair, just like their mother.

Willow smiled at her. "Yours is much easier to keep up with though." When she was born, her mother was thrilled to see that unlike her other children, Willow had inherited her grandmother's curly locks that matched the shade of the sun's golden hour.

Willow twisted in front of the mirror to look at her long

honey-blonde waves cascading down her back. Their mother, Rachel, had taken a curling iron to them, tightening them up a bit more, and now they fell to her midback just the way she'd envisioned. Her mom then braided two small sections and crowned them behind her head, fastening them with a silver hair clip. Whitney had loaned her a pair of sparkly dangle earrings she'd worn at her own prom nine years earlier, matching the clip perfectly.

Whitney now lived in the town next to Terra Cove with her fiancé Jason Wilder, but luckily Martha's Vineyard was so small, it was never far to get to anyone on the island. Despite the close proximity, Willow didn't see her as often as she'd liked since her sister had finished college and went right into teaching kindergarten at one of the elementary schools on the island, so being alone together like they had been all afternoon meant a lot to Willow.

"You know"—Willow leaned closer to the mirror again—"I think Grayson will love this red lipstick. I'll keep it." The high neckline on her long, dark green prom dress made her red lips and golden-brown eyes pop. She'd been dating Grayson Turner for four years now and despite many school dances in the past, this would be the most dressed-up she'd been with him.

"Just wow . . ." Her mom's voice behind them made both girls turn around. "You look stunning, Willow. You and Grayson will be the island's couple of the night. I hope these fit. I can't believe we forgot to buy you shoes." She handed Willow a pair of silver dress heels and held her hand to balance her while she slipped them on. "Sorry it took me so long to get them. Your father needed a hand outside with one of the horses." Rachel Anderson was a full-time homemaker but would often pitch in to help their dad with the family's horse farm—especially with all the office management.

"I'm sure they will be talked about. Everyone from one

end of the island to the next has had the privilege to witness their relationship unfold over the last four years. So we've all been waiting for this night . . . I know I have," Whitney said, bending over to fluff out the mermaid-style skirt after Willow fastened the heels. "Besides, it's not hard to be talked about when everyone knows everything about you around here." Other than a charter school, Martha's Vineyard had one public high school that Willow attended along with the rest of the kids from the five small towns on the island.

"There," Willow said, smiling at her mom and sister. "Perfect fit. Now I'm ready."

"Grayson should be here in about an hour. That leaves me just enough time to head to the flower shop and pick up your corsage," Mom said.

"Thank you for helping him with that." Willow looked sheepishly at her mom. "I know his mom wasn't all that involved with prom."

Nicole Turner was always nice to Willow, but very withdrawn from all of her and Grayson's activities over the years, so Rachel stepped in to help him get the right corsage.

"It won't take me long and when I get back, Dad and I would love to take some photos with just you and your brother and sister before he gets here."

"Did someone mention me?" Her little brother, Wesley, came into the room with a low whistle. "Well, look at you! Going somewhere special?"

"Do you think Grayson will like this dress?" Willow turned around for him to see.

Wesley shrugged. "Don't ask me. A dress is a dress."

"Wes!" Whitney gave him a shove. At fifteen, Wesley only cared about his friends and making the soccer team that year as a freshman. Regardless of his immaturity, both sisters adored their little brother with his round chocolate-brown eyes. Even

Willow remembered how cute they made him look when he was younger.

"Kidding! Geez, you're so uptight." Wesley smiled at her. "You look beautiful. Grayson will love it."

"It's so amazing you two have been together through all of high school. From ninth-graders with braces, nervous about starting high school, to graduating seniors," her mom said with a sigh.

"Thanks, Mom. I think it's pretty amazing too. I love him more as each year goes by. I can't wait to see what happens for us after graduation." A tingle shot through her as she anticipated all the exciting possibilities on the horizon. It wouldn't be the easiest path, but they had a plan.

Willow would attend Connecticut College in the fall, and Grayson planned to stay in Terra Cove to save some money while working full-time and taking online business courses through Cape Cod Community College. The commute from Martha's Vineyard to Connecticut was doable, and they both felt positive about the decision.

"Is Tyler bringing his date to take pictures with you two?" Mom asked.

"Tyler is going solo. The girl he wanted to bring turned him down," Willow said. "But yes, he's coming to take pictures with us."

"I'm sure he'll want some time with you alone," Whitney said, waggling her eyebrows.

"Would you stop?" Willow grabbed a pillow off her bed and tossed it at her sister.

Whitney had teased her for years about her and Grayson's best friend, Tyler Parker. Both boys were handsome in their own way, but the girls at their school pined after Tyler with his striking good looks. Quarterback of their football team, he was a noticeable figure when they walked through the hallways, very tall with blonde hair and blue eyes—but she had eyes for only one of them. Grayson's more rough-around-the edges charm was what captured her, with his unruly brown hair that always spilled across his forehead, framing his mesmerizing bright green eyes.

The three of them grew up together and were inseparable. As kids, they often referred to themselves as the "three island amigos" of Terra Cove. Things got a little awkward when Willow started dating Grayson the summer after eighth grade, but they couldn't blame Tyler for feeling left out. She and Grayson spent more time together without him, but as their high school years continued, everything with Tyler seemed to settle. He began to date and got busy with football alongside Grayson, giving the boys time together without her. Soon she and Tyler grew comfortable around each other again and could talk—just like old times. Yet, for some reason, Whitney always insisted Tyler was jealous of her relationship with Grayson.

"Just wait until Tyler sees you in that dress. 'The look' is coming," Whitney said, lifting her fingers to make air quotes.

"You'll never give up on that. It's just the way Tyler looks at me. It doesn't mean anything." Willow rolled her eyes. It was an argument that had gone nowhere with her sister over the years.

"I'm with Whit," Wesley said. "I've seen that look a hundred times."

Willow shook her head but stayed quiet. While it annoyed her that they always thought Tyler looked at her a certain way, she had to admit she'd seen it too. She would turn or look up and catch him staring at her with a sense of deep admiration. She'd become good at pretending she never noticed and sure hoped Grayson didn't. He was not the jealous type, but there was one night after homecoming junior year at a bonfire party when something was said between them about her, and it was the only time she'd ever seen them fight. The boys saw how upset Willow had gotten after witnessing the two people she cared about the most arguing over her and they dropped it right then and there. As far as she knew, nothing had happened since.

"Okay, you two, leave Willow alone. Whatever 'look' you think Tyler gives her doesn't matter. She and Grayson are together, and Tyler knows that. Give it a rest," their mom said and headed toward the door. "Meet me and Dad outside for pictures in about twenty minutes. I'm off to get the corsage."

An hour and many family pictures later, Willow checked the time on her phone. No text or missed call from Grayson. He was always early, so it was strange he hadn't shown up yet.

"Maybe he's taking pictures with his mother and Abby," her mom said, patting her shoulder. Abby was Grayson's little sister and was in the same class as Wesley. Their father, Jack Turner, hadn't been around since Grayson was twelve years old, and with his alcoholic, abusive nature, it had been for the best.

"Or maybe he picked up Tyler first?" Whitney suggested.

"He was supposed to come here on his own so we could take pictures on the beach before Tyler gets here."

The day before, they'd been running in and out of the rock boulders on their special beach that many tourists missed during the summer, which kept the area quieter than the rest of the island. Coastal Rock Preserve was their favorite place to have picnic dates, trail rides, swim, dive off the large rock lodged in the water, and where Grayson had first kissed her.

"While you figure out where he is, I need to do a couple things out in the barn before dark. That old tractor has been giving me fits today. Your mother wants to get a shot of you two in front of the barn," her dad said, pointing outside toward the horse barn.

Anderson Stables, started by her dad, had become a staple on the island for horse training, boarding, and care. On their sprawling fifteen-acre property a large barn sat behind the main house, complete with spacious stalls and an open arena and paddocks. Dedicated to the health and well-being of his horses, Liam Anderson himself and a handful of expert trainers developed the horses' skills, tailoring to the specific needs of each one. Willow's siblings didn't love the farm, but she had learned to ride and rode well. She had even competed in multiple prize-winning competitions over the years.

As soon as her dad left, a knock sounded at the front door, and she rushed to answer it, a wide smile on her face. But when she opened it, Grayson wasn't the one standing there. It was Tyler, dressed in a simple gray suit, which fit him well. Her smile fell, though she tried to paste it back on, not wanting her friend to think she wasn't happy to see him. "Hey, Ty! I wasn't expecting you yet. I guess Grayson's running a little late, because—"

"Willow," he cut in, his voice on edge. "Grayson isn't coming."

Everything around her spun as her heart picked up its pace. "What?" She didn't want to believe what he'd just told her. Her mom came close to her with a look of concern, and Willow held up her finger, indicating she wanted a minute alone with Tyler. She stepped out onto the front porch.

"He's not coming to meet you for pictures or to take you to prom."

She began to pace. "I don't understand. Is he okay? Did he get into a car accident or something? Or did his dad—" Panic rose. She didn't even want to finish that thought. Grayson's father had been known to show up randomly, drunk, and start fights with him or his mother.

Tyler hesitated. "His dad came over, and they had a fight," he admitted. "He's not hurt or anything. He's okay. But he just can't take you to prom."

Must have been a bad fight. She tried to figure out what to

do next. Should she go see him and skip the whole evening? Even when his dad wasn't violent, the encounters were tough on Grayson emotionally. Tough enough that going to a big party was probably the last thing he wanted to do.

"Right," she said, glancing at Tyler. "Okay. Just let me get changed, and we can go over to his place." Even if he didn't want to be around a crowd, Grayson never minded letting her and Tyler in. And she didn't want him to be alone and hurting. She was disappointed to let go of the special prom night she'd thought they'd share, but she pushed that aside. So they'd miss prom—so what? At least they'd be together. That was what really mattered.

"No, don't change," Tyler said quickly, looking down at her dress. "You look . . . absolutely gorgeous."

Willow flushed and tried to ignore the heat in his eyes.

"And anyway," Tyler continued, "he wanted us to go. He *told* me to take you."

"Of course he'd say that, but I'm not going to a party when he's at home upset. Really, it'll just take me a minute to change," she said, then turned to head back to her room, but Tyler caught her arm.

"No, listen to me, Willow. He doesn't want you to come over. He doesn't want to see you."

That didn't make sense. "Why wouldn't he want to see me?"

"He's . . ." Tyler let go of her arm and fidgeted with his sleeves, avoiding looking her in the eye. "He's extremely upset."

"Well, that's exactly why he needs *me*, don't you think?"

"That was the first thing I said to him too, but all he kept saying was that he couldn't."

"Couldn't what?" Willow waited for an answer, but her mind was going in circles trying to understand.

"Couldn't be with you," Tyler said, the words coming out

in a rush, like a dam had broken. A strange light filled his eyes that she didn't recognize. "Not anymore."

Willow froze. "What?" The word sounded faint and strangled even to her own ears.

"He has wanted to end things with you for a while now. He's brought it up over and over again, but he always talks himself out of it. Then tonight the fight with his dad pushed him to do it. I guess he finally decided he's done with pretending and just isn't man enough to tell you himself. It's over, Willow. You and him. It's done."

"Done?" she repeated, her voice cracking midway through the word. "No, it can't be. He wouldn't. He . . ." A sob caught in her throat, and she couldn't manage to say anything more. A part of her wanted to tell Tyler he was wrong and to leave, but she couldn't. He was her friend. He wouldn't be saying this to her if it wasn't true. But *how* could it be true? How could everything have fallen apart so fast? Had Grayson really been planning to break up with her for a while now? How had she missed the signs?

Tyler pulled her into his arms and let her cry on his shoulder.

"I'm here for you, Willow." He held her tighter as she cried and tried to understand.

They stood in silence for a moment as she buried her face into him, then suddenly pulled back. "No. It's not true." She backed away, holding up her arms when Tyler reached for her again.

"Willow, listen to me. I just sat with him for over an hour. It's true. He—"

"He wouldn't do this to me! You're wrong!" Willow turned and dashed down the porch steps and toward the barn.

There, she went straight for their gelding, Finn. He was the fastest horse they owned, and she led him out to saddle him.

"Willow!" Tyler's voice echoed into the barn as he got closer.

Tears continued to stream down her face as she gathered her tack. The makeup her sister had worked so hard on was ruined now.

"Where are you going?" he asked.

"Where do you think?" She pulled the strap and stroked Finn's neck. "Go on to prom. Have fun. I need to see Grayson."

"I told you. He doesn't want to see you. Not anymore. It's over, Willow. Seeing you will only make him more upset." Tyler pointed to her dress. "Besides, you're in a dress."

"And?" She kicked off her heels and pulled on some tall boots from the corner of the tack room. She led Finn outside while Tyler followed close behind. Pulling up the front of her dress, she hoisted herself into the saddle. "Like that would stop me."

"How about we go to the beach? Just for a little while. Please," he begged. "He doesn't want to see you."

"I don't believe you," Willow turned Finn toward the driveway, clicked her tongue, and dashed off toward the preserve and the trail to Grayson's house.

———

GRAYSON

He was too stunned to move. How could he say that to Willow? That was *not* what he'd asked Tyler to do. But before he could approach them, Willow took off on the horse, not even noticing his old pick-up truck that had made its way up her driveway only a few minutes before he overheard her and Tyler.

When Jack stumbled into his house earlier, he'd shocked Grayson with news that affected all of them, and Grayson needed the night to calm down. He'd asked Tyler to simply drive her to prom so she could go have fun and that he'd see her afterward. There was no way he could show up at a dance with a smile on his face, walking in with Willow and his best friend, who, he'd just learned, was possibly his *half brother.*

Clenching his fists, he rounded the side of the barn and halted when Mr. Anderson walked out and stopped next to Tyler.

"Let her go, son. I don't know what's going on, but I heard enough. If what you said about Grayson is true, let her figure that out." Mr. Anderson strode over to the tractor, climbed up, and turned it on.

"I can't believe you!" Grayson shouted as Tyler turned in surprise.

"Why are you here, Grayson?" Tyler stepped toward him, the sound of the tractor muffling their voices a bit.

"I came to my senses is why! I realized after you left how stupid I was being, but I can't believe you just lied to her like that!" Grayson shoved Tyler, making him stumble into the barn.

"Boys!" Liam hopped out of the tractor, leaving the engine running.

"I didn't lie. You're not in your right mind to be with her!" Tyler got right in his face.

"I asked you to take her to prom so she could go have a good time, not lie!" Grayson tackled Tyler, and both boys fell to the ground, wrestling outside the stalls.

"*Enough!*" Liam got between them and grabbed Grayson's arm before he punched Tyler. "Grayson, *stop!*"

Tyler scrambled backward to get out from under Grayson's grip and stood up. "See? He's unstable, Mr. Anderson. I'm just trying to protect Willow."

Grayson lurched at him again but stopped when Liam

shot him a warning look. "Don't you dare, young man. You want to fight him, go ahead, but *off* my property!"

Thick smoke past Liam's shoulder grabbed Grayson's attention. "Sir? Smoke! I think the tractor is on fire and so is the barn!"

Liam spun around, pausing for a second when they saw the door covered in heavy flames. Hay was quickly burning, and the fire was moving fast.

"*Dad!*" Willow screamed from the other side of the fire. Grayson could just make out her horse through the smoke.

"*Willow!* Call 911!" Liam yelled toward her. "Boys! Out the other side. Now!"

Liam started to usher him and Tyler out of the barn, but Grayson stopped.

"The horses! Let me help you!"

"No! I can't have you two getting hurt," Liam said, but it was too late. Grayson and Tyler ran to the stalls and threw open the doors to get the horses to safety. They managed to get two out, but the fire was intense, spreading quickly.

Grayson's heart hammered as he raced to the next horse, but Liam started coughing, then stumbled to the ground.

"Tyler! Help me get him out of here!" They grabbed his shoulders and carried him out, the sound of sirens in the distance.

———

WILLOW

Sitting on the porch steps a few hours later, Willow looked up at the moon, full and bright. The firemen had managed to put out the fire, but not before more than half of the barn was gone, along with seven horses. How would her parents mitigate such loss with their clients? She couldn't even imagine what type of lawsuit could come of this for them. Her mother was at the hospital with Dad, who was staying for observation overnight. He had inhaled a lot of smoke, and the paramedics wanted him to get a thorough check-up.

Her sudden intuition that Grayson wouldn't be home had proven correct. She only made it to the edge of the road before she'd turned Finn around and spotted Grayson's truck parked up near the house. The shouting in the barn had made the horse uneasy and by the time she got there, the entire tractor and entranceway were already in flames. The flashing lights of the police cars and firetruck still parked in the drive held her attention as her mind raced with everything that had happened that night . . . including her and Grayson. An image of them during one of their nightly walks along the shore over the last four summers pushed the trauma of the fire out of her mind. Were they really over?

"Dad will be okay," Wesley said, dropping to sit next to her.

"It's my fault."

"It wasn't your fault. You know that." Wesley put his arm around her.

"I should have just stayed, then Grayson and Tyler wouldn't have had that fight, and Dad would have seen the fire faster . . ." Fresh tears spilled out.

"The fire was an accident and would have happened either way. Who knows what was wrong with that old tractor."

Willow wiped the tears, just as Grayson and his mother walked away from one of the officers who had been taking his statement. When Grayson turned toward her, she expected him to come over, but shock rippled through her when he only gave her a long stare before getting into his truck.

"See?" a voice near them startled her. Tyler sat down on her other side as Willow watched the truck go down her long driveway. Grayson had not spoken a word to her since the fire was put out. Maybe Tyler had been right after all.

"I'm sure he'll call you," her brother said, unaware of her earlier conversation with Tyler.

Lowering her head, she looked down at her hands. *It was a bad accident. He just needs some time.* After all, he came to her house for a reason, most likely to explain himself. She only needed to wait and give him some space, she tried reasoning with herself, not realizing just how long it would be before she got an explanation.

Chapter One
Eight Years Later

This was it—the day she'd been dreaming about since she was a little girl. Her wedding day. The weather was beautiful, and everything was arranged. All she had to do was walk down the aisle, then she could start the rest of her life. She ignored the itch of doubt she'd been feeling for a while now, the tiny voice deep inside that asked if this was really what she wanted. It was just pre-wedding jitters. Nothing more. She was exactly where she was supposed to be, on the verge of marrying exactly the right man.

"Willow," Whitney called from across the room, but when she turned, Willow realized they weren't in a room at all. They were facing a barn—a very familiar one. She hadn't stood near that barn on her parents' horse farm since before that terrible day.

"Aunty Willow, look at my dress!" her niece, Maya, squealed, so excited she couldn't stand still. The sweet yellow bow in her niece's hair and the ruffled white flower girl dress fluttered as Maya bounced up and down, holding her mommy's hand. Whitney's son, Brandon, was perched on her sister's hip and waving at her with his gummy baby grin.

Why were they all here? Her parents' house was not where the wedding had been planned.

"Would you get yourself into the bridal suite? We need to get going on your makeup!" Whitney said.

The acrid smell was suddenly overwhelming, and when she looked back at the barn, it was in flames. She wanted to scream but couldn't as Whitney tugged her arm to get her inside the house. There, Wesley quietly watched them from the stairs with a somber expression.

"Wesley? Why do you look so upset?" Why didn't her siblings notice the fire?

Her brother looked down, unable to meet her eyes. "He's waiting for you."

"Who's waiting for me?" Was it Tyler? It had to be, right? Who'd be waiting for her other than her fiancé? Smoke filled the room as the barn blazed outside.

"Willow!" her name echoed from down the hall.

Willow froze, immediately recognizing Grayson's voice.

"Are you awake?" Ivy Everett, Willow's best friend, called from the other side of the door. The knock sounded miles away.

Yes, I'm up, she tried to say, but her voice wasn't cooperating. She sat up and brushed some loose hair off her sweaty forehead, trying to pull herself together.

The wedding in the dream wasn't what had her heart racing. In the two weeks since her wedding-that-wasn't, she'd dreamed about it in dozens of different scenarios. Sometimes, it went off without a hitch, just like she'd always imagined. Sometimes, it went wrong in weird ways, like the dream where she got lost in the wedding venue and kept wandering the halls endlessly, trying to find the right room. In one dream, *she* had been the one who'd run away at the last minute, Julia Roberts style. That one was interesting, but she'd never dreamed of the fire being part of the wedding.

In fact, Willow hadn't thought of that day in years. She'd successfully pushed it far into the back of her mind, where it had stayed locked away. Until now.

"Don't do this to yourself, Willow," she mumbled, shaking off the memories like she had since she left Terra Cove right after graduation—leaving it all behind. "That day is long over."

Of all the dreams over the past couple weeks, none had played out the way the day truly went—her hair and makeup done to perfection, stepping into her wedding gown, and receiving the call.

"Willow, the wedding is off. I'm so sorry."
Silence.

It was all he had said before hanging up. Now two weeks had passed since it happened. Two weeks without answers. Two weeks of grappling with the idea of being on her own after being part of a couple for so long. Tyler Parker had been with her for nearly eight years, since their freshman year of college. Marriage was the natural, expected next step . . . *Right?*

She'd thought things were—well, maybe not *amazing* between them, but at least *good*. They fit in each other's lives. They liked each other's families. They had so much history— he'd been part of pretty much every major stage of her life. She loved him. Maybe she hadn't been head-over-heels, butterflies-in-the-stomach in love, the way she'd always thought she'd be with the man she married, but that was how kids thought about love. What she and Tyler had was the grown-up version. At least that was what she'd told herself over and over for the past few months leading up to the wedding. It was the kind of love they could build a life around—or so she'd thought, anyway.

She'd tried to think rationally over the course of the past year since he proposed. Ever since they'd gotten engaged, things hadn't been the greatest between them. Starting with a rough engagement party after Ivy, Whitney, and Wesley confronted her and asked if she was happy. After she responded with nothing but defense, doubts had begun to build, little by little, until it eventually burst out of her the final week of wedding preparations. Snapping at everyone, sleepless nights.

Wedding anxiety, her mom had called it one night on the phone, and as a therapist herself, Willow understood that big life changes could induce all kinds of reactions. She'd dealt with them during many sessions with her clients. It sounded logical enough and for a while that reasoning helped her keep her nerves under control, but by the time her wedding day finally came, nothing felt right. Instead of feeling joyful about walking down the aisle toward Tyler, she woke up with a headache after tossing and turning half the night before finally drifting into a couple hours of fitful sleep.

Perhaps Tyler questioned it all too, and he just had the strength to say it out loud on their wedding day and stop them from making a mistake. But to leave her like he did, without facing her and without talking to her, was wrong. It was a betrayal of all they had shared, not just through eight years of being in a relationship but the years before, too, when they'd been childhood friends. He *knew* how hurt she had been when Grayson ended things so abruptly on prom night—before the devastation of the fire. An accident that she *still* insisted could have been prevented had she not taken off to chase Grayson . . .

"Willow, you know how these machines can be faulty. And that one was old. It was also parked much too close to the barn," her dad had tried to reason with her for months after, to no avail. The fact was that Tyler and Grayson had been fighting over her, distracting her dad when he was normally so careful around his farming equipment.

Ivy's persistent knocking grew louder, snapping Willow

back to the present. Here she was, years later, and she couldn't believe Tyler would do the same thing to her. That, more than anything, was what she struggled to understand—why she kept replaying it in her mind, whether she was awake or asleep.

But none of that explained why her latest dream involved the place she hadn't visited in eight years. Or the man she hadn't seen in just as long. Ever since he never came back for her after that fire. And she never understood why . . .

"Willow Anderson, answer me!" Ivy knocked one final time before the door opened and she came to the bed next to her. "Are you okay? I've been at that door for five minutes."

"Just a hard night, but I'm okay." She tried to give her friend a weak smile, but Ivy knew her better than that.

"Another wedding dream?" she asked.

Willow sat up straight and looked at Ivy. "Yes, but this time . . ." She paused, unsure of how to begin to tell her. Ivy had been by her side since the day they met in their freshman dorm room at Connecticut College. Since then, there wasn't anything Willow kept from her—except Grayson.

"This time?" Ivy gently pressed.

Willow struggled to find the words while Grayson overshadowed her thoughts. "It wasn't at the venue." Her mind reeled through the dream again, Maya's sweet little voice echoing through her ears, and she could almost smell traces of smoke.

"Willow?" Ivy nudged her.

Willow blinked. "I'm sorry, I just—"

"Don't be sorry. I'm not surprised you're having these intense dreams after such a heartbreaking event."

Dreams that replace my fiancé with my high school boyfriend on my wedding day. Willow kept that detail to herself . . . just like she kept a lot of Terra Cove out of their discussions. Ivy knew about the fire, but only at surface level. Her very best friend didn't truly know how that terrible accident had affected her. When asked, Willow used weak excuses for not going home, such as being busy with school or work. The damage from the fire and the emotional scars of everything she lost that night—both Grayson and the horses—remained concealed behind her guarded demeanor. As did her love for riding. It all stopped when she left.

As a therapist, Willow knew that suppressing all those memories was a recipe for disaster, but over the years she'd somehow convinced herself that she'd simply moved on. Yet deep down she knew she'd been hiding and after being so closed about going back home, Ivy must have sensed not to push her. After a couple years, once both women were busy finishing college and starting their careers, any talk around Martha's Vineyard stopped altogether. Her past with Grayson didn't concern her anymore, so there was no need to dwell on it in the present.

How would she bring him up anyway? Tyler was the only man her friend knew to be in her life and besides, what would Ivy think learning Grayson was close to both of them growing up? It was a jumbled love triangle she had sealed the door shut on when she boarded the ferry for college. She'd always figured she'd go home again one day when she was ready, but days turned into years and that never happened.

Ivy stood up and her long brown hair fell forward as she held her hand down to help Willow to her feet. "Come on. How about a shower, and then I'll take you to a late breakfast. It's nice outside, and you could stand to get out of this room." She pulled Willow's much shorter frame up next to her. Ivy was tall and always stood out to men when they'd gone to bars or parties over the years, not to mention how her humor in all those social settings drew their focus.

Yet, her friend was still single, having not met "the one." Ivy always insisted the right man would swoop down from out of nowhere and capture her. Her prediction always made

Willow laugh, especially because Ivy's pickiness hadn't been an exaggeration. She truly had found something wrong with every man she'd ever dated since Willow met her.

"Out to eat? Isn't it a . . ." Willow contemplated with a furrowed brow. She'd lost track of time after the nightmare of a wedding day. She'd officially blocked off these two weeks for her honeymoon, so there was nowhere she needed to be, and she hadn't left since she got to Ivy's. "Wednesday? You need to get to work. I can't make you late again."

"Perks of owning my own boutique. I get away with more than others." Ivy winked at her. "Besides, we're fully staffed and covered today. I was just going to help my manager do inventory, but she can wait a bit, especially for you. Come on, I'm starving and I'm sure you are too."

Half an hour later, a freshly showered Willow stepped outside for the first time in days. The summer sunshine was almost blinding, and she dug through her purse for her sunglasses. "Is it me or is the sun extra bright?"

"It's you."

They got in Ivy's car and when Willow finally found her sunglasses, her phone lit up in her bag. "My brother is calling." Ivy turned on the car and slowly backed up while Willow took the call, curiously glancing at her. Her friend knew how much her family had been checking on her. It was a little annoying but mostly sweet, so she tried to be patient with answering the same questions over and over again. No, she didn't need someone to come stay with her. Yes, she was eating. And no, she hadn't heard from Tyler, despite her family's early predictions that he'd come crawling back on his hands and knees, full of remorse for letting go of the best thing in his life.

"Hey, Wes!" She answered with her best attempt to sound cheery and put him on speaker while she reached for her ChapStick at the bottom of her purse.

"Willow," her brother started, his voice shaking a bit as if he was walking somewhere in a hurry. "It's Dad. He was in an accident."

"What?" She dropped the ChapStick and looked over at Ivy whose mouth was open as she immediately pulled back into the parking spot and reached for Willow's free hand. "What kind of accident?"

"With one of the horses a couple hours ago. He fell off. Well, he was sort of bucked off one of the new colts. I'm on my way to the hospital now. Mom and Whitney are already there."

"Wesley . . ." Willow could hardly take a breath against the pounding in her chest. "Tell me right now. How bad is it?"

Her brother let out a loud sigh through the phone. "It's pretty bad. All I know is they got him stabilized for now. There are injuries to his back and head. Willow, you need to come home."

After a night of heavy dreams and just over two weeks of her life being turned upside down—this was a crushing blow that left her feeling nearly defeated. "I will. I will book myself on the soonest ferry."

"I hope you get a ticket. Fourth of July is a little over a week away . . ." Wes grew quiet for a moment. "Look, I'll fly over and get you if I have to."

Her brother was one of the youngest pilots on the island and a very successful one. He'd traded a degree in business to follow his passion and learn to fly helicopters. Vineyard Helicopter Tours had quickly become a favorite tourist event after he and a fellow pilot started the company a year ago. All while she was away, missing it all. She hadn't flown with him yet, and she didn't want a family emergency to be her first experience.

"I'll get a ticket. Don't worry." June meant the island's population was tripled with tourists, and ferry tickets sold out fast, but they usually ran more often due to the high demand.

It was the middle of the week, which meant fewer passengers compared to the larger weekend crowds.

"Okay. I'll call you from the hospital." Wesley hung up and Willow went blank, unable to move, and barely heard Ivy talking.

"Willow?" Ivy squeezed her hand. "What do you need me to do?"

"I . . . I don't even know." She turned to her friend. She'd been so proud of herself for staying mostly strong after getting jilted at the altar, but this hit her on a whole new level. Losing Tyler had been painful—but losing her father would be *devastating*. She usually thought of herself as someone who had it all together. Heck, she was a therapist—the person everyone else went to when they needed help getting their lives on track. But right now, she felt totally lost at sea.

"First off, you need to pack." Ivy said. "My staff already doesn't expect me for a couple hours. I'll help you. And I'm assuming you need to get more stuff from your condo. The one bag you brought here surely doesn't have enough clothes, right?"

Willow stared aimlessly around her, still trying to process her brother's words.

"Willow?" Ivy nudged her.

"What?" She blinked out of the trance and turned to Ivy. "Oh, sorry. My mind's going a million miles a minute. Yes, I need more things from my place." After her failed wedding day, Tyler had moved out, but it was too strange for her to be there without him. She'd hastily packed some clothes to stay at Ivy's but not enough to travel home. And with her dad's accident, she wasn't sure how long she'd be in Terra Cove.

"I figured." Ivy was still holding her hand as they sat parked outside her apartment.

"I also need to call my mom." She tapped her phone and tried to call both her mom and sister, but they didn't answer.

"I'm sure they will call you back as soon as they can." Ivy put the car in reverse again. "Let's run to your condo and get you ready to leave. And we can pick up something fast to take with you to eat on the way to the ferry."

Willow nodded, still in a daze. A tidal wave of emotions came crashing down, right along with her tears. Her whole family was at the hospital already except her, and the effects of being away so long only made the sobs come out harder the more she tried to pull herself together. What if her dad didn't recover? He'd spent years telling her how upset it made him and her mom that she had never come home. He'd begged her for a trip back to see them and that she not miss out on any more important family affairs—especially after not being there for Whitney with the birth of her niece and nephew. She squeezed her eyes shut, trying to grapple with the deep-seated, long-denied reality of all she'd been absent from. How could she have done that?

Her parents constantly reminded her that they never blamed her for the fire, yet it had been all she could do not to hate herself for what had happened, especially when she had to stand by while they battled lawyers and the clients that lost their horses. Her parents lost a lot but had successfully regained it all back over the years, rebuilding their business and reputation. But none of that made up for her years away.

"I can't believe I haven't been home with my family in eight years!" The words burst out of her. "Now look what's happened."

"The accident was not your fault." Ivy kept her attention on the road. "And remember, it's not like they haven't been here to visit you. They've seen you plenty of times."

Willow stayed quiet, trying to calm herself down. She had to focus on getting herself safely home. Her family didn't need her getting in an accident on the way to the hospital, and while Ivy was right, they visited her and Tyler in Mystic, Connecticut, that wasn't the same.

Through college and until now, her parents were the ones who made the effort and traveled her way. Her brother and sister came when they could, but once Whitney had her kids and her brother started flight school, it was harder for them to get away.

Tyler had even gone home without her, although mostly for work-related reasons. He was the chief financial officer for his family's chain of breweries, and after many failed attempts to bring her along, he, too, gave up trying to convince her. She'd never meant to be gone this long, but as the years went on, it seemed more natural to keep things as they were. Her life wasn't back there anymore—it was here, with her growing practice . . . and Tyler.

But in that instant, it wasn't Tyler's face she thought of. It was Grayson's.

His face flashed across her mind wearing the expression from the very last time she saw him, the day after graduation, in the cove by the ocean staring at the waves. Reminding her of the hurt she'd felt when she left Terra Cove shortly after that. He never came after her, which confirmed everything Tyler had told her before the fire—that Grayson didn't want to be with her. She'd let that hurt deepen the excuse to stay away, ignoring the distance it put between her and her family. She knew her dad's accident wasn't her fault, but it sure felt like a punishment.

Chapter Two

L eaning back in his chair, Grayson Turner stared at the screen on his laptop. It had been almost two hours since he had moved from his office. The new hires for their newest location in Boston were going to be trained that weekend, which meant a lot of preparation. This new brewery would be their largest to date, and he was responsible for making sure the incoming staff and managers were ready and had everything they needed.

Glancing at the clock, he quickly checked over the final schedule for the training, before he'd take off for lunch at home and let out his dog, Monty. With so many people in and out of his office that morning, he was grateful he'd have the midday silence to recharge.

"Mr. Turner?" Jesse Olsen, his administrative assistant, poked her head in.

"Hey, Jesse. I just finished the schedule. I'll shoot it over to your email."

"Thanks. I just wanted to make sure that was set before I leave for lunch. The new manager keeps bugging me for it." She rolled her eyes, making him smile. Their new hire for

Boston came with a lot of experience and was fit for the job, but was already proving to be a little pushy. "Also, Tyler needs to see you."

Jesse walked off and he emailed her the files so she could make sure the dates and times lined up correctly. She was meticulous with proofing his documents and finding errors, which he appreciated immensely. After he was done, he took a deep breath to mentally prepare himself for an encounter with Tyler.

Grayson was still getting used to having his former best friend around every day. For years, Tyler had lived in Connecticut with Willow and worked from home, traveling to the office only as needed. The arrangement had worked well enough as coworkers, but things had shifted now that Tyler had moved back to Terra Cove—without Willow, after he left her on their wedding day a couple weeks prior—an act that boggled Grayson's mind. He couldn't imagine anyone being lucky enough to have Willow want to marry them and choosing to throw away a life with her. Like he did.

But maybe he was biased. Despite everything that had happened, she was still the only woman Grayson had ever loved. Eight years ago he made the biggest mistake of his life and lost her, only for Tyler to push his way into her heart. When she left Martha's Vineyard after high school for college in Connecticut with Tyler, their absence from the island gave him the space to try to move on, but he hadn't been able to. Not really. Willow was it for him, just as she always had been. As time passed, all he wanted was for her to be happy, and he'd assumed she was.

Even though his love life had never really gone anywhere, things had fallen in place for him in other ways. Daniel Parker, both he and Tyler's father and owner of Parker Craft Brewing Co., gave Grayson a job the summer after high school working under Ralph Fletcher, the general manager in their flagship location. He helped with shipments and supplies. Over time, he'd developed a passion for crafting the finest brews and moved his way up in the company to the head of operations for all five of their locations.

While Tyler lived in Connecticut, it gave Grayson time with Daniel, getting to know him more than how he'd known him growing up. Once the truth came out that Mr. Parker was his biological father, it was like the two men made up for lost time and he supported Grayson's growth within the company like a real father would do.

The job was perfect for him, even if it meant working with Tyler after he graduated from college and joined the financial department. Things had been strained between them at first, but for the sake of the company, they found a way to work together—and gradually, it became less awkward. They'd been friends for so many years for a reason, after all. And while they didn't have the same closeness they'd shared as kids, they'd found a new equilibrium and focused on work. Parker's Craft Brewing Co. was one of New England's favorite breweries, particularly on the islands, the Cape, and hopefully their newest location in Boston.

Walking over to Tyler's office, Grayson drew in a breath. He paused outside the door to cool his rising temper. The man had lied to steal Willow from him and then left her behind, ditched her at the altar. Some days, it was all Grayson could do to maintain a neutral expression around him. Emotionally, the ordeal had taken him back eight years to a memory that had played on repeat for two weeks now.

———

"YOU ASKED ME TO TAKE HER TO PROM BECAUSE YOU couldn't!" Tyler shouted as Grayson entered the Anderson's barn, just before Willow's dad got to his tractor—not hearing what the boys had both discovered only hours prior.

"I asked you to escort her to the dance. That was all!" Grayson roared back, quickly glancing over his shoulder to see if anyone had followed him into the barn before glaring back at Tyler. "I'd just gotten the shock of my life when Jack stumbled in and told me my mother had an affair! After learning that, I wasn't up to going to the dance, but I never wanted to break up with Willow. You knew that, but you saw your opening and you took it without a care for how much it would hurt Willow and me."

"I was hurt too, or do you not remember that part? Your mom's affair was with my dad! Forget that little detail, Grayson?" Tyler was seething, his eyes growing dark with anger. "But I didn't leave Willow hanging because of it. You did. And yeah, I might have stretched the truth a little when I told her things were over between the two of you, but I'm still the one who showed up for her, and you're the one who let her down." He stepped closer. "I'll take care of her better than you ever could. And you know that's true."

TYLER SEEMED TO HAVE KEPT HIS WORD ON THAT last point. For a while, anyway. But his friend's words, along with Jack's drunken insults, had halted him in his tracks after that awful night, causing him to let Willow slip away—telling himself it was for the best. That she was with the right guy, the one who hadn't let her down.

But now, after the failed wedding, all of that logic was turned upside down. Grayson didn't know the details, but he couldn't help being mad at Tyler. *What happened to taking care of her, huh?*

On the other hand, picking a fight now with him was a

terrible idea, so Grayson tried to swallow his anger and frustration before he reached the open door.

Tyler was on the phone when he knocked lightly and stepped inside. He glanced up at Grayson and held up a finger.

"Yes, I'll get last quarter's budget report sent over by tomorrow morning," he said, pointing to a chair for Grayson. "Okay, sounds good. Talk soon." Tyler hung up the phone. "Hey, Grayson. Thanks for coming in. I wanted to make sure you didn't have any questions about the expense sheet for the new Boston location."

"Everything looks solid with the budgeting," Grayson said. He paused when Tyler's cell phone rang. Tyler shrugged apologetically and picked up the phone.

"Hold on just a moment, Grayson." He accepted the call. "Drew?" His eyes lingered on Grayson while he listened.

Grayson sat back against his chair, noticing Tyler's grave expression.

"Everything okay?" Grayson whispered, and Tyler held up a finger again as he listened. The only Drew both men knew was Drew Ryder, a buddy from high school who was now a paramedic on the island. Judging by the look of shock evident on Tyler's face, it must have been him.

"When did you say this happened?" Tyler closed his eyes. "Okay . . . and Willow—I assume she knows so she can get here as soon as possible?"

Willow. Coming back to Terra Cove? No, it couldn't be. She hadn't been home in eight years. Whatever Tyler just heard must have been serious.

"Okay, I'm sure they did too. Thank you for letting me know." Tyler ended the call and looked at Grayson. "That was Drew Ryder. He took Willow's father by ambulance to the emergency room earlier this morning. He was thrown off a horse and is in the intensive care unit. It's pretty bad, and Drew doesn't know if he will be okay. Willow should be headed into town—at least, that's what Drew assumes. But I need to call her. Or maybe I'll just go straight to the hospital."

Grayson watched as Tyler stood and began to pack up. "Are you serious?" A part of him told him to mind his own business, but his irritation was building. He had a bigger push to protect Willow.

"What do you mean? There's a family emergency—"

"For a family you decided not to join two weeks ago." The words just came out before he could stop them. Tyler fumbled with the papers he was putting away and paused, locking eyes with Grayson.

"That is none of your concern," Tyler said through clenched teeth.

Grayson threw up his hands. "So you're just going to show up at the hospital? And assume her family will greet you with open arms?"

Tyler continued to glare at him. "Why wouldn't I be going? Did you not hear me? Mr. Anderson is in the ICU."

"Oh, I don't know," Grayson said, standing up to meet him at eye level. "Because you left the man's daughter in her wedding dress on your wedding day? As far as I've heard, you haven't spoken to her since. Do you really think she wants you showing up now during a time when she is hurting and scared?"

Tyler's eyes widened, and Grayson regretted the words when a few coworkers slowed as they passed by the office. This was not the time nor place for this argument, but he'd started it and now Tyler was clearly heated as he placed both hands on his desk and leaned forward, closing the gap between them.

"Like you should talk."

Grayson stepped around the desk and stood inches from Tyler. "I was an eighteen-year-old kid who had been dealing with a rough encounter with who I thought was my dad." Grayson narrowed his eyes. "Then my so-called best friend made a play to steal her and twisted the situation into a breakup after I only asked him to escort her to prom. You know as well as I do that I *never* intended to hurt her or leave her. You, on the other hand, are a grown adult who asked her to *marry* you! Then you abandoned her on her wedding day. And now you think it's no big deal to show up at the hospital?"

"What Willow and I do—"

"Gentlemen!" Daniel hurried in and shut the door behind him. "Sit down, both of you!" When they were back in their chairs, Daniel stood with his arms folded as he stared at them. "Now I just got off the phone with someone I know who works in the emergency room and told me about Willow's father. From the little I heard outside this office, I am assuming you got the same call."

"Yes, sir. I'm sorry for the outburst," Grayson said, ignoring Tyler's scoff.

"Let me finish." Daniel put up his hand. "You are both adults. This pettiness not only needs to stop, but it is never to be played out in this office again. If you feel the need to battle out your feelings, do it outside. The Anderson family is going through a major trauma and needs our support. Whether that is from afar or by their side."

"Which is why I am about to head to the hospital," Tyler said as he stood again. He stopped when Daniel put his hand on the stack of papers Tyler reached for.

"Tyler?" Daniel turned directly to him. "Perhaps Grayson has a point. Willow's dad may be unaware of what's happening since he's hurt, but I know Liam Anderson, and the man is livid with you. I don't think the rest of the family is happy with you either. I'd call Willow before you show up at that hospital."

Daniel straightened up and left, and Grayson shot Tyler a warning look before he walked out as well. Tyler must have received the warning because he didn't say another word to him.

———

HIS MOTHER'S CAR WAS ALREADY IN HIS DRIVEWAY when Grayson pulled in. After hearing about Willow's dad, he couldn't concentrate on his work, and he packed up and let Jesse know that he would be gone for the rest of the day. His mom had called before he made it to his car in the parking lot.

The news about Willow's father was spreading, typical for a small town like Terra Cove. Pretty soon, the whole island would know. Martha's Vineyard may host thousands of tourists each summer, but in the off season the population was low, which meant everyone knew everything about everyone.

Barking from inside caught his attention, and Grayson went to the door to let Monty out. Standing just over two and half feet tall and weighing close to a hundred pounds, his German shepherd was perfect for him. He protected the house and kept Grayson company when the nights got lonely.

His mother got out of her car and hurried up to hug him. She pulled back and the same green eyes as his shined up at him. Her brown hair with a few strands of gray blew across her face.

"This is just so awful. I can't imagine what the Andersons are feeling, especially Rachel."

"Well, she'll have Whitney and Wesley with her, I'm sure. And I've been told that Willow's coming to town." He walked behind his house and over to a bench outside the small barn and sat down with his mom. Monty sniffed around the paddock, circling back and forth.

"Oh my! She is?" Mom was clearly just as taken aback by the news as he had been in the office. "I mean, of course she is. Her father is hurt. It's just been so long."

"Yeah, it sure has." He hoped Tyler would do the right thing and let Willow know he planned to show up. "Tyler wants to go to the hospital. I guess he wants to be there for her."

"For Willow?" his mom said.

"Yeah."

"After *leaving her at the altar*?"

Grayson let out a humorless chuckle. "Yup."

"And he really thinks that's a good idea?"

"Both Daniel and I warned him that may not be the best plan, but I'm not sure if he'll listen."

His mom tsked and shook her head. "I suppose I don't blame him for wanting to go, but it does seem a little thoughtless. I can't imagine anyone in the Anderson family will be very pleased to see him."

Grayson nodded. "That's what Daniel and I told him. We said he should call Willow first and make sure she's okay with seeing him."

His mom studied him, her eyes tender in a way that always signaled she was about to say something important. "If I know anything about Tyler, even if he calls and she says no, he will go anyway."

She was probably right about that, but it was out of Grayson's hands. He'd warned Tyler—that was all he could do. "I can't stop him."

"But you can control what *you* do."

"I don't understand."

"Maybe . . ." She paused before continuing. "You should go too."

He shook his head. "No. That's a terrible idea."

"Is it though?"

"Of course it is. Why would I do that? I haven't spoken to Willow in years. I haven't even laid eyes on her." That first year, he'd counted on the chance to see her again, thinking she would come home for Christmas or the summer, and they could talk, patch things up a little, as friends if nothing else. But she never came.

"That's true, but . . ." She gave him those eyes again. "You still love her."

He blew out the frustration and leaned his elbows on his knees as Monty came over and sniffed his face. His dog always knew when conversations were more serious. Grayson gave him a head scratch.

Was it that obvious? He'd tried so hard to bottle up his feelings for Willow once he learned she was officially together with Tyler. Yes, he was hurt he'd lost her, but he also didn't want to make things harder for her. So he stayed quiet and kept to himself, especially around his mother who worried about him.

"I'll always love Willow. She's . . . Willow." He smiled at his mom, hoping to move the conversation off the idea of him going to the hospital.

"Grayson, you're my son and I observed you and Willow for your entire childhood and then when you were together in high school. I don't care how long Tyler has been with her, I doubt she ever felt for him what she felt for you."

"That's a bold assumption considering she was set to marry him only two weeks ago. He left *her*, remember?"

"Uh-huh, I know. But"—she put her hand on his knee—"we don't know what prompted that. You don't know what had been going on."

"Mom," he said, straightening up and putting his hand over hers. "I know you wish she and I would find a way back to each other, but you have to understand what seeing me might do to her. She'll already be upset over what happened to her dad. Running into me could make things much worse."

"Or much better," his mom said. "How about I go with you? We can go and keep our distance and at least have Tyler tell Willow we stopped by to make sure she and her family were okay. We can leave before we even see her.”

“Then I’d be doing the same thing I told him *not* to do.”

“Tyler is a different story. What happened between you and Willow was years ago.” She shifted to face him. “You were kids then and now you’re adults. If she knows we came, it shows her and the Andersons that you still care. Besides, I’m sure we won’t be the only ones checking on them. The whole town is worried sick for Liam. And the more people who show up to support them the better, I think.” His mother grew silent, but he knew she wasn’t done. “Besides, I’m going whether you come or not.”

“I don’t know . . .” he said. Even the risk of seeing Willow made his heart beat harder. How he’d dreamed of seeing her again, even from a distance. To actually talk to her would be more than he’d ever hoped for, despite the countless times he’d imagined what he’d say to her if he ever got the chance. Standing in a hospital while her father fought for his life was not the ideal place. But his mom was probably right. The more support, the better. Maybe she was also correct about the years having softened the blow of what happened with them. “Promise we can just make an appearance, show our support, and leave?”

“I promise,” she said. “It would be awkward for me to see her too, so I’ll keep my distance if she sees me, but I at least want her to know I care. I hate how things turned out, but we can’t erase all the good years.”

“Okay.” He stood up. “Let me change out of my work clothes and then we’ll go.”

As he walked inside the house, his nerves on end, he hoped his mother’s idea would work out okay. He was about to find out.

Chapter Three

Turning the key and opening the door to her condo provided the next devastating blow. The corner by the front door was empty without Tyler's golf clubs. This was the first time she'd been back since she hastily packed her bag and left for Ivy's immediately after the wedding.

Ivy followed her inside. "Let's just go upstairs and pack as quickly as we can," she said as Willow stood frozen and staring.

Aside from the clubs, he'd only taken his clothes, yet the first floor felt chillingly surreal in his absence. Eight years together and a condo filled with every part of their relationship. Now it was as if it never happened. Going into autopilot, knowing her family was waiting, she hurried up the stairs and pulled out two large suitcases out of a hall closet.

Half an hour later, she was ready to face the two-hour drive to the ferry port at Woods Hole on the Cape. She'd opted for the farther port so she could take her car aboard. For practical reasons—she'd be able to get to the hospital easier—but for other reasons too. Having her car meant she wouldn't be trapped there. Guilt immediately poked at her for thinking of her childhood home as a place where she might feel stuck, but she needed that escape hatch. Despite the emergency bringing her back, she was nervous about facing everything she'd hidden from for so long. One step at a time.

The sun broke through a cloud, brightening the bedroom she'd shared with Tyler for years, and its warm rays drew her to the window. Looking out in the distance, the Mystic seaport sparkled against a variety of vessels on the water. From the majestic to the humble, old and new, each boat whispered its own tale from the high seas of the past and present. The view had sold her and Tyler back when they first bought the place. She looked away before the memory dug too deep, picked up one of the suitcases, while Ivy got the other, and left.

"Okay," Willow said out loud when they got back to Ivy's. "I can do this."

"Of course you can." Ivy gave her a worried look. "Are you sure you don't need me to come?"

"I'm sure." She would love to have her closest friend with her on the trip, but something urged her to go alone. "I'm just relieved I got a ticket for the ferry on such short notice. I'll arrive at the hospital later than I'd like, but at least I'll be there today." The two women embraced in a long hug before Willow got in her car. It was time to face this.

The drive was a blur with her thoughts racing in circles as she built up her emotional shields. When she reached the port, she got her ticket, and seeing the familiar area made her feel disoriented and confused. Her excuses to avoid homecoming all these years suddenly left her reeling as the cars queued up to wait for the ferry's door to open. Terra Cove, her beloved hometown, left in the dust along with the people there who cared for her most—all because of an accident and heartbreak.

———

Less than an hour later, with the gentle lapping of the waves and the flapping of the seagulls wheeling above, Martha's Vineyard grew closer. The ferry was still packed for late afternoon on a Wednesday, and many eager tourists were ready to explore the island. After driving off the ferry and rolling down her windows, Willow was enveloped by the salty air. Living by the water in Mystic didn't hold the same vibe, one that instantly made her homesick as she soaked in the Vineyard's presence. She was home.

An incoming call lit up on her dashboard from Wesley. "Hi, I just got off the ferry." She had texted to let him and everyone else know which one she was taking.

"Good. I'm outside with Whitney getting a little fresh air."

"Any updates?" Her pulse quickened with anticipation.

"Yes. Dad's going into surgery soon. We'll go over more once you get here."

"I should be there in fifteen minutes."

"Actually, I also called because Mom needs you to stop by the house for her cell phone charger. She said it's by her bed. You. . ." His voice dropped. "Still have a key to mom and dad's house, right?"

"I do." Willow glanced down at her keys hanging from the ignition. She'd never taken it off.

"Thanks. Mom's battery is running low from making so many calls."

"No problem. Text me if you think of anything else you all need. I'll be there soon."

The twenty-minute drive up the island consumed her at every site, filling her with a maelstrom of feelings as she traveled from Oak Bluffs' lively harbor through the farmers market in West Tisbury. Time slowed with each passing minute, reminding her of all the wonderous places she had loved so much growing up, giving her snapshots of her past. Her parents' horse farm by one of the island's salt ponds just down the road from the ocean had been nothing short of idyllic—floating between serene pastures and scenic shorelines, Willow had the best of both worlds. But a cloud hung over all those memories, since Tyler and Grayson had been a part of so many of them.

She reached the familiar driveway and stopped, putting her car in park as she stared at the name on the closed gate: Anderson Stables. A text from Ivy popped up on the dashboard and she hit read.

> Just checking to see if you made it okay?
> I'm here if you need to talk.

She sent a quick reply, not wanting her friend to worry.

> I made it. And all good. For now. Will call
> when I can.

Willow gazed past the gate and down the long, winding dirt driveway that led to her parents' house. Her mind continued to muse on her childhood, memories coming back to her at rocket speed. Hiking trails off the beaten paths that tourists never knew about, bonfires at the beach, all the secret adventures at the old Coastal Rock Preserve, including its more secluded beach . . . and the cove.

Releasing a pent-up breath, she rolled her window down and stared at the keypad. It had been so long since she'd entered the combination, but she still had it memorized and started to punch in the code in for the gate when an incoming call on her dashboard stopped her. Glancing at the screen, she nearly collapsed back into her seat when she saw his name. She hadn't heard from Tyler since he told her the wedding was off. Anger quickly overpowered everything else she was feeling. Should she answer?

Before she could decide, the call went to voicemail, and her hands shook while she waited to see if he left a message. A text came through instead, which felt a bit easier to handle than hearing his voice. She pressed read on her screen.

Willow, I heard about your dad. Call me.

Reading the words over and over, she fought the impulse to ignore him. After all, he had it coming after the radio silence she'd gotten from him for the past two weeks. But for him to call and text back-to-back like that, she got the sense that he'd keep reaching out until she replied. Might as well bite the bullet. Tyler picked up after the first ring.

"I'm actually on my way to the hospital. I'm nearly there," he said when he answered. Just hearing his voice again made her feel sick. *Calm down, Willow.* Her family would always be important to him. How could they not be? Her parents were like second parents to him. Of course he was worried about her dad. And there was nothing to be gained from starting an argument with him.

"I'm picking up something for my mom, then I'll be there too," she said. "Who called you?"

"A friend from high school, Drew Ryder. Remember him? He was one of the paramedics that took your dad in." He sounded like he was trying to catch his breath. "I . . . I don't even know where to start."

"What do you mean, 'where to start'?"

The pause made the background noise of his car clear. He must have had the window down. "I don't even make sense," he finally said. "I'm just upset about your dad."

"Well, he doesn't need you to get hurt too," she said the same thing she'd told herself back in Connecticut while she drove to the ferry. "Just focus on the road."

"I don't know much of what's going on. Have you heard any updates?"

"I don't know either yet. Wesley just told me he was going into surgery. I'll know more once I'm there." Willow pressed the code and the gate opened. She drove up to the house and parked.

"Okay. I don't want to upset your family, so I'll wait somewhere away from them."

"That is probably for the best." Willow paused before turning the ignition off that would end the call. "I'll find you once I'm there."

"Willow . . ."

"Yes?" She closed her eyes, trying to stay patient.

"I'm glad you're home."

She didn't respond, other than to hang up and get out of the car, nearly slamming the door shut. That was a bold statement coming from him. Even though she fully knew Tyler was in Terra Cove, she hadn't considered the possibility of running into him.

After dashing through the house to grab the charger, not stopping to take in her childhood home after being gone so long, she hopped back in her car and left. She turned onto the main road that led straight to the island's one hospital back in Oak Bluffs. Annoyance at Tyler's statement continued to build as she picked up speed. Did he forget they were no longer together? Once she got an update on her dad's condition, she'd share it with Tyler because she told him she would, but then she'd tell him he needed to leave. He couldn't help anything by hanging around, and he'd just be an unwelcome distraction when she needed to focus on her dad.

Willow silently prayed the police were not doing speed checks as she pushed the limit to get down the road as fast as she could. When she found the first open spot in the visitor's lot near the emergency room, she barely put the car in park before getting out.

The large doors to the ER opened, and the bright lights above, mixed with the commotion emergency rooms typically held, made the situation all too real. She couldn't believe her dad was there when only weeks before he was dressed in a suit, smiling as he and her mom greeted all their guests before the ceremony that never commenced. Willow put her hand on a nearby chair to keep her balance as her sudden anxiety made the room spin. After collecting herself, she rushed to reception and nearly tripped when she saw Tyler standing at the desk.

"Are you family?" the receptionist asked with her eyes still on her computer screen—completely missing the sunken look on his face. The question nearly knocked her backward as well.

No. This man left me the morning of our wedding, so he's not family. She swallowed the words and shook her head when the receptionist glanced up at her approach.

"I'm not, just a . . . close friend of the family." Tyler turned to her, with a pained look. "She's family though."

"Hi, ma'am. I'll be right with you," the receptionist said to her before looking back at Tyler. "Since you're not, have a seat right over there to wait. Unfortunately, I cannot let you through any more doors."

"No problem." He turned to Willow. "Keep me updated," he said, then went to sit down.

"Ma'am?"

Willow looked at the receptionist.

"If you walk through those double doors, you'll see another waiting area just outside of the ICU with anyone else who is here for Mr. Anderson."

She thanked her and rushed toward the doors. On the other side, she realized she wasn't sure how long Tyler would be waiting and pulled out her phone to tell him it might be a while. The text just above the one he'd sent today made her stomach roil. Those words haunted her for two weeks. The message was the closest thing to an explanation she'd gotten from him since their wedding day.

> Willow . . . I don't even have the right
> words. I know you are in shock. All I can
> say is, I didn't mean for it to end like this.
> Just know that I will always love you.

Frustration pooled in her eyes and a few tears escaped down her cheeks as she quickly texted.

> If he's just gone in for surgery, it might be
> hours before we know anything. Don't feel
> like you have to wait all night. If you need to
> leave, I understand. In fact, it might be
> better that way.

She shoved her phone in her purse and went to find her mom and siblings. They were all seated down the short hall-way, just outside the ICU. When her mother saw her walking up, she jumped out of her seat and threw her arms around her.

"I'm so glad you're here, Willow," she said, pulling Willow in tighter. Her mother's eyes were swollen and red from crying and she was gripping tissues.

"Me too, Mom." Willow handed her the charger and turned to her siblings who both stood and hugged her.

"I got here with zero traffic and no issues with the ferry. The angels above must have paved the way to allow me to get here so smoothly," Willow said, and they all sat down again. "Where is Jason?" she asked Whitney when she realized her brother-in-law wasn't next to her sister.

"Home with the kids. They're too little to understand what is happening and his parents are out of town, so they can't watch them," Whitney said.

Willow nodded. This was not the place for a baby and toddler. "Okay, so what is the surgery?"

"There was some more swelling and bleeding in the brain since he'd first arrived earlier, so they operated to treat that and to allow room for the swelling. He will be in a medically induced coma afterward so his brain can rest and prevent a secondary injury," her mother explained.

"So now we just wait?" Willow asked.

"We wait," her mom agreed, putting her arm around her. Willow leaned onto her.

For nearly two hours they sat in silence or passed the time with small talk, trying to keep the discussion light to distract themselves. Her mother made some more calls until finally the doctor came out to update them. Her mother nearly knocked him over, she walked up to him so fast. Willow had never seen her this distraught and wished she could fix it, but the only thing that would help was her dad getting better and returning home.

"He made it through the surgery," the doctor began, and everyone sighed in relief. "But we're not out of the woods yet. The next twenty-four hours are really telling for his recovery. We will be monitoring him closely overnight for any additional bleeding."

"Can I see him?" her mother asked, and the doctor nodded.

"I can only have one of you back there at a time for now," the doctor said, and her mother followed him through the doors to the ICU.

Willow's knees shook a bit with the news. While waiting, her body had been so tense, and now that she was on her feet, she could feel the strain. She suddenly needed some air—and while she was getting it, she could also update Tyler, provided he'd actually stuck around.

"I'll be right back," she told her brother and sister. "Going to get some fresh air."

"Need me to come with you?" Whitney asked.

"No, I'm okay. I'd rather be alone and walk a bit." It was a poor excuse, but she didn't want to risk having them see her talk to Tyler.

Half expecting him to be gone, she walked back through the same double doors as before and stopped in her tracks. Tyler was coming back into the waiting area from the vending machine side and following close behind him was . . . Grayson's *mom*?

Tyler stood with his back toward her, facing the woman as they continued their conversation. Willow didn't know what to do, so she waited where she was, but when Nicole leaned to the side and locked eyes with her, Tyler turned and did the same.

"Willow . . ." Tyler jogged over and hesitated, clearly restraining himself from hugging her. Unsurprisingly, she didn't share that same urge and crossed her arms over her chest to discourage him from getting too close. His eyes widened and he shoved his hands in his pockets against her flat response. "How is he?"

Willow glanced behind him as Grayson's mom rushed past them, barely giving Willow a nod of acknowledgment, which didn't surprise her. For all the years she'd known Grayson's mother, she'd kept to herself. When they were kids and their parents all got together, Nicole would rarely show up. Willow turned back to Tyler.

"When did Nicole get here?" she asked, trying to understand why she was even there to begin with.

"Oh," Tyler said, glancing past her in the direction Nicole went. "I'm, uh, not too sure. I came back from the bathroom at one point, and she was here. I haven't spoken to her in a long time, so it's been a bit strange."

Something felt off with his answer, but it wasn't important.

"I see. Okay, so my dad—"

"Whatever it is, just know I'm here for you." He pulled his hands out of his pockets, and took a step closer, just as she moved a step backward.

She raised her hand in defense. "Listen to what I have to say about my dad and that's it."

A somber expression settled over his face. "Willow, I hate this tension between us. I—"

"*I said* listen to what I have to say about Dad, and that's it," she repeated with grit and determination. "I'm not here to discuss anything else with you."

"Okay." He stepped back.

"He's out of surgery now," she began. "There was some swelling and bleeding in the brain, so they operated to treat that and to allow room for the swelling. He's in an induced coma. The neurosurgeon warned there might be more surgeries needed but had no clear answers to what that would entail yet. The swelling needs to go down and they're going to watch for additional complications that are very possible within the next day or so."

"Okay . . . so what does this mean?"

"It means for now he's stable," she said. "I'm going to get some air and then go back in there. Since he's okay for now, it's best for you to go home. I'll update you if anything drastic changes."

Just as she was about to leave, he threw his arms up and began to pace in a circle. "Willow!" he nearly shouted, but immediately quieted when a passing nurse glanced in their direction. "I don't even know what *I'm* feeling anymore. These last two weeks—"

"Have nothing to do with what is happening right now with my dad." She kept her gaze on him, showing no emotion. "All we can do now is wait, but again, you can wait at home."

Tyler stopped moving and nodded. "Now we wait," he repeated barely above a whisper, running his hands through his hair. Something he always did when he was frustrated.

Just then, time seemed to slow as Grayson came around a corner and walked toward them from another hallway.

"Tyler, I just need to—" Grayson stopped short a few feet away when he saw her.

Blinking out of the daze that had overtaken her, she looked back at Tyler. Why was Grayson addressing him like they were picking up an ongoing conversation? From her understanding, neither of them had spoken to Grayson since they left for college. But maybe that was something else she'd gotten wrong.

"I can see that you have all the company you need," Willow said to Tyler, trying not to feel pushed aside. "But your choice of company is a bit of a surprise." Avoiding eye contact with Grayson, she turned to leave.

"Willow . . ." Tyler grabbed her arm to stop her but let go when Grayson walked closer and shook his head directly at Tyler.

"Am I missing something?" Willow finally asked. Were they keeping something from her? Something else she wasn't allowed to know—like why Tyler jilted her at the altar? Or why Grayson randomly dumped her on prom night eight years ago?

Tyler pointed to the waiting room seats near them. "Willow, let's chat for a minute. I need to tell you—"

"I'm going to grab a water," Grayson cut in. Hearing his voice again was all it took to break her resolve, and in spite of her best intentions, she met his gaze and could barely breathe against the impact. He'd changed—of course, he'd changed, it had been eight years—but those green eyes were exactly like she remembered. His attention was fixed on her for a moment before turning to make his way to the vending machine.

Tyler reached for her again, and she shrugged him off. "Glad to see you two reacquainted." She took a few steps back when he moved toward her. "Don't!" She quickly turned and left, not looking back once.

Outside, she sat on top of a flowered retaining wall to catch her breath. The summer's late afternoon sun cast a golden light over the bed of flowers, while they soaked up the last of its rays. She closed her eyes toward the sky, feeling her body calm in the sun's comforting orange glow.

"Willow?" a deep, painfully familiar voice said from nearby.

His voice made the past crash into her thoughts before she could stop them. His teenage face smiled at her in her mind, and for a moment, she didn't want to open her eyes, longing for a past that couldn't be recaptured.

"Willow?" he said again, now standing right next to her.

"Grayson," she said without hesitation and opened her eyes. A part of her had guessed he'd find her out here.

He sat next to her on the wall's ledge, his legs brushing against hers while he took a long sip of water. Her body trembled as he put the lid on the bottle, set it down, and placed his hands on each side of him, one beside hers, to steady himself. For a minute, they sat in silence—neither able to begin the conversation.

"Asking you how you're doing is such a stupid question," he finally said, making her smile against the stress. Something he was always the best at doing during hard situations.

"I take it Tyler called to tell you about my dad?"

"Something like that," he said.

Out of the corner of her eye, she watched him lean farther back against his arms to face the sun. It was the first time in eight years she was able to really look at him. His wavy brown hair looked weeks past needing a haircut, his jeans were worn down just as they always had been, and his usual white t-shirt hugged his biceps, which had grown with him over the years. Studying him, she realized Grayson Turner was a man now.

At the same time, all she could see was the teenage boy who fiddled with the sand that first day his lips found hers. Eyes as green as the island's beech-trees staring down at her as he held her close in the cove. Back when everything was simpler, and the world felt endless with opportunities for her future—with him.

"It is a stupid question," she said, poking at him, keeping her gaze straight. She suddenly wasn't sure what would happen if she looked at those green eyes again.

"I just . . . I . . ." He stumbled over his words, although she couldn't deny how awkward he must feel too. "I came to the hospital to check on you and find out what was happening with your dad."

Willow nodded. Like with Tyler, her family had been an important part of Grayson's life growing up. "Well, thank you for coming. It was kind of you."

They fell silent again for a minute.

"You looked upset in there, but that's understandable," he said, and she felt his focus turn to her.

She wanted to ask him what his mother was doing there, but she couldn't muster up the energy to start that conversation. Besides, she was most likely just showing her support for the family too. The intensity of the day weighed on her and all she wanted to do was go to her parents' house and sleep.

"I'll be okay, Grayson," she said, sensing his gaze still on her.

She finally met his eyes, now softer, hinting at the passage of time, despite the vivid memories of that awful night that suddenly passed through her mind. For years when she thought of Grayson, anger was all she'd felt. But seeing him now, it was just the opposite. In fact, the desire to fall into his arms while her world felt out of control overtook her. Willow abruptly pulled herself out of her daze and stood.

She needed some space to get herself together before going back inside. Her relationship with Tyler and their life in Connecticut seemed like a dream she had just woken up from, and she was now back in reality, at home in Terra Cove.

Eight years gone. And her past had just taken a seat right next to her—like it never left.

Chapter Four

After tossing his empty beer can into the recycling bin later that evening, Grayson walked out to his back deck. He ran his hands along the railing he'd just smoothed out earlier that week and forced himself to turn his thoughts toward staining the last of the deck's surface—and away from Willow.

Leaning over, he watched lightning fill the summer night sky in the distance, storm clouds threatening to cover the moon that had taken center stage. Next to the Atlantic in the moisture-rich air, storms were always a little more intense. His home sat high up and overlooked the Vineyard Sound, giving him the perfect view of the lightning illuminating the waves below with each flash. He never took this property by the water for granted, especially since he never could have afforded it if he hadn't inherited it.

His great-grandparents purchased the land in the late 1800s, and it had been two years since his mother handed it down to him, along with all the work it needed. Besides the house, there was a small barn that was still in good shape, where he kept a couple of horses—including one, Nova, that went way back with him and Willow.

As a single mom for most of his teen years, his mother never had time for much upkeep, and the repairs needed on the home were long overdue. A couple years after his younger sister, Abby, graduated high school, his mom was ready to move on from the place. He'd been sharing a tiny apartment with a roommate in Edgartown at the time, so it had been a nice surprise when she gave him the keys, and ever since, he'd been making his way through each room with updates. One remodel he was itching to get to was his mother's old soap shack that sat back behind the barn.

She had worked selling homemade goat's milk soaps when he was younger, but after Jack left them, she was forced to find jobs that brought in more money, since she was the only one paying the bills—even if it meant abandoning her passion.

As the next spark imbued the sky, her words echoed in his memory.

"It's yours now, Gray," his mother had said, standing on her toes to kiss his cheek and lean toward his ear. *"I know you will make this home what I couldn't."*

Heavy footfalls thudded up the steps, and Monty padded toward him after guarding against all kinds of animals that often found their way onto the property. Stroking the dog's dense coat, he fought to think about anything other than Willow. Picking up on his unease, Monty nudged his owner.

"I'm alright, boy. I'm just working through some stuff." That seemed to satisfy Monty's protective nature, but the brewing storm had him just as nervous, and he howled. "For such a big dog, you sure can be a baby during thunderstorms."

They continued to watch the storm unfold, but all Grayson could see was every aspect of Willow's beauty from earlier still etched deep in his mind. How the fading sunlight seemed to enhance the intensity of her stare as they sat on the wall outside the hospital, those honey eyes aglow. How it took everything in him not to give in to an overwhelming old habit to run his fingers through her golden curls, cut shorter to fall on top of her shoulders. Eight years had passed, yet Willow still encompassed every aspect of his heart and seeing her today only confirmed it.

As the first rumble of thunder boomed above, he remembered those summer nights watching storms from her parents' screened-in porch. She'd perch on his lap with her long hair blowing against him in the breeze and blocking his view. But he hadn't cared. Nothing mattered other than the serene happiness he felt at having her so close.

He was lost in his memories until the current storm started pouring rain on him, and Monty's anxious barking pulled him back to reality. He finally pushed off the railing and headed inside. Shivering from getting drenched, he walked upstairs to have a hot shower and wallow in his own self-pity for not being able to say more to Willow.

He'd known that someday they'd cross paths again. That she would make her way back to Terra Cove, and yet today, he'd been so taken aback when he'd seen her, that he felt like he was just thrown off a bucking horse himself. When she walked away, it was like that horse had kicked him in the gut, leaving him drained and defeated all over again. Countless hours wasted, rehearsing what he'd say to her when he finally had the chance, and now that she was home, he knew he wouldn't be able to restrain himself any further. He had to see her again.

He thought about how surprised she'd seemed when he spoke to Tyler inside the waiting room. Did she think that was their first encounter since high school? Did she not know they worked together?

He knew he shouldn't be stepping into Tyler's business with Willow and what he had or hadn't told her, but after years of building a wall of restraint, today just broke through it. He still cared deeply for her, and if Tyler had kept the fact that they were coworkers a secret, what else was he hiding from her—especially about him and Tyler? She'd been through enough between the both of them, and he wasn't going to let this go.

An incoming call drew his attention but only added to his annoyance when he saw it was Tyler. Part of him wanted to answer and yell at him for making him feel like he had to be the one to tell Willow everything she clearly didn't know. It didn't help that he'd seen the sorrow still so clear in her face along with dark circles under her eyes. She must not have been sleeping well since her failed wedding. Seeing her had made what Tyler did to her become real. How could he screw things up with her—*especially* her—their Willow? Despite how Tyler swooped in and deceived Willow to have her for himself, Grayson had still spent eight years hoping Tyler could make her happy. Now they'd both broken her heart. His mood was not right for any conversation, but because of the current circumstances with Willow's dad, he answered.

"Any updates?" Grayson asked abruptly, hoping to avoid small talk.

"Thankfully, no. I haven't heard from Willow again, which is a good thing. She's only going to call if something significant changes," Tyler said.

"Okay. So why are you calling?"

"Other urgent news. Ralph has to have unexpected surgery tomorrow."

"He does? Is he okay?" In addition to Daniel, whom he'd grown close to after learning he was his father, Ralph had also become a good friend and a mentor. He always joked with Grayson that he would be general manager at their Oak Bluffs location until he couldn't stand anymore. The man refused to retire, and no one had asked him to. He ran the business like no one else could and had for as long as Grayson could remember. Both he and Tyler had childhood memories of Ralph always having candy for them as a reward for unloading a few boxes here and there.

"He said it was minor but couldn't wait. I'll check in tomorrow night and find out more. But he will need a few weeks to recover."

"I'm relieved it isn't something major. I, uh . . ." He hesitated. Grayson had planned to take two weeks off starting Monday, but now he wasn't so sure he should. "I feel guilty taking vacation now. I can cut one of the weeks if you need me to."

"You skipped out on having a vacation for nearly two years. Take the time off. My dad would tell you the same thing. I just wanted you to know what was happening with Ralph."

My dad. Grayson blew out frustration. Tyler still never acknowledged that Daniel was his dad too. "Call me tomorrow if you find out more."

"Of course I will find out more. Ralph is very important to my family." *My family.* Grayson winced at the words. "I'll check on him and make sure the surgery went well."

Just like I had to do for Willow today. Follow her outside to check on her after you upset her. Grayson arched his arms over his head, like a protective barrier against his thoughts to keep him from speaking. He was on the verge of making Tyler upset again, but eight years of keeping quiet meant his words were bound to come out at some point—he just hated to disappoint Daniel like they had earlier in the office. Daniel spent the better half of the last few years since Tyler joined the company trying to make him and Tyler resume their friendship, but with little success.

Grayson went to the bathroom and turned on the water for his shower. "If you need me to do anything pressing, don't hesitate to ask during my time off."

"I will, but there won't be anything pressing that I or the staff can't handle while you're out," Tyler insisted.

"Thanks for letting me know about Ralph. And, Tyler?" Grayson closed his eyes, mentally preparing himself for the question that needed to be asked. "Willow doesn't know, does she?"

"Not right now, Grayson. I don't have the energy."

"Then find some."

Grayson ended the call and stepped into the shower a few seconds later, letting his irritation wash down the drain. The steam had begun to fog the bathroom—reminding him of the moments just before the fire. He'd tried to catch Willow, but she got on her horse so fast and took off. Her hair was pulled back and styled perfectly for the dance and bounced behind her as she rode away. *God, she was so beautiful.* He squeezed his eyes shut and tried to will away the memory, but all he could see was her gorgeous dark green gown. And the shock on Tyler's face when he'd asked him to escort her to the dance in his place sliced into his thoughts—a decision he forever wished he hadn't made.

If only he'd known then what Tyler would do that night, he never would have asked him to take her.

"GRAYSON, STOP!" TYLER CUT HIM OFF. "DO YOU *hear* yourself? All because Jack came over drunk and said a few choice words to you?"

With his fists curled into balls, Grayson wanted to punch something—or rather, *someone*. But it wasn't Tyler. "Would you just stop arguing with me!"

"This is Willow . . . *our* Willow. She's been planning this prom night for months. Are you really going to trash all of that for her just because your jerk of a dad came over and made a scene?"

"Stop. Please just be a friend to *me* right now. I know we both care about her, but I—" Grayson dropped onto the couch beside Tyler with his ears ringing so loud he could barely hear himself talk. Something that always happened after an encounter with Jack when he'd been drinking. Like when Grayson had to hold Abby in another room until all the drunken shouting at his mom stopped. Now it happened every time the man came back and caused trouble.

"But what?" Tyler sat next to him.

"I need you to listen to what I am about to say and not lose it."

"Tell me."

"When Jack came over, he didn't just blab nonsense like he usually does. He . . ." Grayson shook his foot, his nerves almost getting the best of him, but he needed to get this out. "He told me my mom and your dad had an affair."

Tyler jumped off the couch. "What!"

"You heard me." Grayson could barely look at him. "I asked you not to lose it, so sit down. I'm not done." When Tyler did, he continued. "And that affair resulted in . . . me."

"Wait." Tyler shook his head. "Are you telling me that *my* dad is . . . *your* dad too?"

"That's exactly what I'm saying. Daniel is my biological father. Which means we are half brothers."

Tyler stood back up and paced around the room. "I don't even know what to say."

Grayson watched him, recognizing the same stunned expression he'd had only an hour prior. "Yeah, that makes two of us. And that's why I just can't imagine going to prom right now. I need some time to just . . . wrap my head around all of this. But that shouldn't keep Willow from going as planned and having fun with you and all our friends."

"And what makes you think she'll be okay going with me?"

"I don't know." Grayson exhaled instant regret, knowing how difficult his absence would be for her. "Just tell her I had a fight with my dad and I'm not feeling it. She'll understand. I'll tell her the whole story later, after the dance. Not right this moment when I'm still coming to terms with it. I don't want to completely ruin her fun night."

"But you were fine unloading this on *me*?" Tyler asked. "I'm just supposed to go on like everything's normal? This affects me, too, Grayson. I—"

"Tyler . . . please. Just do this for me." Grayson pleaded with him. He knew the news wouldn't be easy for Tyler either, and he hadn't thought through how his friend would feel once he knew, but Tyler hadn't just dealt with a drunken madman telling him his mother had an affair and that he wasn't his real father. He was just too shaken up to attend prom.

"You're being a coward." Tyler crossed his arms, glaring down at him. "Besides, Jack probably just drank too much and made it up."

"Maybe so, but since I was the one who was just told, I have to be the one to find out. I'll confront my mom, and I need time to think through how to approach her. I need to be alone for a little while."

"You could have just used Jack's drinking problem as an excuse. Why did you feel the need to drop this on me tonight too, especially before talking to your mom to see if it's even true?"

"I needed to tell someone!" Grayson stood up, glaring at his best friend who was possibly his brother too. "Look, it's bad enough our parents kept it from us for this long. It just didn't feel right for me to know while you were still in the dark."

"Yeah, well, maybe I liked it better in the dark," Tyler said, a thread of anger in his voice.

"Don't get all worked up. It's bad enough that I am. We don't need you getting mad too. I need you to distract Willow tonight while I calm down."

Tyler stared quietly at him before his eyes narrowed in sudden thought. "Wow . . . and all of this is coming out right as my parents are divorcing. Now I know why."

"What? No, Tyler, just stop. You don't know if that's the reason. For all we know, the affair ended after my mom got pregnant—eighteen years ago. Why would that have anything to do with the problems your parents are having right now?"

"Well, what if the affair *didn't* end years ago? What then, huh?" Something had shifted in Tyler's eyes that Grayson would never forget. A look of disgust had fallen over him before he went to the door. "I'll take Willow to prom alright. Someone has to take care of her."

———

THE LOUD, CRACKLING THUNDER RUMBLED through the memory, bringing him back to the present. Grayson turned the shower knob to switch off the water, and dried himself. Lightning immediately flashed again outside, the rain now hitting the windows sideways as the storm passed directly overhead. Perfect timing to drown out his emotions. After changing into a fresh t-shirt and sweatpants, he grabbed his phone and went back downstairs, where Monty was howling by the window.

"Alright, alright. I'm here. Come on, let's eat something." Monty jogged past him, beating him to the kitchen. "Food always does the trick with you." But not with him.

Willow was back in town, her wedding with Tyler was called off, and the truth of everything he'd spent eight years trying to ignore was all landing on him with greater force than the storm's fury outside. He had no idea how to make it right again, but he suddenly had an idea of where to start.

He scrolled through his phone, found Wesley's number, and hit call. He'd really only seen Willow's brother in passing over the last few years. They were close once, but their friendship got strained after he and Willow broke up. Things between them were fairly cordial, though, so calling him shouldn't be an issue—especially because Wesley was a good entry point for reconnection with the Andersons. It was time Willow and her family knew that Tyler was his brother.

CHAPTER FIVE

The crisp Friday morning air out on the trail seemed to offer a temporary reprieve against the relentless stream of thoughts coursing through Willow's mind. The day hadn't started out easy after she'd drawn up enough courage to finally push open those rusty barn doors to assess what needed to be done for her dad. She was determined not to let him down and help, yet the silence when walking through the gate was deafening—even the horses hadn't made a sound at first. It was as if they all somehow knew it had been the first time in almost a decade that she stepped foot inside that barn since the fire.

The pounding in her chest made it even more difficult to focus and when she'd left, she had to catch her breath outside. *A panic attack?* She'd asked herself on repeat while deeply inhaling and slowly letting it out. She'd really needed to get it together. Her parents needed her right now. Not wanting to burden her mom with how uneasy she'd felt, Willow told her that she was heading out for some fresh air and a hike.

After her body began to relax again while walking, she'd tried to give herself a break. After all, she'd just survived the worst forty-eight hours of her life, waiting to see if her dad would make it through without any more complications. The good news was that he'd made it, and the other news that she hadn't exactly labeled fully *bad* yet was that she hadn't been able to stop thinking about Grayson.

Maybe she hadn't been fully present while entering the barn with her mind so consumed by him that it sparked an intense reaction. But hadn't she put the night of the fire behind her? Grayson Turner—she shook her head—once again capturing all her attention. She'd tried to ignore their first encounter outside the hospital by focusing on her clients the last couple days and pushing out their next appointments once again. She hadn't wanted to make them wait when they'd already gone without two weeks of sessions, thanks to her "honeymoon," but they all understood the family emergency. Privately, she was a little relieved not to have to dive back into work when her mental state was so tumultuous. How could she offer therapy to others when her own life was falling apart?

Yet at the same time, how many days could she afford to take off? She was on her own now, which hadn't really occurred to her until the day before when she had to finally answer emails and make calls to her clients. She'd decided to reschedule them for another couple of weeks. Hopefully things with her dad would be more resolved by then and she could figure out what to do next. One thing was certain: Keeping that condo in Connecticut wasn't an option on her salary alone, so she would have to talk to Tyler about selling it as soon as possible.

Willow drew in her breath as she rounded a bend on the familiar path, and the memory of Grayson's face crowded out the peaceful scenery around her. What she had hoped would be a restorative hike ended up only making her more agitated. Grayson hardly spent five minutes next to her outside the hospital the other day, and it resulted in two restless nights.

The late-morning sun broke through the cloud cover just as she finished the turn, halting her worries temporarily as its gentle rays lit up the sky at the edge of the cliff. Looking down, she caught her breath when she saw the canvas of unparalleled beauty unfolding. Overlooking the Atlantic from this point never ceased to amaze her and capture her attention as if it were her first time seeing it. Whispers from her past filled her mind as she gazed at the blue water below.

Martha's Vineyard had been her home for her entire upbringing, and as she took in every detail before her, her childhood came alive, overwhelming her with emotion. Casting her eyes across the endless ocean, she tried to push the memories away. But they were everywhere. Endless days passed down on the sand and swimming in the waves as they caressed the shore. Every corner of Terra Cove and the surrounding towns, this trail, and especially . . . the cove. Where both Tyler and Grayson spent all those years with her. Her two very best friends—now her biggest heartbreaks.

Despite the melancholy in her heart since returning home, she had been reminded of all she still had in Terra Cove. A family who loved her and never left her, even when she moved away without looking back.

The sound of a horse's sudden movement broke her trance.

"It's beautiful, isn't it?" The woman on top stroked the horse's neck while taking in the same view and nodding hello toward Willow.

"What a gorgeous horse," Willow said, admiring the mare. Her mother had insisted she take one of their horses for a trail ride, but not yet. She wasn't ready. "May I say hello?"

"Sure. Her name's Bella." The woman smiled down at her as Willow slowly approached them.

"Good morning, Bella." Willow stayed nice and calm while Bella checked her out. When she raised her hand, the mare stayed still, signaling to Willow she felt safe. She ran her hand down Bella's neck, the texture of her soft mane transporting Willow back in time to the countless rides she'd taken growing up.

As she breathed in the horse's stable energy to try to calm herself, tears stung her eyes. She hadn't been around horses in so long. After they lost those horses in the fire, Willow couldn't bring herself to ride. It had always been an outlet, and she was sad she'd let it go, but like many things on this island, riding also brought her right back to Grayson—and the summer they fell in love at fifteen years old. Bittersweet memories filled her as she caught eyes with Bella.

She took a step back from the horse. "Thank you," she said, and the woman gently squeezed her heels to signal the mare onward. Willow stood still, watching them slowly make their way back down the winding trail.

Maybe riding again would provide her with enough clarity to know what to do next. But did she have to know? For years, she'd told her clients in therapy that it was okay not to have answers to their struggles right away. She chuckled at her hypocrisy and tried not to dwell on the fact that she hadn't had any answers either. Her life was in flux now while waiting on her dad's recovery process, pausing work, moving forward after an eight-year relationship, and not to mention battling the repeated memories that hadn't stopped coming since she returned home. Memories of happiness, memories of heartache.

Continuing her hike, Willow braced herself. She knew exactly what she was about to see up ahead as every inch of this trail was still sketched clearly in her mind. She closed her eyes for a moment as her heart thudded against the unmistakable presence of what she was about to encounter and she prepared herself for the first of its outstretched limbs. When the light morning breeze pushed the white oak's familiar, earthy scent around her, Willow could no longer stop the memory that had been trying to flood her thoughts since the beginning of the hike. The morning after the fire . . .

With swift force, she remembered her hand against one of the large winding branches as she desperately tried to steady her breathing. She could almost feel the makeup still on her face from the night before—the makeup her sister had so carefully applied for her senior prom—still washing down her face with each tear, and the heavy pain from her first breakup weighing against her chest. The aftermath of the fire had hit her hard the moment she'd woken, with traces of smoke still lingering in the humid early summer air. And the fact that Grayson hadn't returned any of her calls . . .

Everything Tyler had told her when he was the one to show up instead had suddenly hit her, and she ran out of the house to get some air and landed right here, where she now stood eight years later.

Willow sighed in frustration, racking her brain as to why all these thoughts from her past with Grayson were clouding her mind. She should have been focused on how to move forward from her recent broken engagement to Tyler.

She quickly moved away from the tree and made her way back down the trail, passing the woman and Bella who were taking a break near the bottom.

"Let's head back now. You must be ready to get back. It's been a long ride," the woman said to the horse. The grunt that followed made Willow smile, easing her tension.

"Nova used to answer me like that too," she whispered without a second thought, nearly startling herself. Did she really just say *Nova*? She hadn't thought about that horse in years, but just saying the mare's name instantly yanked her back into the whirlwind of her past.

Her parents' horse farm had always provided her with an ample choice of horses to ride, yet Nova, who belonged to

Tyler's family, was a very special horse to her. His family didn't own a large farm like her parents, there were only a few horses in their small barn. Unlike Grayson, Tyler had grown interested in riding after watching Willow when they were young, and his parents decided to get him a horse of his own—a mare named Nova. The first time Willow met her, she knew the horse was special and she quickly found out why.

The summer they turned fifteen, a couple years after Grayson's alcoholic father abandoned him and his sister, leaving them alone with his mom to finish raising them, Nova was there—and so was she. Not noticing Tyler's annoyance at first that it had to be *his* horse, Willow convinced Grayson to finally give riding a try with Nova. To her surprise after years of never bothering with it, he took to riding fast. The horse's nurturing demeanor was perfect for Grayson as he coped with the changes in his life. Nova became the steady figure he had needed, helping Grayson heal through his sadness—all while he and Willow began to fall in love.

Years later when she and Tyler left the island and settled in college, she used to ask him how Nova was doing, but she stopped when she caught the jealousy cloud over his expression. He'd known she associated the horse with her past with Grayson. In time, Willow eventually stuffed away the horse's memory, just like she did with everything else—until now.

Before she exited the trail, she saw the almost-hidden entrance to another trail, and she stopped. The path led down to the cove just behind Coastal Rock Preserve beach. Her perfect little oasis, nestled between the towering cliffs against the water, that she and both boys had called their own hideaway. With Nova on her mind and their time together with Grayson, an intense wave of nostalgia overtook her, bringing her mind back to a day she hadn't thought about in years. The last happy memory she'd had with Grayson . . .

―――――

"You wouldn't smell so pretty either if you had been shoveling horse stalls all morning!" Willow giggled, giving Grayson a playful shove as they leaned against a large boulder along the sandy cove at the preserve, still wet from their swim.

"Swimming in the ocean hasn't cleaned you up enough for our date tonight, so I better get you home for a proper shower, Ms. Anderson."

"Ha! If you'll even get to take me now." Willow picked up some rocks and threatened to toss them, laughing as he tickled her, causing her to drop them.

She leaned back against him, and they both looked up. "We have to take some photos here tomorrow for prom," Willow said.

"This will be the first place we go after I pick you up." Grayson reached for her hand.

"We need to get pictures here for every special occasion. Since this is where it all began." She closed her eyes, remembering their very first kiss as the waves swelled around the rock.

"Of course we will. It's our cove. Forever."

―――――

Willow stared at the trail's entrance as she returned to the present. How was she going to get her life straightened out if her mind wouldn't give her past a rest? Moving forward, she made her way to the dirt road and was parallel to the pond until she reached one of the entrances to her family's farm. The short distance across the field that led to the house was only a few minutes' walk, but anxiety began to grip her. The late June summer air had quickly changed from the morning's cooler temps, and the heat wasn't helping her nerves.

Moving through the field, she realized she was still caught up in the flashback, trembling as if she were running a marathon in her own skin. Struggling to keep focus while everything around her blurred, she moved her eyes to her feet and slowly paced herself forward, a grounding technique she shared with her clients to help them relax themselves and something she was only trying herself for the first time now. Unfortunately, it didn't seem to work. Another panic attack? She walked a little farther until she reached the barn, then paused outside the gate to think.

"Grayson is just a distraction," she said out loud, her therapist mind quickly making the conclusion. Instead of facing what had just happened to her, she was trying to divert attention away from it. Glancing at the gate, she put her hands on the latch and tugged. This time when she'd looked inside the barn, she felt stronger. "Yes. That is exactly what it must be." Feeling a little steadier, the shaking easing and relief settling in, she nodded. "I can do this. One day at a time."

With a logical answer, Willow made her way toward her parents' house, hoping her reasoning had calmed her enough for her mother not to notice how distraught she'd been. Before her dad's accident, she'd grown tired of talking circles the past couple weeks around possible reasons Tyler had called off their wedding. How could she even begin to tell them that it was Grayson who was gripping her thoughts, not Tyler?

Reaching the front door, she knew one thing: She needed to get herself through the blow, make sure her dad was going to be alright, then move forward. She had clients waiting for her return in Mystic and a life to resume . . . all by herself.

———

The table was already set when Willow entered the kitchen after her shower. Plates of sandwiches and fruit salad. Her mother was standing at the counter, pouring lemonade into glasses, and looked startled when she saw Willow.

"Oh! Willow, you're back." Her mother filled the last glass and set it down.

"A little while ago actually. I just had a shower."

"Well, just in time then." She gestured toward the table. "Chicken salad, just how you love."

"Looks delicious. Thank you, Mom." She sat down and picked at a piece of melon. "But you did not have to go to the trouble or even wait for me to finish my hike. I know you want to get back to Dad."

"I do, but the nurses were insistent that I come home and nap and take care of myself. I tried to nap but couldn't. I showered and then for the first time in days, I felt hungry. So I made us some lunch. How was your hike?"

Willow chewed the melon, focusing on the scenery beyond the window and allowing it to soothe her against the heavy emotions that kept engulfing her. "I forgot how beautiful it is out there."

"Did you make it to the edge and get some good views of the water? How about that cove you always snuck out to with the horses?" Her mom's back was turned as she gathered some napkins to bring to the table—completely unaware of the loaded question.

"What a sight to see you sitting at the table with us," Wesley said, coming into the kitchen and pulling out a chair to sit next to her, saving her from having to answer their mom. He kept his eyes on her, making her stomach sink at the truth of his words, but she stayed silent in response. It was no time to get into the same old argument about how she never visited them. Besides, her brother had a right to feel the way he did.

Mom placed the napkins in the center of the table. "Don't you start on her. She's hardly been here three days. We don't want to scare her off."

"She knows I'm teasing." He picked up a glass of lemonade.

"When did you get here, Wes?" Willow asked and popped another piece of melon into her mouth. "I thought you had to check in at work today since you've had to cancel a few flights?"

"I did that while you were out on your hike, then came here to check on Mom, to make sure she was resting." He looked at their mom and accepted the plate she handed him. "Which she's obviously not doing."

"Oh, I'm fine. Let's just eat and get back to Dad."

Willow took a bite of her sandwich. "You're not wrong, by the way," she told her brother in between bites. "It is probably strange seeing me sitting here." Willow smiled at him but only got a hesitant stare in return. "Did you want to say something else?"

"Well . . ." He took a bite of his sandwich and finished chewing before finally saying, "Have you updated Tyler any more since he was at the hospital?"

"How did you . . ." Willow hadn't told her family that Tyler was at the hospital that first afternoon, and she suddenly wondered if Wesley knew about Grayson being there too.

The sound of glass banging on the counter caught their attention. "Didn't you just buy those glasses, Mom? Let's not break them yet," Wesley said, trying to joke.

Mom whipped around with a frown.

"So Tyler thinks he can just show up whenever he pleases? He still hasn't given you a real reason why he called off the wedding and completely destroyed your life. But that doesn't matter, right? Let's just show up and forget it ever happened!" Her mom threw her arms up.

"Mom . . ." Willow stood and went to comfort her. "I'm not destroyed. Like I've told you a million times already, I will be okay." She put an arm around her and gave her mom a reassuring squeeze. "Focus on Dad and his recovery. Don't worry about me and Tyler."

Mom turned and placed her hands on the counter, giving herself a moment to calm down. "I know you will be okay," she said, looking back at Willow with sad eyes. "But that's not the point."

"The man does owe you a solid explanation," Wesley said, standing up with his now-empty plate. "But I know he eventually will when he's ready." He kissed Mom's cheek. "That was really good. Thank you."

"When *he's* ready? Do you hear yourself?" Mom exploded again, causing Wesley to nearly drop his plate in the sink. "He left her at the altar and hasn't said a word to her besides a five-second phone call and some silly text message! He is not the man I thought he was."

Willow sighed. Her family was still very upset, which was understandable, but the added stress was not good for her mom during such a difficult time. She was most likely on edge because the doctors told her before she came home that they were hoping to wake her dad up soon from his induced coma, and Mom was nervous about it.

"Mom, again, focus on—"

"He made a mistake," Wesley cut in. "But maybe it's for the better. You don't need a man who could do that to you for a husband." He gave her a sheepish grin. "Sorry, Willow. I know this is not helping you. And to answer your question, I knew about Tyler coming by because one of the receptionists was in my high school class."

Willow nodded. Typical Terra Cove, always gossiping.

"I'm going to head out to run a few errands, and then I'll

meet you at the hospital later. Okay, Mom?" Wesley said, leaning in to kiss her cheek.

"Sounds good," their mom said in a slightly calmer tone, then looked at her when Wesley left. "Sorry I shouted."

"Don't apologize," Willow said. "You're under a lot of stress."

"Thanks for understanding." Mom's eyes now reddened. "I'm going to take a few minutes to myself upstairs." She was clearly too upset to continue any conversation.

Willow cleaned up the dishes from lunch, but before she could go check on her mom, her phone lit up on the table.

Seeing Tyler's name still stung, but she answered anyway.

"What is it, Tyler?" she answered in a hushed voice.

"I'm at the gate."

"*What?* Tyler, no. You should not be here, especially with my mom here. She nearly broke a glass in frustration over us only minutes ago. I'm not letting you in."

"Please, Willow. I just want to talk."

She sighed. "Fine. But stay where you are. I will meet you down there."

After hanging up, she racked her brain to figure out what to tell her mom.

"Mom?" she called up the stairs.

"Yes?" Her mom appeared at the top of the stairs, tissues in hand, making Willow feel even worse for lying.

"I forgot to pack some stuff from my bathroom, so I'm going to head to Maggie's Market. Need anything?"

"No, I don't need anything. Wait, Willow?" She attempted a smile. "I'm sorry for all that. Your brother is right. This is not what you need, or me for that matter. I'm just still really sad about how your wedding day ended is all."

"I know, Mom. I'll be back in a bit and maybe we can call the hospital to check on Dad. If he's okay, we can do something relaxing before we go back to see him."

"I'd love that. There is a new nail salon in town. Any interest?"

Willow was never one to dress herself up and be into any of the girly things her sister and her mom liked, but today she would be. "Sounds like a good idea. Maybe Whitney will come too."

The mention of her sister coming perked her mother right up. "I'll go call her!" She dashed off, and Willow quickly made her way outside to meet Tyler.

Grateful for the long driveway that hid the view of Tyler's car, Willow drove up to the gate, opened it, and pulled up next to him with her own car.

"You should have just called me. I don't need to deal with my mom's reaction if she saw you right now. I have to go to the market and get something to bring back. Follow me there, and we can talk."

Willow pulled out onto the road, feeling like a teenager sneaking out with her boyfriend, and rolled her eyes. She couldn't believe that at nearly twenty-seven years old she had to hide Tyler from her family, but the intensity of their situation was too much for her to bear any harsh responses right now.

As quickly as the word *teenager* crossed her mind, so too did Grayson's face. Her pulse picked up its pace, kicking up her confusion. "He's just a distraction," she quietly reminded herself and turned up the music to drown out her thoughts.

The main road into town was stop-and-go with tourists. To pass the time, she found Ivy's name on her dashboard list and hit call. She'd called her friend the day before, but she knew Ivy was probably anxiously awaiting another update.

"Hey!" Ivy answered, her breath heavy.

"You sound out of breath over there." Willow crawled toward a stop light.

"Just moving stuff around the store to prepare for the

Fourth of July sidewalk sale. But I was just thinking about you. How is your dad?"

"The doctors are optimistic. He officially made it through the first forty-eight hours without any further bleeding or other complications, and the swelling is going down. They are hoping to wake him up soon from the induced coma."

"That's really good news. I'm so relieved. Dare I ask about anything else?"

"It's been . . . quite a bit more than I anticipated," Willow said.

"Oh yeah? I take it you've seen Tyler then?"

Willow realized just how much she needed to catch her friend up on, but she'd have to save some of it for another conversation since the market was just ahead. "Yes, I have. But we still haven't really talked yet—just that quick conversation at the hospital I told you about yesterday." She didn't mention that she was about to meet up with Tyler again, because she wasn't sure how the conversation would go. Like her mom, Ivy was mad still. She'd fill her in later, along with everything her friend didn't know yet about the *other* man who was making her homecoming complicated.

"As soon as you do, I need a phone call."

"I know. You will be called right away." Willow sighed through the phone just as the light turned.

"I'm so sorry you have to go through this. I couldn't imagine. He has a lot of explaining to do." Ivy's voice muffled as she directed one of her sales associates on where to put a box, followed by some more sounds in the background. "Sorry for the noise; I'm unpacking new sale signs that just got delivered."

"It's been rough, but I'm glad to be home despite the reason why. It's been nice to see my family."

"That's good to hear, given the stressful circumstances. You needed to go home anyway. It's been long overdue."

Willow pulled into the market parking lot. "Listen, I have to go. Sorry to cut this short. I just missed you and wanted to hear your voice."

"I miss you too, and I'm here anytime you need to talk."

After hanging up, she saw a free parking spot and grabbed it. When she got out, she looked around. Running into people who knew her in Terra Cove was practically a given, but maybe she could escape it with a fast in and out. Tyler found a spot a few spaces down. When she reached him, he was leaning against the driver's side, waiting with a small smile. A part of her wanted to storm past him and forget the entire conversation, but she couldn't.

"Did you come for an update about my dad? I can give you that, and then I have to go."

"Willow . . ." he said, but stopped when she put her hands on her hips. "I need to say this. It was why I showed up at your parents' house—"

"I said, do you want an update, Tyler?" she repeated, narrowing her eyes at him in warning. Yes, they needed to talk, but this was not the place to have that conversation, and after seeing how comfortable he seemed with Grayson in the hospital, she felt uneasy. Like there was something more she needed to know—but not without mentally preparing herself for all she had a feeling she was about to hear.

His gaze lingered on her for a beat before he reluctantly broke eye contact and stared past her at a woman walking by. "Yes."

"He's stable still and made it through the last two nights without any new complications. The doctors are optimistic about taking him out of the induced coma soon. I'm heading back there later this afternoon, so I may have more information then, but again, a phone call would have been just as easy to share all this." With that, she nodded and started to walk toward the market, but he gently grabbed her arm before she shrugged off his grip. "Tyler Parker, this is not the place for this. If you want to talk, then we need to plan it—when my mom isn't waiting on me to return from a short trip to town."

"Willow, I love you!" he blurted, running his hands through his hair before holding them on top of his head in angst.

"You sure have a funny way of showing that!" Now she was yelling and she decided she didn't care who heard. The audacity—to tell her that after what he did astounded her.

"Willow, please." He lowered his arms and pointed to his car. "Let's get in my car. I need to get this out."

Curious shoppers whispered as they walked by, slowing down to hear more.

"I'm not getting in your car," she said, taking a step toward him as anger boiled, ignoring what she'd previously said about planning this discussion. It *would* be smarter to talk somewhere else, somewhere more private, but she was too angry to let this drop. "If you have something to say, then just say it right here. Why did you call off our wedding?" Her jaw burned from biting down so hard as she waited for his answer.

"Tyler!" A voice startled them both, and when they turned, Willow saw a man she recognized from one of Tyler's work events at their Cape Cod location. He stopped short when he noticed her. "Willow . . . Hi. I didn't know you were in town." He looked nervously at Tyler. "I didn't mean to interrupt."

"It's okay, Sam. I'll call you in a bit."

"No need. I just wanted to let you know that I had a conversation with Grayson, and everything is all set for Monday's meeting when he starts his vacation. And I just got word that Ralph is recovering well from his surgery, which is good news." Sam glanced at Willow as he was leaving. "Good to see you."

Too stunned to respond, she looked at Tyler. "What does

he mean he talked to Grayson? When he starts *what* vacation?"

"We have a lot to discuss." Tyler nervously looked at Sam just as the man turned to leave. "Let's go sit in my car and talk. Please, Willow."

"Does Grayson . . . *work* with you?" Her eyes grew wide with disbelief, her uneasy feeling proven correct. Tyler's hesitation was enough of an answer. "And when were you going to tell me this? What else have you been keeping from me?"

"Nothing!"

His sudden outburst had her immediately questioning his response. Why did he look so guilty? "I don't believe you . . ."

He stepped toward her, which only ignited her anger further. "Willow, you know me. I—"

"Apparently, I don't know you at all. Don't you dare follow me." Tears now streaming down her face, she stormed off.

For eight years Grayson had been out of their lives. Or so she *thought*. And in so many ways, Tyler was the reason the break had been so complete. He'd gotten jealous any time she brought up anything connected to Grayson, and eventually, she'd just . . . stopped. As the years built up, so did the silence.

It was Tyler who pushed her to drop him completely from their lives. And now this? Telling her it was best they just let Grayson go and to keep her distance from him. All while he was secretly working with him?

Without even going inside the market, she left and decided to take the long way back home. Her mom would surely notice she came back empty-handed, but at this point, none of that mattered.

What did matter, she decided as she drove along the road that hugged the shoreline, the ocean breeze whipping through her hair after she rolled the window down to breathe it in, was trying to understand which man she was truly crying over.

CHAPTER SIX

The knock at his door was louder the second time. Grayson had stepped out of the shower and dried off as fast he could after the first faint knock. When he reached the bottom of the stairs, he peeked out the window and saw his mom's car.

He patted Monty who was already facing the door. "I know you hear her." The dog's tail wagged excitedly as he circled Grayson's legs before Grayson swung open the door. "Hey, Mom."

Her grin spread quickly. "Good morning!"

"Come on in." He moved aside for her. "I just made a fresh pot of coffee before my shower. How'd you know I'd be home on a Monday morning?"

"I saw Jesse at the gas station last night, and she told me you were taking a couple weeks off? You never told me." His mother stepped through the door, holding a shopping bag, and he led her to the kitchen. Monty excitedly followed them, sniffing the bag.

"Yeah, it's been so long since I took a vacation that it

didn't feel real." He chuckled, glancing down at her. "What were you up to, out on a Sunday evening?"

His mom's face reddened. "I was with Daniel . . ."

Grayson waggled his eyebrows. "Oh yeah?"

"Stop it." She smiled shyly. "I'm glad to see you taking time off finally."

Seeing her light up with such happiness was wonderful to witness. "Me, too, except I don't know what to do with myself." Monty kept his nose glued to the bag, nearly making his mom fumble over him. Grayson snapped his fingers once, and the dog obediently lay down.

"I love how well you've trained him." She smiled down at Monty who was not moving from his position, but his eyes stayed on the bag. "And you'll fill in the time. It's Martha's Vineyard, after all. Plenty to do." The first thing she pulled out of her bag once she'd placed it on the kitchen table were chocolate peanut butter cups. "Here, eat these so I don't. They are left over from last night. They are Daniel's favorite." She paused, looking content in thought. "We used to—" She stopped herself, but he didn't press her. How happy she looked told him enough.

Her seeing Daniel was relatively a new thing, and he was truly pleased for them—even if Tyler wasn't. It had been so long since Grayson found out Daniel was his biological father, but the reality of it still caught him off guard. Maybe because for a long time after the news broke, his mother continued to keep her distance from Daniel and gave him time to process his divorce from Tyler's mom. All while his own mom was still emotionally healing from how bad her marriage to Jack had been. More recently, both she and Daniel seemed ready to move on—with each other.

"What else did you bring?" Grayson nodded toward the bag.

"I picked up your favorite from the café at Edgartown

Books. An heirloom tomato, egg, and scallion cream cheese breakfast sandwich."

"Thank you," he said and poured them both coffee before sitting down. His mother pulled out his sandwich and one she'd gotten for herself.

"Have you seen Abby lately?" she asked him, opening the paper the sandwich was wrapped in.

"Not in a few weeks. I know she's been busy with work." His sister had just been promoted from a news assistant to reporter for *The Vineyard Times*. "Her hours are all over the place now. Why do you ask?"

"She called me yesterday to see if I had any updates about Liam Anderson, but she had also heard a little rumor that you and Willow were seen talking outside the hospital the day we went. Must've been right after I left." She took a bite of her sandwich, and her gaze flickered with curiosity while she chewed.

"Well, isn't she already the top island reporter?" Grayson laughed, putting his sandwich down to take a sip of coffee. "How'd she even hear that?"

"I asked her the same thing and all she said was she had 'connections everywhere.' She's already sounding like a reporter for sure."

"Well, she's right. I did talk to Willow outside the hospital."

"And?"

"And nothing. I talked, then she talked." Grayson shrugged, and his mom rolled her eyes as he picked up his sandwich.

"Don't be coy with me, Grayson Turner. This is Willow we're talking about." His mother leaned forward like she was bracing herself for some intense news, but there wasn't any juicy gossip to tell. Their first conversation was a flop in his mind, and he was still beating himself up over it.

"We didn't say much. It was like two strangers making small talk. Honest." He sat back against his mother's questioning stare. "I went outside to check on her because her conversation with Tyler in the waiting area looked stressful, which is understandable considering what just happened between them. Once I was next to her . . . Mom, I don't know. I just . . ."

"Got overwhelmed?" she said. If anyone knew how much pain losing Willow had caused him, it was his mother. She was there by his side the first few months after graduation when Willow took a celebratory trip with her family to Europe for a month—a much needed break for the whole family after that devastating fire. She'd urged him to go after her when she'd returned from Europe before she left for college, but he didn't, and ever since, that decision sat heavy on his heart.

"Yes, exactly. I lost my words once she looked at me. I had practiced what to say to her for years if I ever saw her again, and my mind went blank."

"I feel bad about the way I ran past her in the hospital," his mother said, crumpling a napkin on top of her nearly finished sandwich.

"You did?"

"Yes, I did. I was chatting with Tyler right before you came back from the bathroom. I got so nervous when I saw her."

"I'm sure it's no big deal. None of us were in our right state of mind because of the accident."

His mom reached over from under the table and patted his knee. "Then you shouldn't beat yourself up for not saying what you had planned. It's not like you prepared for seeing her again under such circumstances. I'm sure she appreciated the gesture of you coming at all."

"Or she couldn't get away from me fast enough." Grayson blew out some air and set his sandwich down again. "Which was how it appeared."

"Grayson, give yourself a break. I know it was hard. It was hard for all of us, probably for Tyler, too, especially with what just happened between him and Willow, even though he brought that upon himself—"

"Then the same goes for me." He cut in. "As far as I know, she still thinks I wanted to dump her on prom night out of nowhere after four years together. I broke her heart too."

"I remember alright, but what I'm trying to say is . . . It's clear you still care about Willow. She's finally back in Terra Cove, and that means there's still time to see her again and talk to her. I feel like I need to do the same. When she saw me at the hospital, she didn't exactly look happy, which was why I got so nervous. I figured I'd made a mistake going and dashed off."

"I almost did too, but I ended up following her outside when she walked out. I'd love to talk to her again, but only if she wants to. I'm not asking for her back. That's probably the last thing she'd ever want, but I just don't want another eight years of silence. We've known each other since we were babies. That has to mean something."

"Of course it does."

"Well, I'm not going to push her." Grayson shrugged. "If I see her again, I'll judge then how she responds. She has a lot on her plate with her dad and this mess she's in with Tyler."

"So I take it he hasn't talked to her yet?" The Turner family did not attend the wedding; however, his family all knew how it ended. Everyone who lived on the island knew.

"I don't think so . . ." He shifted forward. "And there's more. Willow had no idea I worked for the brewery and had been working with Tyler all this time."

"What? She was *engaged* to him. She didn't know you are the head of operations?"

Grayson nodded. "A coworker ran into them outside of Maggie's Market and told me her face went red when he mentioned my name and my vacation time. And she still doesn't know about you and Daniel and—"

His mother's mouth gaped; her eyes widened as she sat back in silence for a moment.

"She doesn't . . ." Mom could barely get the words out. "She doesn't know? Are you *serious*? Does Daniel know this?"

"I don't know. I think if Tyler doesn't clear things up and face her with the truth, then I might need to."

"I don't understand why he'd keep that from her. Or you, for that matter. One of you should have told her this long before now."

"I know."

"It's strange to learn she's been in the dark with this." Mom crossed her arms, glancing up toward the ceiling for a moment. "You know, I never knew Willow's parents very well, so I never spoke to them about any of this either. When the truth came out, I pulled away even more."

"I know you did, but there's no need to hide the past anymore."

Her face relaxed. "No, I suppose not. It's wild to me that the entire town of Terra Cove doesn't know by now. Even Daniel's ex-wife didn't say anything."

"I don't think she's even come back to visit since she moved to New Jersey and remarried. I know she and Daniel had their ups and downs during their divorce, but Daniel did tell me once that his ex didn't want to stir up any trouble for Tyler with this news back then, so she kept quiet about it. Which is probably a good thing in this small, nosey town."

"Daniel and I have never talked about that before."

Grayson chuckled. "Discussing his ex-wife is probably not good dinner talk while out on dates."

"This is all too much." His mother shook her head. "And I'm partly to blame."

"I meant what I said." He reached for her hand. "No more

hiding. Besides, I like that you are talking to Daniel and seeing him. You seem . . . livelier."

A glint of excitement lifted her expression. "You know, it was great seeing him last night."

"I hope it continues."

"And I hope it continues with Willow." She squeezed his hand before standing up. "I wish I could stay longer, but I have to get going. I have some errands to run."

"And I better get started on my first day off." He thought about the soap shack. "Guess what I might do?"

"Hmm . . . kayak? Surf? You haven't done either in a long time." She walked with him to the front door.

"Actually, speaking of kayaking, I reached out to Willow's brother after I got home from the hospital that day. We're going camping and kayaking the weekend of the Fourth." He kept the part about spilling the truth to Wesley to himself as he didn't exactly have that plan all figured out yet or know how he'd even begin that conversation. Besides, their camping trip was more than just sharing the truth about his parentage. Grayson was tired of the distance that continued to grow between them after being such close friends.

"You are? That's wonderful you two are reconnecting. I remember how much you both loved doing that together."

Grayson looked away in thought, imagining he and Wesley gliding across the pond—just like the old days. The ocean was always spectacular to be near, but the island offered over a dozen great ponds all throughout the island, making it perfect for kayaking. "Yeah, I'm looking forward to it."

"I don't mind keeping Monty for the weekend while you two catch up and camp."

"That would be great." He looked back at his mom. "It would save me a lot of money from having to hire a dog walker for two days. Thanks, Mom. And surfing isn't a bad idea either. My surfboard definitely has cobwebs on it, but it would be fun to get out on the waves. But what I was referring to isn't as exciting as either of those. I'm thinking about clearing out around the outside and inside of that old soap shack of yours."

"Oh yeah? What will you do with it?"

"Not sure yet, but something is pushing me to finally do it."

She kissed his cheek. "Good luck with that; it's probably a disaster in there. I always assumed you'd knock it down. But I know you'll do something great with it."

He watched from the doorway as dirt spun up behind her car until she was gone. Then he stepped out onto the driveway and faced the path that led toward the soap shack. It was overgrown with weeds, and his mom was right. He really had no idea what kind of clean-up he would face inside it, but he meant what he'd told her. Something had sparked him to clear it out, so it was time to get started.

———

TUESDAY MORNING ARRIVED WITH OVERCAST SKIES and dense humidity. This summer was proving to be hotter than normal, but that only made tourist season busier—which meant good business for the brewery. Grayson was still a little torn about taking time off in the middle of it all, but the time away from the office, and particularly Tyler, was genuinely needed to clear his head.

Grayson woke later than usual, but after a day of clearing weeds and assessing what equipment he'd need to effectively clean up the area around the shack, he'd needed the extra sleep.

He took his coffee to the back deck and sat down to think about the day ahead. Monty sat next to him enjoying the view, until something caught his eye and the dog sprinted down the steps to chase whatever it was he'd seen.

"Leave the animals alone, boy!" He whistled and Monty came padding back up the deck stairs. A gust of wind moved the thick air around. "The waves today will probably be good for surfing." He thought about his mom's comment the day before and clicked on his phone to check the wave reports. Just as he suspected—perfect for surfing. Monty barked. "Why not? It's my time off and Mom was right. We live on Martha's Vineyard, which means vacation year-round. Time to ride those waves."

An hour later, he had his surfboard tucked under his arm, his wetsuit on, and was standing in Squibnocket Beach, one of his old favorite spots to go surfing, since it was a private beach for residents. A thrill ran down his back as he held his board, observing the waves. Two other surfers were already out in the water. It had been at least a year since he'd gone himself, and watching them glide on their boards made Grayson's body spring into action.

The ocean's energy propelled him toward the breakers as salty spray misted his face. When the perfect wave approached, like a towering wall of blue-green water, its crest glistening, he popped up onto his board and onto the wave's shoulder. The wind blew through his hair and the rush of exhilaration was intoxicating as he danced across the water. Every worry seemed to dissolve in the white water behind him as he cruised. It was the perfect escape and something he needed to make more time for. Whether he was surfing or kayaking, the ocean was his therapy.

The skies darkened a couple hours later, and the wind picked up as cooling rain began to fall, bringing relief to the sticky air. Grayson dashed to the truck, pulled off his wetsuit, tossed it in the back along with his board, and hopped into the driver's seat to towel off some more. The dry clothes he'd brought instantly warmed him as he started the truck, and clicked the windshield wipers on high against the rain that was now pouring down in buckets.

After honking at the other surfers he'd gotten to chat with a bit before the storm hit, he waved and headed to town to grab lunch at Stella's. When he arrived, the line wasn't long—probably because of the weather—and he was able to get a parking spot right in front. He quickly made his way under the awning and got behind the other patrons. Stella's was a popular outdoor seafood restaurant and had the best fish-and-chips on the island in his opinion. After he ordered, he stepped aside to wait.

"Hey, Grayson," a male voice said from behind him, and when he turned, Tyler stood there holding a take-out bag.

"Tyler, how's it going?"

"Fine. How's your week off been so far?"

"Just went surfing, so it's going well." Grayson shoved his hands into his pockets, trying not to look irritated. Making small talk with Tyler was the last thing he wanted to do while waiting on his order.

"Did you? Wow. When's the last time you did that?" Even though they rarely talked outside of work, Tyler managed to know a lot about his life. Looking at the man who once was his very best friend for most of his life, now reduced to barely an acquaintance, Grayson suddenly wished it didn't have to be that way. Despite what had happened the night of prom, he missed his friend. A part of him wanted to make amends, just like Daniel had wanted for his two sons, but so much had happened since Tyler and Willow left Terra Cove—together, as a couple—and he wasn't sure how everything could be resolved at this point.

"About a year. Getting up on my board again felt amazing."

"I bet." Tyler moved the bag to his other arm. "I better get going. I was just with my dad. We have some work to do before we make a trip over to the Cape Cod location tomorrow for the day."

You mean our dad? Grayson clenched his jaw. "So it's busier than usual this week?"

"A little. It's just busy work, but I better go." Tyler turned to leave but Grayson grabbed his free arm to stop him.

"Tyler . . ." Grayson gave him a stern look and lowered his voice so the other customers couldn't eavesdrop as easily. A few familiar residents were already watching them, including a mutual friend from childhood, Ethan Bradley, who looked away when Grayson noticed him. "I meant what I said the other night. Tell Willow the truth."

Tyler didn't say anything. Instead he gave Grayson a long stare before he walked away. Grayson's number was called soon, and after he gave Ethan a quick hello, he took his food back to the truck. Tyler's silent response only drove his irritation deeper as he pulled out of the parking lot and headed home. He couldn't wait for his camping trip with Wesley. This secret couldn't go on much longer.

Chapter Seven

The flash of lightning outside the window in her dad's hospital room caught Willow's attention, but as the rumble of thunder boomed, she turned her attention back to the medical team gathered around his bedside. His eyes fluttered open again. No one else in her family noticed the Tuesday afternoon storm and they all joined hands while they waited for the doctors to finish their checks.

Almost an entire week had passed since his accident, but it seemed like years. Or perhaps it only felt like that since she truly hadn't been back in years. After her argument with Tyler outside Maggie's Market, her life had been a whirlwind as she helped her family sort out the duties on the farm. The horses were always Dad's job, with a little help from Willow and her siblings when they were growing up. But now that they were all adults with careers and lives separate from the horse farm, her dad ran it solo other than a couple part-time stable hands and another trainer he hired here and there. The good news was that business had continued to be successful. Every stall in Anderson Stables was filled.

After the fire, Dad worked hard to rebuild his barn and his reputation. In time, he'd became known again across the islands and the Cape for his skill in training horses. However, their thriving family farm would need to hire extra workers for the next stretch of time while he was recovering and her mom was spending most of her time at the hospital with him. Willow was glad she was there to help out, especially since Wesley couldn't easily find other pilots to fill in for him, and Whitney had small children to care for.

Rain pounded on the roof and windows, drowning out the beeping of the machines that kicked up with Dad just beginning to wake. He was hooked up to so many wires that he was still hardly recognizable. Willow fought the tears that threatened to escape. Her dad had always been such a strong man, and seeing him so vulnerable was the hardest part for her.

"Remember what we talked about in the hallway?" asked the neurologist overseeing his case. Whitney put her arm around their mom who was wiping tears as they washed down her face. Mom was nervous and so was Willow, but she needed to stay strong for her.

"I do," Mom said, barely above a whisper. "This is a slow process." The doctor motioned for her to come toward him. It had been two days since they started reducing the sedatives, and today the family was called in because his eyes finally opened.

"Liam, my darling. It's me," Mom said as she sat in the chair next to him and picked up his hand.

Whitney stifled a sob as she watched their parents and her husband, Jason, put his hands on her sister's shoulders to steady her. Wesley came over to Willow and took her hand as their dad continued to silently look around the room. The doctors had informed them thoroughly about how this process would probably go, how long it may take to hear him speak, and they were pleased with how he was progressing, especially now that his eyes were open.

Each of her siblings took turns talking with him in a calm and reassuring tone. When it was Willow's turn, she sat down in the same seat her mom had been in and swallowed the lump that kept pushing up and the tears that continued to build.

"Dad? It's me, Willow."

Liam made a slight grunting noise, and Willow sat back in surprise.

The doctor walked over to the other side of the bed. "It's okay, this is a good thing," the doctor whispered toward her. As she looked back down at her dad's face, her tears finally spilled when she saw that he was looking directly at her.

"I'm home, Dad." She stood up and leaned over him to kiss his forehead. "And I'm not leaving until you are running circles around the farm again."

After a few more minutes, the doctor advised that they leave him to rest again. Too much stimulation could stress him this early in his waking up. Out in the waiting room area, her niece, Maya, and nephew, Brandon, were sitting with Jason's mother.

"Aunty Willow!" Maya jumped off her seat and ran to her.

"How's my little mini-me?" Willow bent down and scooped her up, burying her face in her niece's curls that matched her own. When Maya was born, she came out of the womb with a head full of thick curls the color of honey, just like Willow's. It surprised everyone that she didn't get her parents' brown hair, and ever since, Willow referred to her niece as her "mini-me."

Just thinking about that made her eyes sting, reminding her yet again that she hadn't been by Whitney's side after the birth. Maya looked at her with big brown eyes that she got from her dad with such adoration. Even though she was unaware of Willow's absence at the time, the unconditional love and acceptance that her niece showered her with helped ease the painful regret.

"Did you see Grandpa? Is he still asleep?" Maya asked, looking past Willow toward the door to her dad's room.

"I sure did," Willow said, and Whitney came over, holding Brandon on her hip.

"Can I go see him?" Maya asked her mom. At four and one, her niece and nephew didn't understand much of what was going on, but Maya at least understood that her grandpa had gotten hurt.

"Grandpa needs to rest a little longer, then you and your brother can see him," Whitney said, taking Maya's hand with her free one. "It's getting close to dinner. How about some pizza?"

"Only if Aunty Willow comes!" Maya looked up at Willow with pleading eyes.

"Of course I'll come." Willow laughed as Maya jumped up and down with excitement.

"Excuse me, little miss?" Wesley cleared his throat and bent down. "I think you forgot an invite."

Maya giggled and touched his face. "You can come too, Uncle Wes."

"Alright! Pizza it is! Let's go!" Wesley stood back up and started to march off in an exaggerated fashion, pulling their mom to do the same. "You, too, Grandma. Pizza time!"

Maya let go of Whitney's hand and copied her uncle, laughing hysterically now. Even baby Brandon smiled and clapped.

"Maybe we can bring Grandpa back a piece?" Maya looked up at Willow's mom.

"Hmm . . . I'm not sure the doctors will let him have pizza yet, but I'll tell you what . . ." Her mother swung her arms, joining them as they marched along, with Wesley leading the way. "Once he is out of the hospital, pizza will be the first thing we go get for him."

"Yay! Pizza twice!" Maya jumped again.

Willow smiled as the family made their way outside. Despite how long it'd been and everything that had happened—it was good to be home.

———

"I'M SO HAPPY TO HAVE MY SISTER BACK," WHITNEY said the next day, looping her arm through Willow's as they made their way down Terra Cove's main street. Filled with independent small businesses and a few brand name stores, it was the best shopping area on the island. Boutique clothing, art galleries, home décor, souvenir shops, and coastal outfitters lined the street. The sun was shining brightly and since it was the middle of tourist season, shoppers were plentiful for early afternoon. The people who passed them were smiling and enjoying themselves as they bobbed in and out of stores.

Willow laughed. "And where exactly did I go?"

"You know what I mean." Her sister gave her a playful nudge. "Having you back home."

"I'm happy to be here with you too. It's been quite a visit so far."

After Willow had checked on the horses that morning, she'd gone for a nice long swim in the pool before meeting Whitney for lunch and shopping. They walked inside a clothing store and started to browse the sales rack. Willow was stuffed from lunch and wanted to walk it off with a little retail therapy.

Her sister glanced at her with a worried expression. "It's been quite a *month*. We both needed this day of fun, and I'm happy Mom is taking time to be with Maya and Brandon."

Whitney looked through a few shirts. "And I hope being home has helped you cope with the breakup."

"Yes and no," Willow said truthfully. "Being with you and the kids and Wesley and Mom has definitely helped. Even sitting with Dad as he's waking up has too, but I've been avoiding everything else. Which I knew would happen by coming here and having my family to hide behind. Not to mention Dad's accident. That has pulled a lot of my focus away from my own life." While her dad still wasn't fully coherent yet, just seeing his eyes open the day before had brought them all such relief. He wasn't out of the woods, but his progress continued each day.

Whitney sighed and picked up another shirt to study. "I feel like it was time for you to face it, and I don't mean just Tyler. Eight years away from home was too long. And before you start in on me, I'm not ignoring what happened that night with the fire. It was terrible for all of us. But by not coming home, even for visits, it felt like you blamed us in a way."

"Yeah . . ." Willow swallowed. She knew her family hadn't been happy about her staying away, but Whitney hadn't quite expressed it like that before. Maybe she had been inadvertently blaming her family in order to hide. While going into the barn and helping with the horses had become easier as the days passed, Willow realized she should have done this years ago. "I can see why you felt that way."

"Sorry, we're supposed to be having fun. I shouldn't have said that." Whitney moved down the clothes rack.

"It's okay. This needs to come out."

"Yes, it does, Therapist Willow." Her sister flashed her a cheeky grin. "Couldn't help it."

Willow chuckled. "I deserve that. I should've known better after all, as a therapist, and looked at things from your perspective. I was in my own bubble." She paused her own browsing and glanced at Whitney. "I'm real sorry, Sis."

"You're here now, so we move forward."

"Yes, that's what we do." She eyed her sister, wondering if it was a good idea to bring up Grayson, but since Ivy didn't know about him yet, she wanted to talk to someone. "But seeing Grayson the other day has made moving forward feel like a giant shove backward."

"I'm sorry I didn't talk to you about seeing him last week at the hospital, but between visiting Dad, Maya's ballet camp, and Brandon coming down with that summer cold, it's been a week so far. Sometimes I think it's busier when I'm off teaching for the summer with the kids versus during school year."

Willow had immediately told Whitney about seeing Grayson when she'd gone back inside the hospital that day, but so much had been going on, they hadn't talked about it in detail yet. Her first conversation with Grayson had been awkward, to say the least. Despite how busy she'd been with taking care of the stables and figuring out her clients, every-thing about him had lingered in her thoughts for the past week. The way he'd fumbled his words, the stolen glances back and forth, but even more than that, she'd been struck by a sudden longing to collapse into his arms—as if eight years and a whole other relationship had never taken place.

"It's okay. I know mom life is busy. It was just . . . Seeing him." Willow chewed her lip, pretending to be interested in a maxi dress so she could gather the right words.

She'd so badly wanted to tell Whitney how good he still looked, how caring he still was to come find her like he did, and the way his eyes found hers, sending her heart back to where it left him all those years ago. Her strong emotions had her head spinning ever since. Despite her expertise as a thera-pist—she had no idea what to do with her feelings. What would she tell one of her clients in this situation? She still didn't have an answer to that question and turned from the dress.

"It was interesting," she finally said and noticed Whitney had stopped flicking through the clothes and was watching her. "And we didn't really talk about much."

"Why don't I believe you? When you sat back down next to me in the hospital and whispered that you'd just talked to Grayson, you had nothing but pure astonishment all over your face."

Willow winced and looked over her shoulder to make sure no one she knew was near them. Whitney knew her better than that, but their encounter really was short and to the point.

"I'm serious. He came out to see if I was okay. But before he could really say anything, I left."

"I don't blame you, but . . ." Whitney touched her arm and leaned closer to look her in the eyes. "Do you *want* to see Grayson again while you're here?"

Her stomach twisted in knots at the question, and her mind and heart went into an instant battle over an answer. Seeing Grayson and perhaps patching up their abrupt ending from eight years ago felt like a good thing, yet she was cautious at the same time—ignoring the fact that her heart seemed to want her to scream yes.

"I think . . ." Which answer should she give? Her sister would know if she was lying, so she decided the truth was best. "I think I do."

Surprisingly, her sister lit up, then cupped her smile with her hands. "Okay, I know that shouldn't excite me, considering you just got out of a relationship with Tyler, but honestly, Willow, everyone in this town would have the same reaction as me." They moved around the sale section, letting other shoppers have a look. "I know, I know. You two were old

news from years ago, but it's hard to forget. You and Grayson"
—Whitney shook her head—"were something."

"You're right, that shouldn't excite you at all." Willow brought her voice to a whisper. "Whitney, I was *engaged* less than a month ago."

"You know I supported your relationship with Tyler," Whitney whispered back, "but you also know how I feel about you and Grayson, how I've *always* felt."

Her sister didn't have to explain further because Willow did know. Especially since Tyler proposed, Whitney had become louder with her concerns about her and Tyler, sharing over and over that they didn't seem truly happy together. Her parents also had mentioned it to her from time to time. In fact, the more she thought about it, it occurred to her that Wesley had too. Did she really seem that unhappy?

"I know, but this feels like it's going to turn into a bigger mess. I think it's perfectly fine that I want to see Grayson again, but that's because of all the unresolved issues from our past. I don't want to hide from him or Terra Cove anymore. But getting excited about it . . . will just make everything more confusing. Please don't make this a bigger deal than it needs to be."

"I can respect that, and besides, both Tyler *and* Grayson owe you a conversation. Two men who were your closest friends, both loving you and then—"

"I don't want to talk about this anymore in here." Willow looked at the door. "Let's go check out the rack I saw at the store across the street."

Whitney didn't say another word about it. She must have sensed Willow was maxed out on heavy conversation. The rest of their shopping trip was filled with lighter topics and the sisters found themselves giggling as they joked around each store. It was a perfect day to de-stress after such a hard week.

———

WHILE THEY WERE TAKING A BREAK ON A BENCH IN the shade with milkshakes from their favorite ice-cream shop, Willow saw a missed call from Ivy.

"Ivy called. It's the second time since last night and I haven't called her back yet. She's probably just checking in. Mind if I give her a quick call?" Willow held up her phone and Whitney stood.

"No problem. I'm going to head to the general store down the street. They always have great deals on party stuff like paper plates and cups. I need to get some for our Fourth of July pool-side barbecue at Mom and Dad's."

"We're still having a barbecue with Dad in the hospital?" Willow asked.

"I originally didn't want to, but Mom insisted, especially for the kids. She said she would join after she spends some time with Dad, but for us to go ahead and have some fun."

Their parents normally hosted a small barbecue and swimming party every Fourth of July with a few close friends and their family. Willow instantly looked forward to finally not missing it this year. After Whitney walked away, she called Ivy who practically answered on the first ring.

"There you are!" Ivy said.

"I'm sorry I didn't call you back last night. It was a long day helping with the horses." Which wasn't a lie. "And visiting my dad who is still waking up. He opened his eyes yesterday."

"Oh, Willow, I'm so relieved to hear this."

"Me too. But I had a headache by the end of all that yesterday and went to bed early once I got home from the hospital." That part she fibbed, but she kept the pizza restaurant part out so Ivy wouldn't feel ignored, especially with how worried she had been and feeling helpless in Connecticut.

"It's okay. I just wanted to make sure you were alright. I know the horses are probably a lot of work though."

"They are. Definitely more physical labor than seeing my clients."

"Wait . . . physical labor. Does this mean you've ridden?"

A rush of emotions got the better of her with the question. Even though Ivy didn't know about Grayson yet, or just how deep the scars from the barn fire that night still lay in Willow, she at least knew how getting back on a horse had been too difficult for her.

"Not yet, but I'm working on it." She really hadn't been, as helping to take care of them was hard enough for now, but Ivy would push her to try knowing she was now surrounded by horses daily.

"That's great to hear. I take it then, that with your parents needing your help, you'll be home for a while?"

Willow paused and realized she didn't have an answer. "To be honest, I really don't know. I'm kind of taking it day by day."

"I understand. Remember, you and Tyler have that condo to figure out too."

Willow watched a couple walk by, holding hands and content in their world. It felt like a slap in the face when her life was all over the place. "For now, he gave it to me, but I can't afford it on my own. I'm going to tell him we need to list it to sell."

"Better do that soon."

"Yeah, I need to at least get that conversation with him over with as soon as possible."

"By that statement, I'm assuming you still haven't talked to him?"

"Not beyond an argument we had in a parking lot last week."

"Oh no, really? I'm sorry you had to deal with that. I wish

you two would just talk it out, figure out the condo, and move on from each other."

Hearing Ivy say that made her sad. Like Grayson, Tyler was a special part of her upbringing. Just because things didn't work out with either man romantically didn't mean she wanted to move on from her friendships with them completely. Maybe she was being overzealous, but a part of her was still nostalgic about when their trio was best buds. Or maybe it was because being back home in Terra Cove kept her in memory lane. Those days were long gone.

"I'll fill you in as soon as more comes. I know I'm absolutely not going anywhere until my dad is much more stable."

"That's understandable. Well, I better get back to closing up this shop."

"I'll talk to you soon."

Willow hung up and was starting to make her way to the general store when she ran right into someone. When she looked up, she saw Gracie, an old friend from childhood, who had moved away just before they started high school.

"Gracie, hi . . ." Willow said and noticed the woman's eyebrows scrunch together. "You may not remember me—"

"Willow Anderson?" Gracie pulled her to the side to let people walk by them. "Of course I remember you. I heard you were in town." She threw her arms around Willow, and the hug from an old friend felt good. "And I also heard about your dad. I am so sorry. Ethan and I have been praying for him. How is he?"

"Thank you. He's recovering, slowly, but the good news is that he is making progress each day. Did you say Ethan? As in, Ethan Bradley who—"

"Yup!" She held up her hand with her engagement and wedding rings.

"Wow! That's so wonderful!" Willow smiled at her old

friend, ignoring the pang of guilt that shook her for not knowing this news already.

"I was just heading to my barre class, but how long will you be in town?"

"Not entirely sure. But I'm here until my dad is much better."

"Great! Let's try to catch up at some point," Gracie said, eyeing her. "You know, speaking of Ethan, he saw Tyler and Grayson at Stella's yesterday. I'm so sorry to learn what happened between you and Tyler." She frowned before continuing. "But Ethan told me they looked upset about something he couldn't quite make out. I hope everything is alright."

"Oh . . . I'm not sure what they were upset about. It was probably just work-related stress." Willow was guessing, but secretly she was just as concerned as Gracie.

"Hmm . . . maybe. Whatever it was, Ethan said they both looked irritated."

"They are probably fine by now. Who knows what they were bickering about." Willow shrugged, and Gracie's face instantly lifted.

"It was good to see you." Gracie leaned in for another hug.

"You too."

Willow walked into the general store and tried to shake off what Gracie had told her. She had no desire to get into another conversation with her sister about either of the men for the rest of the day. Whitney waved at her from the check-out line, holding a basket filled with all kinds of Fourth of July paper goods for the barbecue.

"I hit the jackpot with all this and it's half off today." Whitney pointed to the basket. "Mom just called and said Brandon woke from his nap a little weak still from his cold and asking for me. I think it's time to end our sisters' day out."

That was fine by Willow. All she could think about now

was what Tyler and Grayson could have been arguing about. She pulled her phone out to send a message and paused on Tyler's name. If he had wanted to share, he would have called her about it already. It must not have concerned her, and they did work together after all—something she'd still been trying to get used to.

When they got in Whitney's car, she was happily chatting about the barbecue and Willow began to relax again. Whatever the men's problem, it was their issue.

Chapter Eight

After spending the following Tuesday morning clearing an overgrown bush from outside the door of the soap shack, Grayson paused before going into Liam's hospital room and wiped dirt off his jeans. Sweat beaded at his forehead and he had no choice but to wipe it with his t-shirt.

June had given way to July, and the summer heat settled right into the new month. He had rented a brush mower for the weekend and made a huge dent in the weeds around the shack. Most of the road leading up to it was also cleaned up. He was about to start on the next brush pile when he received a phone call from Liam, asking him to please come see him as soon as possible now that they had moved him out of the ICU. Too stunned to shower and change clothes, he'd hopped right into his truck and headed to the hospital. It was the first time Liam had contacted him since high school.

Liam was scowling at the nurse administering his medicine just as Grayson walked into the room. Running Anderson Stables required a lot of hard work and to be tied down in a hospital bed on medications must be the last thing the man had patience for.

"There you go, Mr. Anderson. All done. I know you don't want to take all that, but managing the pain and swelling is our main focus right now." The nurse smiled brightly and nodded at Grayson before wheeling her cart out.

He'd heard through the gossip chains that after nearly a week since coming out of the medical coma, Willow's dad was talking and had lost none of his memory. All good improvement, according to the doctors. He had yet to get out of bed, so they weren't sure of the extent of the injury to his back yet, which was their biggest worry after the head damage.

"I can't take one more pill." Liam folded his arms across his chest, his tone gruff.

"I can imagine, sir. Hopefully you won't be here too much longer, especially once they get you moving and out of this bed. I saw the doctor out in the hallway." Grayson took a seat next to him. "He saw me walking toward your door and said he'd be here in a few minutes."

"You know I hated when you called me sir back then, and I still do." Liam moved his eyes toward the ceiling.

Grayson chuckled. He knew all too well how much Liam hated formalities, but it was a habit his mom instilled in him and one he wouldn't break. "Blame it on my mom."

Liam's focus drifted back to him. "How is your mom?"

"She's doing really well."

A knock sounded at the door, and the neurologist came in, followed by Tyler.

"Tyler, what are you—"

"I called him too," Liam said, closing his eyes. "Okay, Doc. Let's hear it. Go ahead and speak in front of these men, it's okay."

"Good morning, Mr. Anderson," the doctor said and looked at both Grayson and Tyler. "Hello, gentlemen."

"He seems to be recovering well from what I can observe," Grayson said, and the doctor nodded in agreement.

"He is much better. I am very happy with his latest scan. On the scale of things, he's not quite where we want him to be for discharge and home care, but he *is* improving. Besides, we still need to assess the pain in his lower back to create an outpatient plan for later. How was breakfast this morning?" The doctor pulled out his light to run over Liam's eyes.

"Crappiest eggs I've ever had."

The doctor smiled. "Well, you ate them with your fork and were able to hold them down. All great signs."

"When can I get out of this bed?"

"Soon," the doctor told him. "I know this is frustrating, but I really am glad to see you passing many tests and gaining strides toward healing. Be patient with yourself. You had a bad accident."

"So they tell me."

Tyler grumbled something under his breath and by his stern expression, he must not have been finding the banter with the doctor amusing. Grayson couldn't say how much of the worry was due to Liam's condition and how much was because of the continued tension between him and Willow. Rumors had been flying through town about their argument outside of Maggie's Market. Even ol' Ms. Maggie herself had gone out to see what the commotion was about and witnessed the shouting.

"Get some rest, Mr. Anderson. It's the best thing for you." The doctor finished his exam and left the room. The three men stayed quiet.

"Well, Liam, this is good news about the scans." Tyler broke the silence and walked closer to the bed and took a seat.

"You'll make it after all." Grayson reached over and playfully patted him on the shoulder.

The corners of Liam's mouth twitched up. "I've missed your humor, Grayson."

"Speaking of Grayson, you didn't tell me he'd be here, Liam. Why did you call us both to come?" Tyler asked, ignoring their interaction.

"I don't want to drag this conversation out too long. Rachel will be here soon and I don't have a lot of energy still. Just talking makes me tired. But I needed to look you both in the eyes as I say this. Especially you, Tyler."

Tyler fidgeted. "I know I owe Willow an explanation about why I stopped the wedding, and I promise you I am trying. She's not wanting to talk yet, but perhaps that's from the stress of your accident. But I will talk to her, don't worry."

"You sure will. Which reminds me. We never really got to that point in our conversation the night before the accident."

Night before the accident? Grayson wasn't following, but this was on Tyler to answer.

"I . . ." Tyler steadied his hands on his knees. "I don't have an excuse for what I did. There just simply isn't one. I never should have let things go that far. But, Liam, the fact of the matter is, she doesn't love me. Willow was unhappy and I needed to let her go. But I don't know, maybe if I just worked on our relationship harder, or . . ."

Liam stared at Tyler, clearly trying to follow the man's rambling. "Or you let her go and quit playing games with her heart."

Grayson tried to keep his eyes to the floor, so Tyler wouldn't feel more pressured than he already appeared to. "Maybe I should step out of the room so you two can talk more about this." He pointed to the door.

"No, stay. That isn't the reason I brought you both here. Grayson, the night I was just referring to, I was at the brewery with Tyler. We were talking about the fact that you two men are brothers."

A shockwave jolted through him but kept himself calm. He didn't want to stress Liam. Besides this was what he'd wanted and why he'd called Wesley the night of the accident, so the Anderson's could know the truth. "I see," he said.

"And when I woke up early the next morning, I was angry. This information was kept from Willow by both of you, and I stupidly decided to work out my frustration on one of the colts that had just come in and got on him too fast. They can sense your moods, you know, and it made him go wild. Since I wasn't paying attention properly, I got tossed right back off him."

"So you told him?" Grayson asked Tyler.

"No, he didn't tell me," Liam answered. "His father did. I saw him with your mom, Grayson, a few days before the accident, and they were . . . rather close. I knew Daniel would call me eventually to talk about it because he could tell I was taken aback to see them together. But when he did, I was not prepared for everything else he shared about the affair. Once we started talking about Tyler and Willow and the wedding, it all just came out."

Grayson glanced at Tyler who began to look flushed in the face. "Tyler, relax. Don't upset Liam in his condition."

"Yes, please take a breath. I know when I called to confront you, it really upset you, but I meant what I said to you that night: Enough is enough. My daughter has the right to know everything that has been kept from her for the past eight years so she can move forward. Besides, now that Nicole and Daniel are . . . Well, whatever they are . . . she's going to hear about it anyway. It should come from you two, not the town's gossip train. If you don't tell her, I will." Liam looked at Grayson again. "And this includes you, too, young man. Enough of this. Enough of all the secrets."

"But, Liam . . ." Tyler stopped when he saw the serious expression on Liam's face.

"Quit making excuses, Tyler," Grayson said, then looked directly at Willow's dad. "There is no excuse for either one of us keeping this from her. None. I will see to it that it's taken care of. No more secrets."

"Thank you, Grayson. You know . . . I've missed seeing you around."

Grayson could feel Tyler's eyes hook into him, but he avoided the glare. He could only imagine how hard it must be to hear that from the man who was supposed to be his father-in-law only weeks ago, but he had nothing to hide. He missed Willow and her family.

"I've missed you too, *sir*," Grayson said and Liam smiled.

"I want you to come visit me again. Don't be a stranger anymore," Liam said, and Grayson nodded, swallowing the emotion that suddenly caught him off guard. "Now, off with both of you." Liam leaned back on his pillow, and Grayson and Tyler left the room.

"Wait, Grayson." Tyler pulled him to the side of the hallway.

Grayson crossed his arms, trying to hold in his impatience. "What is it, Ty? I've got some things I want to finish in these next couple days I have off. Like clean out my mom's soap shack."

"The soap shack?" Tyler's brows raised.

"Yes. I've been clearing around it, and I can now get through the path leading to it with my truck. Before my time off ends, I'd like to finish the project."

"Any plans for it?"

"No. Once I clean everything up, then we'll see."

"I imagine just clearing around it will make it look nicer back there." Tyler looked past his shoulder at the door to Liam's room before he began again. "Listen, I know you must have heard by now what happened outside of Maggie's Market."

"The whole town knows." Grayson eyed him, wishing he'd get to the point.

"Yeah." Tyler glanced down at his feet. "I'm still ashamed I did that. I let my emotions get the best of me and that wasn't fair to her. It was not the place to have a conversation like that."

"Then you need to find the right place for this conversation, and soon."

Tyler looked up. "Yes, I know."

"Is that all you wanted to talk about?" Irritation grew despite his best efforts to keep his response even.

"I just wanted to let you know how sorry I am. It was all I could think about on the drive over here, and I didn't know you'd be here, so I have to get this out."

"Sorry about what?"

"What you told me that night . . ." He hesitated, trying to keep his voice low with the hospital staff all around them. "Prom night."

"Tyler." Grayson threw his hands up. "You bring that up *here*, in a hospital? I don't want to get into this with you anyway." That was a lie. The fact was, he *did* want to talk about it. He wanted Tyler to know how hurt he had been and perhaps still was. He still couldn't believe his best friend had lied and made a move on Willow like it meant nothing. But it had been years and what good would starting a fight do?

Let her go and quit playing games with her heart . . . Liam's words suddenly jumped at him. Maybe he should finally do the same.

"I know, I'm sorry. I just needed to say that."

"I have to go. But, Tyler, I meant what I said to Liam. Tell her everything."

"Just give me a little more time and I will."

Grayson locked eyes with him for a beat, the tension between them palpable. He'd wanted to say more, but rumors were already buzzing about Tyler and Willow. He didn't need to get thrown into the gossip.

———

The cold shower was just enough to cool off how heated he'd been after talking to Tyler. Monty met him at the bottom of the stairs, and ran circles around his legs.

Stopping for a minute, he bent and patted the dog's head. German shepherds were known to be protective, but Monty was also exceptionally good at sensing when something was bothering him.

"It's all good, boy."

Perking up, the dog followed him into the kitchen. When Grayson opened the cabinet and saw he was out of coffee, he glanced down at the dog. "Come on, let's head to town."

The air was so thick with humidity when he hopped out of his truck outside the coffee shop that it was like breathing through a damp sponge. Monty jumped out, and Grayson tied his leash to a bicycle rack in the shade just outside the door. Passing people instantly recognized him and stopped to pet him.

"I'll be right back, boy. I'm sure the ladies in there will have a treat for you."

"Morning, Gray!" one of the baristas called out to him when the door jingled to signal a new customer. Being one of the smallest villages on the Vineyard, Terra Cove only had one coffee shop, and the staff knew just about everyone who walked in. "Usual?"

"Yup. Black and hot."

"You're the only one who has ordered a hot coffee today in this heat. Sure you don't want to try it iced?" she asked, trying to cover the knowing smile across her face. It was a question she already knew the answer to, but the staff enjoyed teasing him.

"It should be a crime to put ice on perfectly good hot brew."

Laughing, she turned to the register to ring out the customer in front of him before getting his coffee. She placed a bag next to it.

"Monty's favorite. Blueberry scone. On us, as always."

He handed her cash for his coffee. "Put the change in your tip jar. Stay cool, ladies."

With a wave he headed back out and nearly collided with Monty who couldn't keep his nose off the bag.

"They sure do spoil you. Let's go have a seat over on the bench, and you can have your snack."

The light ocean breeze caressed his face, offering momentary relief from the heat. Monty chowed down his scone in record time and was already sitting and facing him as if he had more to give him.

Grayson still couldn't fully shake off his annoyance from the hospital visit with Tyler in the hallway, so he pulled out his phone to get his mind moving in another direction. After scrolling through his contacts until he found his mom's number, he hit call, but she didn't pick up and he left a voicemail.

"Hey, Mom, it's me. Just checking in. I visited Liam this morning, believe it or not. He asked me to come. He knows everything about the affair and Tyler and me. We can talk more about this later, but Daniel told him everything after he saw you two together. Did Daniel tell you already? Anyway, I'll talk to you later."

He hung up and looked down at Monty. "That's all I got, boy." His stomach growled as he watched the dog sniff around for more crumbs. Glancing across the street, he saw that the deli had just opened its doors for the early lunch crowd. "The Fletchers never mind if you sit out on their patio. Come on."

He stood and his phone buzzed with a text from his mom.

> Sorry I couldn't answer. In the hair salon.
> No, Daniel didn't mention talking to Liam,
> but maybe the accident distracted him from
> telling me. Talk soon.

He tugged Monty's leash to cross the road but instantly froze when he saw Willow walk out of the drugstore next to the deli and pause next to her car. He stayed still, debating if he should approach her as he watched her rummage through her purse. Her beautiful curls blew across her face and when she leaned back to shake them off, he was already walking toward her without another thought. It was his first time seeing her since their encounter outside the hospital. He'd been waiting for this moment, and now that it was here, his nerves were firing.

Don't blow this again. "Willow!" he called out when he got a little closer.

She looked up at him, and he almost stopped in his tracks because the smile she gave him was both striking and unexpected.

"Hello, Grayson," she said.

"Hey!" he greeted her with added enthusiasm when her warm expression remained in place. In a fleeting moment, it felt like their complex history was put to rest.

Whistling, he walked up next to her car. "Look at that fancy ride."

"And proud of it."

"I bet," he said, admiring the black Audi. An image of her when she got her license at sixteen, coming down his driveway in her old Jetta that didn't have much sound left in the stereo speakers, almost made him laugh. She'd gotten her license first that summer after their sophomore year. Her current, upscale car was nicer, but he'd give anything to be back in that Jetta riding through town that summer—with not a single worry.

"Hot and sunny today, huh?" She nodded up toward the blue sky.

"Sure is. Summer is here to stay for a while. Might head over to the beach for a swim later."

"Definitely a good day for that." Her focus stayed on him, making it harder for him to remain steady.

Silence fell over them as she continued to study him, clearly waiting on him to say something else.

"I heard your dad is awake and talking." It was a lie to say he'd heard about it, as if he hadn't just seen Liam, but Grayson wanted to make sure she knew he was thinking of him and keeping up with his recovery without disclosing their private discussion.

Nodding, she held up her phone. "Yes, he is. I've been updating people all morning and just texted Tyler a minute ago too."

"I see," he said, trying to keep his aggravation at bay. Tyler was allowed to be kept up to date, but just hearing his name come out of her mouth triggered him. He decided to switch tracks. "Listen, I'm heading into the deli with Monty here."

Willow looked down. "He's very handsome." She reached out, letting Monty sniff her hand. His tail wagged as he moved closer to her, and Grayson tugged the leash.

"Down," he commanded, and Monty immediately lay down.

"Wow! I'm impressed. How old is he?"

"He just turned two."

"Well, you've done a good job training him it seems." Monty's tail thumped on the pavement as she bent to pet his head, but the dog stayed in the position Grayson had commanded him to.

"Thanks. It helps that he's such a good student." He watched Monty kiss her hand. "He sure likes you."

"I see that." She beamed up at him and he felt himself tremble against the undeniable impact she still had on him. "So you're both heading in the deli for lunch?"

"Oh right, yes . . ." He stopped, questioning if inviting her to come was too much too soon.

"Mind if I come? I skipped breakfast and was just about to figure out what to eat before you found me."

That answered that. "Great. As long as you don't mind Monty joining us."

"Not at all," she said, patting Monty's head once more before straightening up.

They walked over, and Grayson held the door open, breathing in her citrusy scent when she passed by—it suddenly reminded him of all their firsts. First date, first night they fell asleep together under the stars on the beach, first kiss at the cove at the preserve. One sweet, familiar smell transported him back to it all yet also slammed him with a bitter reminder of the time that had passed. Now they were together again. This time as adults, with lives neither truly knew about—not like before when he'd known everything about her. All he wanted to do now was learn who Willow Anderson had become.

As he walked up to the counter with her to place their order, he reconsidered if this was the right thing to do, but even as heads turned at the sight of them walking in together —he didn't care. This was his second chance, and as Willow greeted Mr. Fletcher behind the counter, her face lighting up at a shared joke, he became determined to give everything he had to making sure her happiness remained in place . . . whatever it took.

Chapter Nine

As she stood in line at the deli with Grayson, Willow felt like she was part of a paradoxical spinning time lapse of the past and present. On the one hand, nothing had changed with Grayson. From the way he stood with his hands in his pockets to his demeanor, he held the same comforting familiarity. When he ordered his sandwich, she found herself whispering his favorite along with him: honey ham with Vermont cheddar and sliced apples. Yet at the same time, he seemed different—like a whole new version of him she hadn't met yet.

Settling on the day's special of warm barbecue pulled pork that Mr. Fletcher insisted one of them try, she then followed Grayson and sat on the patio at one of the umbrellaed tables while Monty laid down under it for some added shade. Out in the distance, the harbor served as a good fill-in for some of the awkward silence. Sailboats of all hues bobbed in the water, their hulls glistening with a soft pearlescent sheen under the hot summer sun. A woman stepping off a boat and onto the dock caught her attention, and Willow shielded her face to get a better look.

"It's Gracie," she said. "I saw her last week while I was shopping with Whitney."

Grayson looked in the direction of the dock. "Good eyesight. She and Ethan bought that sailboat last summer. I've been out sailing on it with them a handful of times. Now that he's the deputy chief at the fire station, his hours are scattered. Doesn't stop Gracie though. She's always out there."

"She told me she married Ethan. I'm happy for them."

"You didn't know that?" he asked in surprise. "You really did disappear from Terra Cove."

"No, I didn't know." She scrunched her face against his stare. "And now he's working in the fire station?" An image of the fire chief, Mr. McKenzie, from the night of the barn fire flashed into her mind. He'd rushed to Grayson and Tyler to wrap fire blankets around them.

"Yes. He started as a firefighter over in Edgartown about four years ago and moved his way up."

"Is . . ." She almost held back, but his gentle gaze put her at ease. "Is Mr. McKenzie still at the station?"

"No, he retired last year and moved to New Hampshire to be close to his grandchildren." Grayson's eyes lingered on her for a beat, as if he suddenly understood that discussing Ethan's occupation had triggered her. "Anyway, he and Gracie just got married this past Christmas up in Vermont where she moved after middle school."

Willow smiled. "I remember that. We wrote a few letters back and forth before we lost touch. I used to be jealous of all the snow she had for sledding."

"Yeah, we did some sledding the day before the wedding. Like we were all kids again sliding down the snowy hills up there. It was the most beautiful holiday wedding with all that snow in the background at a lodge. Such a fun trip."

"Sounds it." Willow squirmed a bit in her seat, feeling more like a stranger in her own town for not knowing any of this. She wondered if Tyler knew about the wedding, but even if he did, he probably kept that to himself too. Outside of talking about their families, they rarely talked about Terra Cove. "It's so great that you went to the wedding."

"Yeah . . ." He drew his brows together. "Wait, didn't you see some of the pictures they shared on social media?"

Willow felt his gaze on her, but she kept her eyes focused on Gracie who was walking down the dock toward town. Willow's cheeks stung with shame. She'd missed so much with everyone she had once cared for. Flashbacks of her and Gracie riding together on her parents' horse farm and all the sleepovers they had flooded her memory. They were close until the end of middle school when she and her family moved away, so it was nice to see her back in Terra Cove.

"No . . ." Willow searched for an excuse, knowing his eyes were still on her. "I must have missed them." But the truth was, the only people from Terra Cove she followed on social media were her siblings. Aside from them, it was like the entire island completely vanished from her life. As she watched Gracie disappear around the corner, her reasons for not keeping in touch felt selfish.

"Well, who has time to stalk people from the past on social media anyway?" Grayson's forgiving smile made her eyes well up.

"That's not an excuse. I . . ." She quickly wiped the tears that kept building, feeling foolish for getting so worked up. "It's just that the fire that night. Well, it was like I couldn't face anyone anymore. My town, my own family, our friends." Courage suddenly gripped her. "What happened with us and—"

"Willow, it's okay. I was going through my own mess back then, but I want you to know that I *was* aware of how hard all of that was for you. I should have been there for you after the fire. I didn't handle any of what happened well. I wish . . ." He closed his eyes with an exhale, reaching across the table. "Well, I wish a lot of things went differently."

Been there for her? His words instantly threw her off guard, especially as he gently touched her shoulder, sending her hurtling into the past when they were just a couple of love-struck teens—making her now question everything. Hadn't he wanted to end things? The way Tyler had phrased it at the time made it seem like Grayson couldn't run from her fast enough.

"Order number nine!" A woman's voice boomed out from inside the deli, shattering through the tender moment.

"That's us." Grayson let go of her shoulder and stood up. "I'll go get our food."

She watched him walk inside, curious to know what he meant. Did he really wish things were different? Or was he just trying to soften a rough ending to how things had gone? Maybe she shouldn't have said anything.

"Thank you," she said when he returned and handed her the sandwich. "Sorry to bring all that up while we're having a nice lunch."

"Never apologize." He sat down and shifted toward her, meeting her eyes. His gentle gaze helped her relax. "Maybe we can talk about all of this another time? And not wait eight more years to do that?"

Her smile grew. "I'd like that."

"Speaking of jobs before"—he leaned back again, lightening the conversation—"I heard chatter through the years that you're a therapist now?"

"You heard correctly. I have my own practice in Connecticut, which has been on pause for weeks now. I need to figure out things with my clients soon." She now knew where he worked but saved that sensitive topic for another time.

"Considering the circumstances, your disappearance is justifiable." Grayson studied her, his empathic stance instantly reminding her just how attuned he had always been to her—something Tyler could never quite manage—before pointing to their food. "Let's eat before your pulled pork sub gets cold."

Within minutes, his quick wit had her relaxed and laughing. As they finished their lunch, he told her about a time when a skunk kept getting into his garage after he first moved back into his mother's house. His arms flared as he shared the story, making her giggle. While taking a sip of her water, she nearly choked in laughter as he explained how he had tried to pour bleach along the garage door so the smell would push the skunk out, and how the whole plan failed when Monty came rushing into the garage, getting them both sprayed. At the mention of his name, Monty's head popped up from his nap.

Grayson looked down. "We smelled for days, huh, boy?"

"I bet!" she said, still chuckling.

"I think the bleach did work in the long run because he never came back," Grayson said, then took a swig of his water. "Or Monty scared him off."

"That's so funny. I would have just run away from it and let it have the garage."

They both laughed and were so absorbed in their conversation that it took a while before she noticed the locals staring at them. Willow looked around and saw a familiar woman nearby from her mom's old book club, watching her with a smile.

"Nice to see you, Willow," the woman said when they caught eyes. "And you too, Grayson." The woman slowly turned back to her lunch, but her hesitation spoke volumes. She knew about their relationship as kids—and based on all the rest of the stares on that patio, the others did too—and most likely what had happened between her and Tyler.

Suddenly feeling uncomfortable with so many people staring at them, she looked back at Grayson. "I think I'm full."

"Me too."

They stood and threw their garbage away before walking back out to the sidewalk.

"Any plans for the rest of the day?" Grayson asked, tugging Monty's lead back so he'd sit.

"Hmm . . ." she said, thinking about the day ahead. Whitney had texted her earlier about coming to their parents' house for a swim with her kids. "I'm meeting my sister for a swim soon up at my parents' pool. Then I will probably go see my dad and eat dinner with him at the hospital."

"Your parents installed a pool?"

"Finally, right?"

"I have clear memories of you begging them to put one in all those summers we were growing up. They always turned you down with the same response—"

"Why put a pool in when you have the whole Atlantic Ocean steps away!" they said in unison.

"After all that asking, all it took was one look at Whitney's daughter, Maya, as a baby, their first grandchild, and they started adding all kinds of fun things around the property, including a large inground pool complete with a waterslide."

"At least you all can enjoy it now," he said. "How old are Whitney's kids?"

"Four and one," she said, thinking about her niece and nephew. "They are so adorable."

"I bet." He looked away, watching a car pass by before his eyes found hers again.

"It's been so fun watching Whitney and her husband put Maya up on one of the horses on the farm and walk her around." He smiled and Willow's pulse sped up. All it took was one glance and he had her buckling. "Th-the happiness on her face while she's up there reminded me of . . . me. I need to get myself on a horse again. It's been years. I hope I didn't forget how to ride."

"What?" His mouth dropped open. "Did you just say *years*? Horseback riding is half of who you are."

"I know . . . I really don't know why it's been that long." That was a lie. The thought of getting on a horse after the night of the fire brought anxiety and . . . *It's because being on a horse brings me right back to you.* Willow bit her lip and shrugged. "I guess work has just taken up most of my time."

He narrowed his eyes at her. "How come I don't believe you?" He knew her so well. She'd tell him eventually, but not while standing in a parking lot. His stunned expression faded into a small smile. "Say, listen, this made me think of something. I don't know if you have a lot going on the rest of the week, but I have someone up at my house who would love to see you, if you can squeeze in some time for us."

Intrigued, she almost said yes instantly, but a pull in her stomach fought her. They'd had a nearly perfect lunch together reminiscing about old times and catching up, but perhaps she shouldn't push it. This wasn't what she had come home to do, but as he patiently waited for her to answer, his gaze seemed to cast a hypnotic effect over her—pushing her doubts right back out.

"Okay." She drew her brows together against his sly grin. "But I feel like I need a warning."

"No, you don't need one." A playful glint crossed his face. "She's been waiting a long time for your return."

"She?" Now her mind was racing as she tried to guess who he was talking about.

"Yup." He grinned again, clearly enjoying keeping her guessing. "Would tomorrow work?"

"I have to do a few things tomorrow at the farm for my dad. We've hired two new people to help out and they start tomorrow. I have a lot to do to get them set up. It'll be nice to have the extra hands around, especially when I have to juggle my clients soon on top of the horses. Is Thursday okay?"

"I'm glad you got more help. That farm must be a lot of work. Thursday is perfect." He nodded toward his parked truck. "Why don't you meet me here, and I'll drive you up? My gravel driveway still needs to be restored, and I don't want your fancy car to get its wheels dirty."

"Don't knock the Audi." She gave him a playful shove. "Took me nearly two years of saving to get that car!"

He opened his truck and put Monty inside before following her to her car door. "And ten years of wishing for it." He winked at her before she climbed in, and a rush shot down her spine. She should have known he'd remember it was her dream car. "I'll see you here Thursday. Does noon work?"

"Yep. See you then."

As his truck disappeared from her rearview mirror, Willow remained parked, her thoughts lingering on a replay on their date at the deli. Was it a date? Or an obligatory invite since he ran into her on the street? Now that he'd truly extended an invitation to his house, that wasn't what had her gripping the steering wheel. Rather, it was how quickly she'd accepted that invitation. Was he just being nice? After all, *he* was the one who had ended things.

As she turned on her ignition, she couldn't help but wonder if all these old feelings were one-sided. He seemed to want to at least be friends. She backed up and pulled out onto the street and realized how ridiculous she'd been to spend years hiding in Connecticut. Sure, some time had to pass to let the wounds heal a bit but *eight years*? All while trying to make a relationship progress that hadn't been going anywhere from the start. If only she had faced Grayson years ago—and everything else she'd been afraid to face since that night—she wouldn't hold such guilt for staying away from Terra Cove so long. And maybe the three of them could have mended the special history they shared. Or was that just wishful thinking?

Driving through the winding back roads toward Anderson

Stables, Willow held on to that thought, praying for a miracle, but also reasoning with herself that maybe there was still time to do just that. It would be a shame not to try.

But as she continued to entertain that notion, Grayson's mesmerizing expression broke into her mind, leaving her to wonder: Could they truly be *just* friends?

———

HER DAD PEEKED HIS EYES OPEN WHEN SHE BENT down to kiss his forehead Thursday morning. It was just before noon, and her mom would be there soon for his afternoon appointments with various doctors. The quiet had been just what they both needed: a peaceful time together. She filled him in on everything she'd done the last couple days at the farm, reassuring him that she had the duties handled and the new hires were working out very well for their second day.

"I don't know what I would do without you, Willow. Helping me as you are with the horses."

"Of course, Dad. I'm happy to help." The upkeep was tough but, despite being away from the farm for so long, she knew horses better than both her siblings and was glad to be there.

"Any plans for the rest of the day?" he asked when Willow picked up her purse to leave. "It's . . . Thursday, right? Are you still off from seeing clients?"

"Yes, I'm still not seeing clients, but next week I need to get that all figured out. I can't keep pushing them off." She put her purse on her shoulder and thought about her day planned with Grayson. An impulse to lie quickly vanished as she looked at her dad's vulnerable stare, but she had nothing to hide. "I'm actually going to meet Grayson." She braced herself, but a smile formed on his face, throwing her off a bit.

"Have fun," he said.

"You're not upset?" She didn't want to wear him out with any more conversation, but his response surprised her.

"No, I'm not." He closed his eyes, and she didn't press him. She kissed him on the cheek once more before leaving.

The drive to meet Grayson was a blur as her mind went through a million different thoughts. She didn't know what to expect, but as she hopped into his truck, nostalgia engulfed her. Monty was in the back seat but leaned forward to sniff her. As she greeted the dog, Grayson wiped away sweat that had gathered on his brow, and she was curious if he was just as nervous as she suddenly was. The cold breeze from the truck's vents helped settle the mix of emotions that flipped around in Willow's stomach when his arm rested behind her as he backed up. She kept her focus on who she could possibly be seeing at his house to avoid staring at him. After a minute, she pulled out her phone to keep herself distracted and sent a quick text to her mother.

> Hi Mom, hope everything goes well today with Dad's appointments. Fill me in later. I'll meet you back at the house for dinner. XO

She turned off her phone before her mother could ask anything, but then it occurred to her that her dad would probably share the information about her meeting Grayson, which meant a lot of questions later. Clicking on the radio, Grayson turned up a popular song, breaking the need to find something to say—yet for Willow, there was so much she *did* want to talk about. Like when did he start working for Tyler's dad? Where did he live before he moved back into his mother's house? Where were his sister and mom now? And the one burning question that was none of her business: Was he dating anyone?

As they continued down the narrow back roads, she sat in a daze watching the landscape go by. The familiar scenery reminded her of when she used to stick her feet out the window in the old Ford F-150 he drove back then. She fidgeted with her hands to keep from rolling the window down, then crossed her feet to keep them in place.

"Don't even think about it," Grayson said.

"What am I thinking?" She shot him an innocent side-eyed glance, running her hand along the window's frame.

"That." He slowed to make a turn and quickly looked at where her hand was along the window. "It may not be as extravagant as that Audi, but this Dodge is an upgrade from that old beat-up truck you rode in back then, and I don't want your feet smudging up my side mirror." His eyes crinkled in the corners when he turned to grin at her. He pulled onto his road, and it was like they were walking down memory lane at the same time.

"Oh, you say that now. But you can't say no to me," she said and had to catch her breath against the flutter in her chest. She couldn't believe how amiable they were, as if the last eight years hadn't happened at all—much less that awful night when he sent Tyler to tell her it was over between them. But being in his truck and on his road—where he used to pull over to sneak kisses before they continued to his house—it was almost impossible not to.

Grayson laughed to himself and glanced out the window. *Is he thinking of the same thing?*

When they reached his driveway, she bit her lip as her eyes suddenly welled up. She was actually pulling into Grayson's driveway, something she thought she'd never do again. Drawing in a breath, she forced herself to calm down, but not before Tyler popped into her mind. Even though he had ended their engagement—and entire relationship—a wave of guilt overcame her about being there with Grayson. It was as though she was still stuck in the middle between them, just like she'd felt when she first started dating Grayson.

He drove slowly down the long driveway that was surrounded by fields. Willow never got to know his mother very well, and after his father left, Nicole worked around the clock to keep food on the table and this property. The land had been in their family since his great-grandfather purchased it, and his mother was determined not to sell it. Willow looked around at the gorgeous landscape, every inch of it holding a part of her memories, and she understood why Nicole fought so hard to keep it.

Black cherry trees spread along the driveway caught her attention when he slowed the truck to ease it over the bumpy dirt. She could almost see herself, Grayson, and Tyler as kids again running in and out from behind the tall thick trunks. They'd loved to run through just about any field, trail, or sandy beach, but the way the branches dipped low made these trees one of their favorite places to play hide-and-seek. That thought prompted one day in particular to pop into her mind.

Fifth grade had just ended, and it was the first day of summer. Closing her eyes, she could almost taste the grape popsicle she'd just finished.

———

HER HAIR WAS STILL DAMP FROM SWIMMING IN THE ocean and over her bathing suit she wore her favorite blue sundress that she wore nearly every day.

"Stop it, Gray!" Willow burst into laughter when he jumped up behind her, now strong enough to hold her, and raised her up.

Grayson was especially happy. His father, Jack, had taken them all to the beach that morning, a rare occurrence the last couple years since he'd started making more time for his drinking than his family.

"You can't hide from me!" Grayson shouted, gently shaking her, which only made her giggle more.

"No fair! You didn't even count to ten!" she said when he placed her back down. "Give me a chance to hide!"

"Yeah, I call for a redo," Tyler said, coming over to them.

"Okay, okay. I'll restart! One-Two-Thre—"

"*Grayson!*" his father roared near them and all three of them froze, not having realized the man had stumbled down the driveway. "*Get inside!*"

"But why, Dad? You knew we were coming out here to play."

She and Tyler exchanged knowing looks and jogged over to Grayson, taking up protective stances on either side of him. The tone Mr. Turner had was the one they'd become used to, and they knew he must have spent the last hour since they got back from the beach drinking.

"You left the box of popsicles on the counter melting!" Jack was now standing in front of him, steadying himself against one of the trees in his drunken stupor.

"I'm sorry, I'll go put it away." Grayson looked at them. "I'll be right back."

"No you won't, young man!" Mr. Turner glared at her and Tyler. "Go home!"

"Come on, Willow, let's go to my house." Tyler had tugged her arm, but she'd hesitated, watching Mr. Turner shove Grayson to walk, wanting somehow to make it stop when she saw his eyes grow watery.

———

Grayson's truck bumped over another pothole, jarring her back to the present. Of all the days to think about, it had to be one of the bad ones, but the importance of that day was something she'd forgotten over the years.

Watching Grayson start crying while his father held the back of his shirt to force him to the house was the moment she'd told herself that when she grew up, she would do something to help people. Like she had wanted so badly to do for Grayson in that moment. When his father officially left them a few years later, that was when she knew for certain that she'd become a therapist one day.

"I keep meaning to fix these holes." He smiled in her direction. "Sorry for the bumpy ride, but that's why I wanted to keep the fancy car parked on the pavement." They reached the house and when he parked, his eyes were bright with excitement when he turned to her. "Ready to see Nova?"

Willow drew in a sharp breath. "You . . ." She could barely get her sentence out and grew dizzy from her thudding heart as Grayson reached over and put his hand over hers. "You have Nova?"

He gave her hand a gentle squeeze, his eyes momentarily falling to her lips before he nodded. "Yes. I have her and my other horse named Max to keep her company. And, Willow . . . please don't feel obligated to ride her. I just want you to see her."

"How?" she asked, trying to understand. "She belongs to Tyler's family."

"And he never told you?"

She shook her head, a mixture of frustration and happiness swarming her at feeling his grip on her hand. Before she could stop them, the words came rushing out.

"I feel so lost with everything. Gracie and Ethan now married. You working for Tyler's dad. Tyler and me. You and me . . ." Tears welled in her eyes. "How did we get here?" She pulled her hand away to wipe at the tears that slipped out.

Grayson moved his hand to her shoulder. "Willow, just breathe."

"I can't believe it's Nova I'm going to go see. I was just

thinking about her the other day." She didn't add that she had also been thinking about that summer she taught him to ride Nova.

"Daniel sold her to me a few years ago when I asked him for her," he explained. "Let's go see her. That is, if you want to . . . But you know as well as I do that she makes everything better during stressful times."

And so do you. She caught the words before they slipped out. After getting out of his truck, she opened the back door for Monty to jump out, and her mind went into overdrive trying to unravel the last eight years, setting off her anxiety that was mounting by the second.

Regardless of how weak her relationship with Tyler suddenly seemed, she'd been set to *marry* him only a few weeks prior. Her wedding dress still hung in her closet in their condo. She'd known their relationship wasn't where she'd hoped it would be, but it had been comfortable. Getting married was what she thought was supposed to be the next step, but as she caught eyes with Grayson, all she could think was: two men and two dresses gone to waste—but was her heart truly broken over both? Looking back, she knew the answer to that question was no.

She followed Grayson to the five-stall barn. After Jack first left, his mother had sold their one horse they had at the time for extra money, and Grayson always told Willow that one day he'd put another in it. That day had arrived, and that horse was Nova. As she stared at the back of him as they got closer to the barn, the moment was almost surreal. In the blink of an eye, eight years were rewinding right before her.

Chapter Ten

Grayson kept imagining reasons to turn around and tell Willow that this wasn't a good idea, but the words never left his lips. Fact was, he'd asked her to come, and he wanted her here, and she said yes. Tyler would surely have something to say once he found out, but Grayson would deal with that later.

For now, he had to fight with everything he had not to reach for her and stroke her golden hair, falling so perfectly around her face, and tell her everything was going to be alright —something he had no business doing but should have done years ago when he'd had the chance. No matter how smoothly things were going between them now, there was no denying that their past still lurked over them.

The large barn door stuck as it always did, and he positioned himself to pull harder. "Step back, this old door needs replacing."

Willow got behind him. "It's definitely aged."

Grayson gave the door a final tug and it slid open. Monty trotted past them inside the barn. "Yes, it has, but I've got plans."

"To remodel?"

"Expand. This property is so large that the plans are endless, but I have time. No one to distract me except . . ." He caught himself before the words slipped out. Willow was back in town and there was no bigger distraction.

She stayed still, watching him with curious eyes.

His jaw clenched as he tried to keep his focus from moving down her face to those pink lips that made him nearly lose control. "What? I know that face."

"Except?" she asked, immediately looking down at her hands.

Willow Anderson was many things, but shy wasn't one of them, especially with him all those years ago, and it really touched him. "Except my work stuff. It's just me and Monty," he answered. The dog barked when he heard his name, coming back out of the barn and sniffing around their legs.

"I see," she said, her voice hardly above a whisper. She faced him again, her flushed cheeks adorable. "No one at all to distract you?"

"No . . . I'm not seeing anyone, if that's what you're wondering."

Her eyes widened as she nervously fidgeted with her hair, drawing it behind her ear. "Well, that's none of my business if you were."

Grayson hesitated, which only made her seem more edgy. "You can still ask me anything, Willow."

The subtle and endearing way she chewed her lip in response took him back to the first time he pulled her close inside the cove with the sound of the waves crashing close by. How her mouth had twitched when he leaned closer.

A loud whinnying from inside the barn snapped them both out of the trance.

"Is that her?" Willow looked past him.

"She must hear you." Another chuff echoed from the stalls. "And that is my other horse, Max."

"Do you think she remembers me?"

"Horses have a keen memory, you know that," he said, looking toward the stalls. "Besides, how could she forget someone like you?" He wasn't sure if he was still referring to the horse anymore as he walked into the barn, but Nova's loud calls kept him distracted. "We're coming, girl, and I have a surprise visitor, which I'm sure you already know."

Willow walked past him and cupped her mouth when Nova popped her head over the yoke gate. Her beautiful brown coat against the striking white patch on her forehead still gave her that sweet and endearing look that she never forgot. After bobbing her head up and down, the old mare immediately relaxed when Willow approached her and gently stroked her neck. Grayson kept his distance and let them have their moment. Tears slid down Willow's face as she silently petted the horse and leaned her cheek closer to Nova's head. Chuffing in response, she relaxed against Willow. Seeing them lean on each other made his own eyes sting.

"She's happy to see you too."

Willow kept moving her hand up and down Nova's neck. "I don't have any excuse," she told the horse, and Nova stayed perfectly still listening. "I should have come to visit. You must have thought I abandoned you."

Nova pulled her head up, eyeing him as he approached them. "The forgiving nature of horses is one of their most beautiful qualities. And once they love you, that never stops."

I know I haven't.

An immediate need to hold her nearly knocked him to his knees as he continued watching her with Nova. Not chasing after her when she first left Terra Cove suddenly hit him harder than ever before. He'd been so consumed with learning about his mom's affair and that Tyler was his brother, not to mention trying to work through all the years of Jack's alcoholism and abuse. All of it had clutched him back then. Yes, his mom had pushed him to fight for Willow, but at the time, he couldn't hear her. All he heard were Jack's words from prom night when he'd shown up drunk. *"You are no better than her or me, and you never will be! Willow will see that soon enough."*

Willow's shoulders drew up, and she turned away from the horse and looked up at him, snapping him out of the flashback before it took hold of him. He wanted to tell her everything. He reached for her hand.

"Grayson—"

"Willow!" A female voice burst through the barn. "Is it really you?"

Abby's footsteps thudded as she ran toward them.

"I should say the same to you, Abby Turner! I can't believe it's you!" Willow let go of his hand and hurried over to collide with his sister in a long hug.

"I didn't know you were coming over." Grayson stood near the two women. It had been so long since he'd seen them together.

"Umm, do I need a special invite to come see my big brother? Besides, I brought you one of your summer favorites —watermelon fresh off the farm." Abby chuckled and pulled back from Willow. "And anyway, yes, you *did* know. I told you I'd come help you tackle Mom's old soap shack today since you were still off from work. So here I am!"

"Yes, but I didn't know that would be today. Your new schedule at work is so random. Giving me a more concrete heads up would be nice."

"I can see why." Abby glanced at Willow.

Willow put her hands up. "I'm just here for Nova! You two can carry on your plans."

"Just for Nova, huh? Sure you—"

"Abby!" Grayson nearly shouted and didn't miss the amused expression Willow gave him. "You know I'm messing with you. You're welcome here anytime, Abs." He ruffled his sister's hair, just like he always did when she was small.

Moving away, she rolled her eyes and looked at Willow again. "Enough about why I'm here. More about *you*, Willow." Abby leaned into her. "How's your dad?"

"He's improving every day and the doctors continue to be happy with his progress."

"That's wonderful. I've been praying for him, and Grayson has been keeping me updated." Abby smiled again. "Gosh, I've missed you!"

"I've missed you too."

"I'm sorry his accident happened, but it's what finally brought you home." Abby nodded toward Nova. "Taking your old best friend out for a ride?"

"I was just getting reacquainted with her," Willow said, noticing Nova intently listening to their conversation. "But ... May I ride her?" she nearly whispered.

He couldn't believe it. She was going to have her first ride in years, with *him*. And what better horse to do it on than Nova? The mare had been there for him all those years ago, and now she was there for Willow.

"This is Nova we're talking about. You don't need to ask!" Abby walked over to the horse and gave her a pat. "She's probably itching to get out there with you. Come on, let's saddle her up and catch up a little before your ride. I have about a million questions to ask you."

Willow smiled. "I have about the same amount for you."

The women embraced again before opening the stall to lead Nova out, picking up right where they left off as if no time had passed.

When Jack left them, his mother was too distraught for a

while to notice how hard Abby was handling it. She was only nine at the time and didn't understand. That was when Willow stepped in, becoming the female support she needed until his mother got stronger. He could still clearly hear the first night his little sister finally let out her cries. Abby had tried so hard to keep her emotions to herself so she didn't further upset their mother, but when Grayson confided in Willow about it, she came over to hold her, allowing his sister to let it all out. His heart thudded as he remembered the sobs Abby released in Willow's arms. That was the exact moment he'd fallen in love with her.

After heading out of the barn to give the women a few minutes to chat, Grayson made his way to the opposite edge of the paddock—his favorite spot. Leaning on the fence, he cast his eyes over the vast blue water of the large pond below that led out to Vineyard Sound. Both he and Willow's parents shared the same view, being so close to each other, and he remembered many times gazing at the rippling water and wondering if Willow was watching it too. The current had always made him feel linked to her in an odd way after they first broke up, like she'd come back and find him next to the water, waiting.

Gathering clouds shrouded the sun, casting a rich blue hue over the water. The salty air filled his lungs as he saw the soft ripples move forward—a reflection of the ebb and flow in his heart since seeing Willow again.

He pushed off the fence and turned to see them leading Nova through the gate. There was no denying what his heart had been telling him since she'd come home. But was it too late? Jack had been long gone from his life and while that turmoil in his younger years caused him to push her away, perhaps he'd needed those years to grow and heal from his childhood.

To almost unload this on her only minutes ago before

Abby interrupted them had him pause in thought. Did those excuses even matter anymore? Willow was going through enough as it was—the last thing he wanted was to make anything worse for her.

———

"I HOPE SHE COMES BACK TO VISIT NOVA AFTER this," Abby said, dangling her arms over the fence as Willow got herself comfortable with Nova in the pen. "I haven't seen her this lively in years, even for an old mare."

Nova stomped in a small circle around Willow. "Easy, sweet girl. I know it's been a long time, but let's take this slow." The horse's nostrils flared in response.

"She's taking in your scent!" Grayson called out to Willow before looking at his sister. "It's like Nova can't get enough of her."

Abby peeked over at him. "You sure it's just Nova who can't?"

"There you go," Grayson said to Willow, cupping his hands so she could hear him as the horse began to ease. He left Abby guessing with just a smile in response.

He watched as Willow took her time, unsure if he should go stand next to her for support or stay back. This was a big moment for her. When Willow slowly stroked the side of the horse's neck, maintaining soft eye contact, he knew his answer and stayed where he was—Nova had this. Just like the seasoned horse always did.

He held his breath as she finally put her foot through the stirrup and swung her leg over. She looked over at him with astonishment. Grayson didn't know the extent of how she felt to be on a horse after so long, but when a grin spread across her face, he could guess it must've been exhilarating.

With an exhale, he watched her slowly move the horse

forward and within seconds, she'd picked up Nova's pace, and they trotted around the paddock. The horse's ears perked up, and they moved with ease. The gentle sway of Willow's soft curls beneath her helmet mirrored the smooth, graceful way she handled her old friend. Grayson was mesmerized by the beautiful view of rider and horse rebuilding their bond. He wanted the scene to last forever, a special moment he'd been privileged to witness.

The fact that it was Nova who helped Willow get back on resonated deeply for him and he hoped it was the same for her. Grayson studied her every movement on the saddle, her body relaxed, and he sensed nothing but relief as she leaned forward, picking up speed as if time had never passed. Nova may be relishing in the Willow she remembered, but the teenager they'd both known wasn't riding on the horse now. The young girl who once danced under the stars with him late at night after sneaking out to the beach was a woman now. His eyes stayed fixed on her as she continued to circle Nova around the pen—leaving him eager to discover who Willow had become.

"So great to see," Abby said, interrupting his daze, but his eyes remained on Willow.

"You have no idea," he mumbled.

"Since Willow is here, I'll leave you two alone and come back another time to help with that shack. The watermelon is on your kitchen counter." Abby shifted away from the fence. "Grayson?"

"Hmm?" He was completely absorbed in Willow and Nova.

"I said I'm going to take off." Abby chuckled.

Grayson finally looked at her. "Sorry, it's just so nice to see them back together."

"Uh-huh," his sister said and nudged him. "Some things

never change, no matter how long it's been. Just remember though, what happened with Tyler is still pretty raw."

The truth of his sister's statement put reality right back in its place, front and center. Glancing at them, Willow led Nova around the bend, but this time they headed toward a small jump. She grinned wildly after they went over it. Seeing her face light up quickly overshadowed his hesitation as his heart took the lead once again, wanting to enjoy this with her. Maybe he should saddle Max, who had become Nova's charge since Grayson bought him as a colt. The mare's motherly instincts had her taking Max in right away, offering protection and mentoring as the young horse grew. Both horses would love a short trail ride.

"Bye, Willow!" Abby waved.

Willow guided Nova over to them. "Taking off?" she asked. "I still have about a million more questions to ask you."

Grayson could feel Abby's eyes dart toward him, but he stared at his feet so he wouldn't make Willow nervous.

"Let's plan a lunch, just me and you, before you leave again," Abby said.

"You got it. It's a date."

Abby waved again and headed off.

Leave again. Grayson could not put his mind there. The thought of Willow leaving Terra Cove again made him uneasy. *I just got her back here.*

Before Willow signaled Nova, he held his hand up. "Before you go back at it, I'm going to saddle up Max. Would you like to go on a trail walk around the preserve? Max and Nova are buddies and will make for a relaxing ride together." He eyed her, unsure if he'd just triggered her. "You . . ." he slowly continued. "You know, down the old trail that overlooks the cove."

"That sounds perfect."

He knew by the look on her face she was thinking the

same thing: *their* cove. The path ran behind both his house and Anderson Stables and served as their favorite trail since Grayson first learned to ride. It was a private entrance to the preserve and led them right to the perfect view of the cove.

"The heat is picking up, so let me slice some of that watermelon Abby brought, grab some extra waters, and I'll be back out here in a bit with Max."

"Sounds like a plan. I'll let Nova get some water and have a rest before we go."

After dismounting, Willow pulled off her helmet and shook out her golden waves, which immediately matted to her face. He could hardly tear himself from the sight of her, especially when the sun moved out from behind a small cloud and bathed her face with radiant light as she walked Nova out of the gate and peered over at him. Her eyes locked him in place, shining like the bright, bold petals of a marigold flower—the same eyes he could only dream about for eight years. The mysterious allure she gave off as she walked Nova to the water trough made her impossible to read, but that didn't matter. When he finally forced himself to move, he heard the scraping of Abby's tires slowly going down his driveway, his sister's warning now long forgotten.

He was still lost in thought once he got inside. The joy of seeing Willow so content had made him seemingly oblivious to the complexities of what had just transpired with Tyler. Her relationship with him was beginning to feel like a distant illusion, like it never happened—at least that was what he wished. Regret over what he'd done so long ago panged him once again, growing stronger with each hit.

"It's just an innocent trail ride," he told Monty who had followed him inside and now looked up at him with a head tilt. Even his dog couldn't be fooled. "Don't look at me like that."

He chopped up the watermelon and loaded it into a lunch

bag with some ice bricks before grabbing a few water bottles from the fridge and some extra frozen ones he always kept on hand for these hot summer days. Making his way back outside, he ignored Monty who was still giving him a questioning stare. Grayson was well past trying to pretend he had moved on.

CHAPTER ELEVEN

Nova stayed at the trough for a while, giving Willow time to absorb the fact that she'd just ridden a horse again. Leaning against the fence, she drew in some slow, deep breaths and let the thrill continue to course through her system. There was no better way to recapture something she'd thought lost forever than through Nova. The trusted steed who played such a pivotal role in both her and Grayson's life had been there for her once again. Without her, Willow wasn't sure she'd have been able to muster the courage to ride again.

Even as a therapist, she'd been having such a hard time getting past the root of her fear. It had always been easier to ignore it, which kept her nerves at bay. She understood that horseback riding had been a trigger from the trauma of the fire, but no matter how much training she'd had, she couldn't face it, until now. Her family would be so relieved to learn she'd finally pushed past it and got on.

Now thinking about the trail ride, she felt like it would be a perfect ending to such a special day. She glanced at Nova, and the mare had a faraway look in her eyes. Willow guessed she'd been sensing other emotions about the upcoming ride with Grayson and Max.

"Are you up for a trail ride, girl?" Willow asked the horse. Nova eyed Willow, as if she needed to contemplate the question. "Don't worry. I know it's hot out here. It'll be a short one, promise." No matter how hard she tried to appear innocent against the horse's knowing look, it was useless. Nova knew exactly what was going on with her and Grayson, but did Willow? What *was* going on?

Earlier in the barn, Grayson had wanted to tell her something before Abby got there. She hoped he'd try again. It had to be about their past, and as she stood there next to Nova at his childhood home, she realized she felt no more remorse or anger. She knew, as she met Nova's stare, that she had finally let go of what had happened between them back then. Being in Connecticut had allowed her to not only avoid riding again. . . but also to avoid Grayson. As the years had passed, she knew now that the hurt she'd thought was still there, was only an assumption, and the truth was—the heartache had long ceased.

They were just kids when they were together, but she couldn't deny that it had been more than teenage "puppy love." Otherwise, she wouldn't be sitting here wishing they would talk. She needed to do the same with Tyler and put that relationship behind her—but what would it mean with Grayson? Better yet, what did she *want* it to mean? Did she want to put them fully behind her too?

Willow stood up from the fence as Nova gave her one last long stare before she bowed her head back down to the trough. "I see that look." Thinking about Tyler again made her frustration build, along with her nerves. Needing a distraction, she walked over to the bench outside the barn where her purse was to check her messages.

Her hands trembled a bit as she clutched her phone. *I'm*

just overthinking as usual. Until coming back to Terra Cove, she had never *truly* combatted anxiety . . . not like this. Sure, the idea of getting up on a horse before she'd finally faced it with Nova always put her on edge, but she'd always handled that by just simply not doing it. It wasn't that easy now. Between the failed wedding, nearly losing her dad, and dealing with the emotions of coming home for the first time in so very long, she'd felt totally out of control in her own skin. Just like when she was taking a hike by herself the morning after the accident, the anxious feeling really bothered her, especially since her entire career was built around helping others with this very thing.

Nova let out a loud whinny, now hanging her head over the fence and watching Willow again—instantly easing her nerves. The horse's graceful, calming gait as they rode earlier was still as strong as it was the day she'd met her.

"Thank you," she said to Nova and looked back down at the phone, wiping her sweaty hands on her jeans before swiping through the messages. The early afternoon heat had intensified, and while her longer pants were necessary for riding, she couldn't wait to cool off in the pool later.

Whitney's text was first, confirming that Willow was still coming to swim and to say she was heading to the store to get a bunch of food to lounge and eat later. Firing off a reply, she told her sister she was looking forward to it. Next up was her mother telling her that a few of Dad's appointments got moved to next week and that she would be heading home soon to go help Whitney shop. The last text made Willow's pulse surge reading his name, especially when she saw that he'd tried to call her too. She quickly opened the message from Tyler.

> Just trying to reach you. Willow, we still really need to talk. Call me.

Closing her eyes, she leaned back against the bench and

thought through a response. They were nearly a month past the disaster of their wedding day, and Tyler was finally pushing to talk to her—and she was sitting in Grayson's driveway, missing his calls. She could almost hear what Ivy would say if she were next to her. *Who cares! Go enjoy the trail ride!* An urge to call her best friend halted when she remembered she'd have to run through her entire history with Grayson. Ivy still didn't even know his name.

Her eyes popped open, a scowl twisting her face in sudden annoyance. Nova's focus was still on her. Tyler was in the wrong, and she had every right to saddle up and have some fun. But she couldn't keep going with that notion. No matter how much she wanted to keep blaming Tyler for the failure of their relationship, it hadn't been his fault completely.

Reuniting with Nova, relishing in an activity she had spent eight years refusing to do with Tyler—even after he tried multiple times to get her on a horse—was eagerly welcomed the first chance she got with Grayson. Tyler must have known for years her heart hadn't been in it. Slowly exhaling, she'd started to accept the fact that she had been equally to blame for how their relationship ended. Grayson still had a hold on her, and Tyler knew it. *But is being here the right thing to do? And better yet, who's to say Grayson could even be trusted again?*

Glancing over, Nova's stare still hadn't wavered from her. "I don't have an answer either, girl," she whispered at the horse. "And I can't believe I let riding go like I did. I don't know if it was you who got me to ride again or—"

The sound of Grayson's footsteps padding near her caught her attention, and when she looked up, his smile as he walked toward her pierced through the tight self-reproach, releasing its grip. *Or him?*

"Max is ready so let me grab my saddlebag to put all this in. Here's some water for you now. I'm sure you need it after that warm-up with Nova." Grayson handed her the water bottle. "And, Willow? I'm so proud of you for getting up there." He disappeared into the barn to get Max, and she opened the water bottle.

The cold liquid was the calming antidote she'd needed for her jangled emotions, and as she started to type a response to Tyler, her fingers slowed.

Despite waiting for days after the wedding for a response from him, the silence between them had been a blessing, giving her time to process some more, especially since arriving in Terra Cove. Staring at the blinking cursor on her phone, she began typing again.

> I know we do. Just give me a bit of space with this, Tyler. I will be ready to hear what you have to say soon.

Nova's loud snort broke Willow's concentration from the screen, and when she looked over at her, the mare was fidgeting and tossing her head. Laughing, she hit send and shoved her phone back in her purse, then placed it on the bench again before walking over.

"Alright, alright. We're just waiting on your friend Max. But I know I have a lot to catch you up on." Nova bobbed her head. "Shh, no need to get all huffy. I know your feelings are still hurt." She ran her hand slowly down the horse's neck. "I won't ever leave you like that again. You're my home, Nova. But being here at Grayson's house sure is making my life even more confusing."

A low whinny from behind made her jump. When she looked, Grayson stood a few feet away holding Max's lead. She had been so absorbed with Nova that she must not have heard them come out of the barn. Heat rose into her cheeks. She wasn't sure how much he had heard.

"We're, uh . . . all ready. Are you?" Grayson tugged the lead and they walked closer. His voice was calm and steady.

"Yes, we are." She met his eyes, her heart pounding as she fought to maintain her composure. She opened the gate to get Nova and latched it behind her. Grayson was still watching her when she glanced back, and she knew by the look on his face that he'd heard everything.

"Good," he finally said, his smile subtle, leaving her senses tingling in anticipation. He placed his foot in the stirrup as she did the same, and they both swung up onto their horses. "I'd say stay close behind until we can be side by side on the trail, but you know that trail well," he said with a wink, his face shifting into a grin before he and Max walked off.

Nova huffed.

"Yeah, I agree," Willow whispered. "He definitely heard us." She signaled the horse and followed right behind them.

———

"Let's stop here, take a break, and then pivot back." Grayson tugged Max to slow beside Nova. "I know you love this view as much as I do, but we can always come back to enjoy it. I bet your family wants to spend some time with you too."

"Yeah. It's been so long since I've been home. I'm sure they do," Willow said, a small smile spreading across her face. "But it's okay we took a while." The corners of his mouth lifted as they locked eyes. "I'm just meeting them for a swim later. Too bad we can't go for a dip now down in the cove." Willow broke their gaze, lifting her helmet to wipe away the sweat. "But we can save that for another day on the beach without the horses." She moved ahead and dismounted, then walked over to the edge of the railing and cast her focus across the tiny strip of sand below, sensing his eyes on her.

"So that's guaranteed more time with me then?"

"Maybe," she said, turning to him with a raised brow. Some things with him hadn't changed at all, like how he was always fast to respond. Yet his stance felt different . . . more confident. When they were kids, his quick wit had often made him tremble, like he hoped she'd understand his humor, otherwise he'd blow it with her. Now, he seemed more direct. More mature. And the tables had turned, leaving *her* shaking a bit.

Sunlight moved across her face, pulling her back to the scenery, specifically the diving rock poised perfectly in the middle of the cove. Images flooded her mind of her, Grayson, and Tyler jumping off the rock every summer. It was always the first thing they'd do when school let out for summer break.

Moving her focus to the wooden steps that led down to the beach, she closed her eyes as a breeze blew and ushered in their past.

SWINGING AROUND THE TREE, SHE STOPPED WHEN she saw his teasing look and knew exactly which game he wanted to play.

"We're too old for tag, Grayson. We're going to be sophomores in a month." Giggles erupted when he reached for her but missed as she swayed in the opposite direction—colliding with him on the other side.

"I don't want to play tag." His strong arms reached for her, and she released her grip from the tree. "And yes, we are, which means—"

"Tag! You're it!" Willow ducked out of his arms and hurried to the steps and down to the small beach. Maneuvering through the boulders in the cove, she felt him closing in on her.

"You don't have a bathing suit on, so what's your plan here, Willow?" Grayson called from behind her.

The rushing sound of water hitting the shore captured her attention, slowing her enough for him to gain on her. When she got to the water's edge, she turned her head.

"Who said we need bathing suits? But you're still it!" She dove in just as he nearly caught her.

Under the water, the crash of Grayson joining her brought a wave of bubbles her way. Moving her arms, she swam toward the rock, and popped up just next to it—and face-to-face with him.

"Got you," he said, both of them bobbing against the waves that hit the side of the rock. Hoisting her with one arm, he gave her the first shove up the side, and they both made their way to the top. The wind whipped across her face once she was perched up high on the boulder while a seagull hovered over them. His arms immediately found her again, turning her to face him. The strength of his hands covering her waist made her gasp.

"Game over." His lips found hers.

———

"IT'S BEEN YEARS SINCE I DOVE OFF THAT THING." Grayson's voice broke through the memory, as he sat atop his horse, watching her.

"I can't believe I'm standing here again looking at it after so long," she said, wanting to run down the steps out of habit.

She turned away so she wasn't tempted to swim out to the rock and feel herself glide through the air and into the ocean. Another familiar sight from the flashback caught her eye. Running her hand along the trunk of the sassafras tree behind Nova, she paused, taking in every detail, still so clear in her memory.

"We must have ridden past these trees a million times back then." She pulled off one of the leaves, then glanced back out at the expansive blue ocean again as the sunlight danced across the water's surface. Grayson stayed silent—both of them drawn to the stunning vista of the sea.

"Yeah, we did," he finally mumbled.

"Know what I love about trees?" Willow hooked her arm across the trunk and swung around until she faced him again. "Especially this one?"

Grayson smiled, got off Max, and met her by the tree. "What's that?"

"Most are strong and supple, bending in the face of seasonal change without breaking. They stay in one spot, enduring so much." Something she should have done. Stayed in Terra Cove. Instead, she took off because things got hard in the aftermath of trauma. Her family needed her, and she turned her back, all while sulking over the heartbreak of both the fire and Grayson.

He may have been the one to break things off, but maybe she should have allowed herself to just be in the midst of it and pushed him to talk to her. There was a lot she could have done, and even though she couldn't change how the last eight years had played out, she could make new choices from this point on. Which was, ironically, the same thing she always told her clients.

It had seemed so easy, guiding her clients through the steps they'd taken in the past and how to proceed differently, but now that it was all falling on her own shoulders, the task was proving more and more difficult to navigate by herself.

"Nature is powerful like that." His tone was soft and gaze steady.

So is love. His eyes held fierce passion, drawing her in. "I also love that these trees, this scenery, all of it"—she waved her hand around—"doesn't change." Like how they seemed to be picking up right where they had left off.

"Trees don't"—Grayson stepped closer—"but people do. They grow . . . and learn."

Willow studied the face she'd known her whole life, now etched with lines of experience and wisdom gained through time. The flutter in her stomach took hold and she shifted her attention back to the tree.

"This exact spot and every untouched detail, including this sass tree, is so unexpectedly . . . comforting." Or rather, his presence was. She crumbled the leaf still in her hand before smelling the sweet, fruity fragrance sassafras trees were known to give off.

"Yes. That's why I love this place." His gaze moved past her as he looked around.

"Coming back here, I now understand why. I didn't realize how much I missed all this. Or that it was just what I needed." *Or seeing you.* The words almost slipped out as she dropped the pieces of the leaf from her fidgety hands. "There's no place like home."

Her earlier veil of confusion started to lift among the familiar surroundings, offering respite as she and Grayson enjoyed a piece of their history together once again. It was becoming clearer that the foundation of what they had remained intact, just like the scenery around them, but now that they were grown, something about their energy together felt more profound. And she'd need to get to know Grayson all over again. Where did they start? And more importantly, why did she continue to sense some kind of mystery hiding behind his gaze, making her keep her guard up. What did he want to tell her?

Willow didn't have all the answers, but when she peeked at him, something in his body language, he was evidently lost in his own thoughts, suggested that perhaps she hadn't been alone in her questioning. Yes, he'd changed and grown, they both had, but what was he holding inside?

"That tree has certainly heard it all," he finally said, sending a chill against the heat of her back. He pointed back to Max. "Want some watermelon while it's still cool enough to eat? The ice bricks in the lunch bag are probably warm by now."

"That sounds like a perfect idea." Willow wiped more sweat off her forehead.

He turned his face toward her. "Are you okay? Overheated?"

"Yeah, a little. It's been a while since I've ridden in the summer."

"Here, have a piece." He retrieved the lunch bag from the saddlebag on Max, and she reached in. They sat under the tree in the shade and ate the melon without talking, but she sensed his mind was just as scattered as hers by how often he shifted around. She smiled as he moved again.

"Is it . . ." He trailed off, shaking his head. "Never mind."

"Oh, come on. Spit it out, Turner. Is it what?" She glanced up at him, noticing his eyes widen.

"I haven't heard you call me that in years."

Shrugging, she took another piece of watermelon. "Just came out." Her attempt to act casual felt useless. The impact from memory lane since riding these trails with him was much too intense to keep herself composed, and by the look on Grayson's face, he saw right through the cover-up.

"You think I can't see it?"

"See what?"

"When your thoughts are troubling you."

His direct gaze made her feel more vulnerable, but she couldn't go there with him. Not yet anyway. "I've just got a lot on my mind."

"I'll say." He leaned over, giving her a nudge. "At least you got to see Nova *and* you rode her."

Turning around, she saw Nova patiently waiting and suddenly felt so proud of her ability to finally ignore the internal battle that had kept her from riding. She needed to do that now—ignore the constant fear and just ask. There was no better time than the present.

"So, what were you about to say before?"

"Before when?"

"Back in the barn."

Grayson dropped his head, appearing as though he immediately started to struggle with an answer. "Willow, I think you need to talk to Tyler."

"That's it?"

"There's always more I can say to you, but Tyler needs to say it first."

"Say what first?

"Just talk to him. Ignoring the inevitable won't help you. You two need to have a discussion."

Is he serious? "And here I thought you wanted to unload some things off your chest," she said, looking out in the distance at the water so she didn't blurt out more frustration.

"I think . . . We will have our time soon to say what we both want to say." He glanced at her.

She didn't believe him. There was something more behind his tight-lipped response, but her emotions were already running high enough, so she let it go. "I must have misread you earlier."

"We better get back." He pulled out his phone, ignoring her statement. "It's nearly three." Grayson stood up and held his hand down to her.

"Okay," she said, taking his hand, and found herself inches from his face when he pulled her up. "Th-thank you for the watermelon." The stutter in her voice seemed to make

Grayson more curious as he watched her continue to move past him to get on her horse.

Nova, sensing her unease, seemed to take control of the reins. Willow hardly paid attention as they made their way back. All she'd wanted was to have a nice trail ride, but she wasn't so sure she believed that was possible anymore. She knew what coming back to these trails with him would do and her suspicions proved correct. It brought out this part of her life that she'd run from when she left the island.

———

Grayson pulled his truck right next to her car outside the deli and just as she shut the door, Whitney and her mother walked right in front of her on the sidewalk. There was no hiding the fact that she had been with him and, by the looks on their faces, she wasn't sure if they were upset about it or surprised.

"Rachel, what a pleasure to see you." Grayson was already on the sidewalk before she could figure out what to say. Her mother took his hand and leaned in to kiss him on the cheek.

"What a nice surprise," her mom said, quickly glancing at her.

"It sure is," Whitney said, her mouth dropping open briefly over his shoulder toward Willow when he hugged her too.

"I hope she's not late to your swimming plans. Willow wanted to take Nova out for a quick reunion ride, and well, you know how it goes out there on the trails." Grayson smiled at the women, clearly oblivious to their gaping mouths.

"Time gets lost out there." Willow shrugged.

"It's quite alright," her mother said with a stunned expression and Willow wanted to melt into the storm drain. "Willow, you got on a horse?"

Willow stepped closer to her and put her arm around her mom. "I did, and I can't wait to tell you all about it at the pool."

Rachel slowly nodded, still taken with surprise over the news.

"Mom and I were just grabbing some stuff for later and to barbecue for the Fourth tomorrow," Whitney chimed in against the awkwardness. "I'm so happy it falls on a Friday this year, so my husband can take a nice long weekend off."

"Oh right, the Fourth is tomorrow. Wow, I didn't even realize how fast this week went by." Willow's weak attempt at small talk made Grayson smirk.

"You've had a lot going on, honey," Rachel said to her, before turning to Grayson. "So any Fourth of July plans?"

"Just my annual camping and kayaking over by Lagoon Pond this weekend."

"Wes was mentioning something about wanting to go kayaking again last night," Whitney said, pausing in thought. "I hope he goes. He hasn't done that in years."

Willow noticed Grayson cast his eyes down at her sister's mention of her brother. Perhaps it was too hard for him to hear his name since they used to be so close.

"You sure look hot, Willow. Ready for a swim?" her mom asked.

"Absolutely. I'll just be a few minutes behind you." Willow gave her sister a long stare.

"Oh . . . right!" Whitney tugged their mom. "Let's get this ice cream back in the freezer before it's a puddle."

Turning to Grayson, she saw him eyeing the exchange and looking like he was about to break into laughter.

"I guess you were aware of how strange that was for them after all," Willow said as soon as they were gone.

"It's suddenly rather amusing is all. The looks on their faces when you got out of my truck was something I'll never forget." Grayson chuckled, stroking the stubble along his beard line.

"I'm glad you see the humor in this. I wish I did." Willow pulled her eyebrows together as she stared at her feet.

"Willow." Grayson stepped closer. "There is absolutely nothing funny about seeing you hurt or sad. Don't think I'm laughing at that."

"I know," she said with a sigh and nearly staggered back a step when he lifted her chin up to look in her eyes.

"Come on, your mother's face was like she'd seen a ghost." The corners of his mouth turned up, and he held her chin for a second before letting it go.

A smile escaped her. "No, you're right. And honestly, even though you all have been in the same town all these years, seeing you like that must be like seeing a ghost from their past."

Grayson put his hands up, taking a step back. "I better keep my distance, never know who else we will see out here."

Willow smiled, feeling the tension release. "Thank you for today. Seeing Nova was really nice. I hope to see her again soon." For a moment she wasn't sure if she was truly referring to the horse. Despite the old memories that had poured out of her up on the trail, in an odd way, it felt good. She nearly laughed thinking about all the times she'd told her clients to do exactly that—find a way to let the feelings move through them. Now she was practicing what she'd preached to them all these years and she was suddenly grateful to experience this. When she resumed her sessions, she'd truly understand a little more.

"I'm glad to hear that," Grayson said, seeming to want to say more but didn't.

Willow watched him, trying to gather what he'd been thinking. Sometimes Grayson Turner was easy to read and other times, impossible.

"Well, I better let you get going."

"If I take too long to meet them back home, who knows what conclusions they will drum up," she teased.

"Yeah. Better go join in on the gossip." They both laughed. "Hey, listen, are you planning on going to the summer festival next weekend?"

Terra Cove's agricultural summer festival was one of Martha's Vineyard's most beloved events. An old-fashioned skillet toss, carnival rides, shucking contests, a woodsmen competition, livestock shows, delicious food, pony rides for the kids, and equestrian contests for the adults gathered a large crowd every year. Standing there with Grayson and thinking about the festival was as if she'd suddenly been transported back in time to those carefree summer days.

"Maybe," was all she could think to say, not wanting to commit in case her parents decided not to do the pony rides because of her dad's accident. "I'm not sure my mom will be doing our booth this year since my dad won't be there."

"Well, there's no rule that says you can't attend if your parents aren't doing their usual pony rides," he pointed out. "Besides, Nova and Max are both in the equine contest this year. You have to come watch."

Willow tried to think of a rebuttal, but his eyes held her in a hypnotic grip.

"True . . . I'll just have to let you know," she managed to say, forcing her attention off him to open her car door. "Talk soon?"

"Anytime." He closed her door after she got in and waved as he backed away.

Something in her suddenly wanted to drive away and never look back, ignoring the opposition that thudded in her chest. Her heart had made it clear up on those trails that Grayson Turner still had a place in it, but this tiptoeing around all of their feelings kept spiraling her back to utter confusion. She heard him loud and clear when he said that people change, learn, and grow, and she believed him. But not what he'd said about talking to Tyler. That could *not* have been what he'd wanted to say back in the barn earlier. Even though they were just teenagers then navigating the challenges of young love, it wasn't easy to bring it up after so long. She didn't blame him for not being able to say what he'd wanted.

On the other hand, she thought about the fact that Grayson worked for the Parkers, something Tyler, her *fiancé*, had kept from her. Why keep it from her? It all felt so strange. No wonder she felt so weighed down. She just couldn't shake the feeling that there was something else she was about to find out.

The heavy burden suddenly overwhelmed her. Tyler, Grayson . . . and unraveling everything all at once. Maybe she just needed to get herself back to her clients in Connecticut once her dad got stronger and put everything in Terra Cove to rest again. She had done that once and she could do it again . . . right?

Chapter Twelve

Sunday morning's golden light gradually intensified as the sun climbed higher in the sky. The pond's water appeared still, bathing in the warmth of the rays. Grayson took in a deep breath, holding his thermos of hot brew and savoring the peacefulness of chirping birds welcoming the new day. Martha's Vineyard's beauty never failed to remind him of the majesty nature provided.

"Please say that wasn't in my dream and that's coffee I smell," Wesley said as he came out of his tent.

Grayson motioned behind him. "You weren't dreaming. There's another thermos near the electric burner. The coffee is on top in that pot."

Wesley picked up the cylinder-shaped pot. "What is this fancy contraption?" He opened the top and peered in.

"A Christmas gift from my mom a few years ago. I used to always complain I couldn't get a decent cup of coffee on my camping trips."

Wesley poured himself some in the extra thermos and took a sip. "Wow, that's good. Nice and hot," he said and took a seat next to him.

"Yup, leave it to my mom to find the best camping coffee maker there is." Grayson looked out across the pond again. "How'd you sleep?"

"After the fireworks stopped, I went right out."

"I'm glad my dog is with my mom, otherwise those fireworks would have spooked him too much." Grayson had taken up his mom's offer and let her have Monty for the weekend.

"I bet. Well, once they died down it was so peaceful. I haven't slept that good in months."

"Nothing like the fresh air out here."

"Nope." Wesley looked up as a flock of birds flew above them. "And I know I've already said this, but thanks again for inviting me. It was good to talk through everything last night. I'll make it up to you with a free helicopter ride. I can't wait to have you fly with me."

"Looking forward to it." Grayson stood up to refill his coffee before sitting back down.

They watched the daylight continue to light up the pond's edges as the woods became alive. Being surrounded by total silence and the beauty of the outdoors usually made it easy to forget the stresses of the world.

The men had spent the Fourth of July weekend camping, and the night before, while sitting by the fire with beers in hand, Grayson told Wesley everything. They had an honest conversation, as he let go of the built-up tension over what had happened with him and Willow and his mother's affair with Mr. Parker. His quiet camping trip had turned into a night of reconnecting and a lot of discussion—which had been exactly how Grayson hoped it would go.

When he called Wesley the night of the accident and told him there was something important he needed to tell him, Wesley didn't hesitate—especially when he learned they'd go camping and kayaking like they used to years ago. Wesley had been a great listener and in return, Grayson let him share his own frustrations about all that had happened—particularly about losing touch with each other. They had been close friends for many years.

"I will say," Wesley started, pausing to take a long sip from his thermos. "When you first called me, I was really taken aback. But it was perfect timing. I had been sitting outside the hospital by myself, trying to collect my thoughts from such a hard day. I was pleasantly surprised to see you calling me."

Grayson hesitated, watching a magnificent great blue heron glide gracefully overhead. The heron's blue plumage glistened in the sunlight while its sharp eyes scanned the water for its next meal.

"I bet you were," he finally said, keeping his eyes on the bird. "I'm glad you came. No reason for us to continue the silence with each other, especially now with . . ." He paused, not wanting to bring up any hard feelings again by reminding Wesley of what Tyler had done on the day of the wedding. Willow's brother had already displayed a lot of anger toward Tyler the night before. "Well . . . It's just been a long time."

"Sure has," Wesley agreed. "Now when I go to the brewery and see you there, you can come have a drink at the bar *with* me." Both men laughed. He was right though. Grayson had come in so many times to get a beer and sit near Wesley like they were strangers.

"I can't wait to get out there for our last day." Grayson nodded toward the rippling water. "And it's been great to have your company again. But listen, thanks for taking the news so well last night."

"That's what friends are for, even friends who haven't spoken in years." Wesley chuckled. "But it's not you I'm mad at, it's Tyler. It's probably time to let it go, I suppose."

"I know." Grayson looked over at him. "Me too, although

I don't think I have a right to be. After all, I was the one who started the whole mess the night of prom."

"You asked him to escort her to prom, not take her off the island and steal her from you." Wesley let out a long breath. "You know, I tried for years to get on board with the two of them, but I never fully could. And now that I understand what you went through with Jack that night . . . I get it, man. That was a lot to process in one night for anyone."

"Yeah, it certainly was." Looking back, the days and weeks following that night were a blur, but somewhere in the mix of it all, Grayson had stalled. "But I just let Tyler get away with lying to her. I just felt so . . . confused after learning about the affair."

"Of course you were. Jack's addiction, always being in and out of your life growing up and treating you and your sister the way he did . . . and watching your mom struggle." Wesley shook his head. "I don't know. I guess what I'm trying to say is I understand what transpired that night a little better now. You found out some shocking news. I don't think I would have handled hearing something like that any better than you did."

Grayson stayed quiet, and before he could stop them, his father's drunken words from that night reverberated deep within his thoughts.

———

"Boy, you're so quick to protect your mother. And she's nothing but a—"

"Don't you say another word about her!" Grayson shouted, stepping closer, unafraid now that he had grown to stand eye level with him.

Laughing, his father staggered back, his legs weakened by the booze. "Alright, alright." He put his hands up. "Nothing more from me. But maybe you can ask Tyler to explain. Being that he's your brother."

"What do you mean Tyler is my brother?" Grayson asked, barely able to comprehend what he'd just heard.

"Why do you think I left your mother?" his father hissed through his drunken snicker. "And you think you're better than me? You're not. You're just like her: a fraud! Willow will see that soon enough!"

———

Grayson blinked out of the memory. "Well . . . not telling Willow what I was feeling and what happened with Jack that night wasn't the right way to deal with it at all." He glanced at Wesley. "That was wrong. Instead, I let what Jack said to me take over. For years I believed him to be right . . . that I was no better than him because of my mom's mistake. It's taken me a long time to work through that man's abuse."

"I think you've done better than you realize. Worked your way up at Parker Craft Brewing Co. and everything. You seem to have turned out alright, unless there's some other deep secrets I don't know about." Wesley grinned.

Grayson laughed and put his hand up. "My mom's affair is it; I hope."

The mention of Parker's Brewing reminded him that he had to get back to work tomorrow and he blew out some air. He enjoyed his job, but with all that had happened, and especially having Willow back in town, it would make it harder to concentrate.

At least working for Daniel made up for it. Daniel had begun to refer to him as "son" after they started spending some time together, which had helped soften the sharp edges of his past with Jack. Eight years of working for Daniel and getting to know him more as an adult had brought great healing—except for one thing. Tyler still hadn't come around to the idea that they shared Daniel as a father.

Grayson hadn't known what a true father was like growing up, but his relationship with Daniel since he'd graduated high school had shown him. He also didn't know it was something he needed until it was in front of him. Once Grayson discovered the truth, Daniel went out of his way to connect with him and provide, as if to somehow make up for lost time. Offering to pay for college if he wanted to go, giving him a job and promoting him to where he was today at the brewery, lending an ear to listen and wise words to help guide him. Daniel Parker had stepped up more than Grayson would have asked of him, all while Tyler continued to distance himself further.

Grayson's only conclusion for that was because Tyler was with Willow, a relationship that started on a lie and continued that way—all while keeping her in the dark. All that had done was enforce her reasoning for staying out of Terra Cove.

Wesley touched his shoulder. "Hey, man. You might have kept that news from Willow, but so did Tyler. He was with her for the last eight years and about to *marry* her. You were a kid back then and dealing with trauma from your childhood and couldn't figure out how to filter that. What teenager could? You were vulnerable, understandably so. What's Tyler's excuse as an adult for keeping from her the simple fact that you're brothers?"

"I'm not sure." Grayson watched the heron swoop by again. "Thanks, Wes. I never really looked at it that way. That was helpful to hear."

"Anytime." Wes squeezed his shoulder, then gave him a playful push. "I just wish you came to me sooner, so we could have avoided years of distance."

"Yeah . . ." Grayson smiled at his old friend. "I do too."

"We could have talked this out, and I definitely would have urged you to go after Willow to fix everything."

Grayson nodded. "It might have saved me from years of silence between me and her. I just hope she won't be too mad finding out now, all these years later, and throw us back into non-speaking terms."

"Remember what we talked about last night? Learning about the affair doesn't affect Willow directly, except maybe it'll be a bit shocking like it was for me. That part won't make her upset. It's the keeping it from her and for so long that will. She trusted both of you, so you might need to earn that back, but you can."

"I'd love to be in her life again, in any capacity, but I also want her to move forward in peace. If that means saying goodbye again in order for her to do that, then so be it."

"I don't think she will." Wesley shifted toward him. "Look, you two share so much history. Regardless of how she responds, the truth needs to come out in the open so you *all* can move forward."

"You're right." Grayson shook his head. "I still can't believe Tyler didn't find at least one opportunity in the past eight years to tell her."

"Yeah, I agree. Which tells me there must be some reason why."

"Who knows. But they have a lot to talk about, so I'm trying to respect that and be patient, to give him a chance to spill the truth. Otherwise, I will. But me jumping too quickly just doesn't feel right. I've been out of her life for so long. I want to be careful how I approach this. Once they have a conversation, then I'd like to talk to her about my side of things."

"Fair enough. But I wouldn't give him too much longer. He's only had eight years after all."

"Exactly." Grayson chuckled, glancing up at the sky. "I feel like all I've done for years now is give him space to do the right thing, and look where it's landed us."

"Quit being so hard on yourself. It's landed Willow back home, and we're all happy about that. But if he can't face her, I'll make sure this time you do. Get everything out in the open so my sister can let it all go and be happy again."

Grayson looked at him. "Are you saying she was *never* happy with Tyler?" He remembered Tyler saying the same thing to Liam in the hospital the other morning.

"She cares about him. That was never a question. Happy? Yes and no." Wesley stood up, turning toward the water. "It's just always been you. She's never stopped loving you. Everyone knows that." He nodded toward the pond. "Come on, man. Enough of this heavy talk. Let's get out there."

Wesley's words struck right through him. *Did* Willow still love him? He couldn't answer that. But to know she'd been unhappy? That instantly troubled him. Happiness was all he had wanted for her and why, after years had passed, he'd let her go. Or tried to. He thought Tyler was what she wanted, and stepping in to destroy that for her had been the last thing he'd wanted to do. But if that wasn't what she wanted . . . That changed everything.

———

Monty's excessive barking finally drew his attention away from the leftover debris outside the soap shack the following Friday. It was lunchtime and the end of a thankfully busy first week back at work, and he'd decided to take the rest of the day off to get his horses moved to the fairground for the summer festival. Despite his workload, he'd found time throughout the week to notice one thing while in and out of town—no sign of Willow. He tried not to let it, but his heart sank each time she wasn't at any of their common spots in town where he'd hoped to run into her.

He'd wrestled in his mind all week with whether he should call her, but he'd meant what he said to Wesley while camping—he wanted to keep a respectful distance so Tyler could talk to her first. Grayson knew the more he saw her, the less likely he was to keep quiet.

He had, however, been talking with Wesley more since their camping trip, but he often found his mind lingering on Willow during their conservations. Not wanting to pry, Grayson kept it all to himself, but her brother did finally share that Willow seemed to be in a very confused state and kept pushing Tyler away. It took all of his willpower not to rush over to her house and be there for her. Time was ticking, and he grew more irritated as his patience waned.

Looking at the shack again, he scratched his head. He'd worked on the area for the two weeks he was off, and the outside was cleared and looking much better, but the inside was still such a mess. He still had no clue what he would do with it once it was cleaned out. There was no time to dwell on it with the festival the following day and he'd needed to get that horse trailer cleaned out for transfer.

An hour later, sweat saturated his face in the rising heat, and he decided to head inside to cool down once the trailer was ready for Nova and Max.

"Come on, boy!" He whistled in the direction of the barking. Monty quieted and fell into step with him moments later. "Find yourself a squirrel to chase out there?" The dog jogged ahead of him, nose to the ground, then dashed off to follow a new trail.

Checking his phone, he saw a text from Wesley.

Let me know if you need help getting your horses to the festival later. I'd be happy to help.

He smiled at the gesture. Even though their first camping trip in years included a lot of serious discussion, it was nice to now rebuild their friendship and move forward. He just hoped it could be the same with Willow. Something Wesley had said from their camping trip popped into his thoughts for probably the tenth time that week. *"I don't think I would have handled hearing something like that any better than you did."*

That statement had stuck with Grayson for days as he buried himself in work, letting his mind sort through the mix of feelings that accompanied the words. For years he'd called himself a coward for not going after Willow, making him feel less and less adequate, especially as more time passed and she was with Tyler. What Wesley said was the first time anyone had given him true perspective on the situation in that manner—prompting him to reflect on it in a whole new way.

Now grown and looking back, Grayson understood the accuracy of Wesley's words. What Grayson had been dealing with at the time was more than any eighteen year old could handle. Maybe he'd inadvertently pushed Willow away as a means of dealing with the lingering effects of Jack's abuse. The time to himself over the last eight years had certainly paved the way for more healing as Grayson grew into adulthood, but it left out one important part of his recovery—what could have evolved between him and Willow. No matter which way he thought about it, it felt like a vicious loop he couldn't get out of.

Whistling toward the woods again, Monty came running out. "What a mess," he told the dog once they got inside. The other thing he realized as he'd spent time reflecting since the camping trip, was that he also needed to give Tyler some slack.

While his mother's affair wasn't new for Tyler or him anymore, it would be for Willow. Not to mention her learning that no one told her after years of knowing. That was going to make sharing that they were brothers a lot more difficult for Tyler.

But still . . . eight years, and *nothing*? That was the part that boggled Grayson's mind the most, and now that everything was coming to a head, he hoped to get a chance to learn why. And despite his feelings for Willow, he and Tyler were brothers. Perhaps Daniel's attempts to mend their friendship could finally come to fruition too.

This is certainly a tough mess to sort through, he thought and grabbed a bottle of water out of the fridge. He leaned against the kitchen counter while his circling thoughts carried him back to another day he'd worked hard to forget.

———

"IS THIS WHY JACK IS SO SCREWED UP, MOM?" Grayson shouted, making his mother shudder as he paced the kitchen.

"Jack didn't know about the affair until a couple weeks ago," she whispered, looking away from him. Tears escaped her eyes, and she let them fall as she stood leaning against the kitchen counter. "I didn't want you to find out like this."

Realizing there was zero excuse for Jack's drinking problem and leaving his family when he did only ignited Grayson's anger. Was it because of something he'd done while growing up?

"So you had a one-night stand with Mr. Parker before Jack ever had an issue with alcohol? I don't understand you!" he continued to roar, but instantly regretted the words when his mother stifled a sob. After the fire, he'd spent a week in his room by himself, unable to confront her until now.

"Daniel and I have loved each other for a long time, Grayson. You are too young to understand," she said, trying to reach for him, but he shrugged her off. He knew Mr. Parker grew up with his mom in Terra Cove, but that didn't make their actions right.

"What you did was wrong."

"Yes. It was very wrong. We all make mistakes, Grayson—"

"And I understand plenty!" He was in no mood to hear her reasoning. But was he really that mad at her or was he still reeling off what he had done to Willow the week before with prom and the fire that destroyed so much of her family's livelihood. A fire that would not have happened if he had just controlled his anger and hadn't picked a fight with Tyler. How could he ever face the Andersons again? Maybe Jack had been right. He *was* a fraud.

"Grayson . . ."

"I understand the person I love is no longer in my life, and I don't even know why now. I lost her from my own stupid mistakes." Grayson sat down at the kitchen table, realizing his rage wasn't about his mother's affair anymore. "I started that fight with Tyler . . . I started that fire."

"Grayson, stop it right now. The fire was an accident and no one's fault."

"If I didn't shove Tyler and cause Mr. Anderson to have to get off that tractor and distract him, he would have seen the fire much sooner." He buried his face in his hands, trying to contain his fury.

"Go to her, Grayson. Explain what happened," she said.

"I couldn't face Willow that night; I can't face her now." He squeezed his eyes shut remembering how he walked right by Willow when she'd sat crying on her front porch with her brother—not saying a single word to her. The devastation on her face when he, instead, got in his truck and drove away had haunted him for days.

His mother instantly went to him and placed her hands on his shoulders. "Willow loves you. Go to her." She gently pressed him again.

He didn't have the energy to tell her it was no use—he'd found her kissing Tyler at the cove . . . their cove. That was it for him. He had lost her and the thought made him crumble against his mother's embrace, Jack's words cycling through his mind all over again.

"You think you're better than me? You're not. You're just like her: a fraud! Willow will see that soon enough!"

Sitting up, Grayson slammed his fist on top of the table in rage at himself. Willow had gone straight to Tyler, and he didn't blame her. He'd destroyed so much for Willow and her family. And now it was too late to fix it.

———

MONTY WHINED BY HIS FEET AND GRAYSON BLINKED out of the flashback. "I know, boy," he said. "I need to stop drifting off like that."

The sound of a car caught Grayson's attention, and Monty dashed out of the kitchen. Grayson followed him to the front door where his dog stood waiting and wagging his tail. A car door shut.

"Must recognize who it is if you're not barking." He opened the door and froze as Monty ran to greet her and she came up the front steps.

Willow squatted to pet his head. "Hey, buddy." Her hair was pulled back in a cute ponytail, the curls sticking out in every direction, and she was wearing a long denim skirt with a cropped white top and matching white sandals.

"Hello, Grayson," she said, staring up at him bright-eyed and vulnerable. Her gold bracelets jingled when she stood and reached up to push her black sunglasses on top of her head.

"Willow? This is a surprise." He opened the door wider, mustering all his willpower not to reach for her as her light brown eyes stared into his, the sun highlighting the features around her face. *She's more stunning than ever.* He tightened his lips.

"May I come in?"

"Yes, of course." He stepped back from the door, breathing in the sweet citrusy tones of her scent as she walked past him.

She took a moment to observe the room, lost in her own thoughts. "It's been a long time since I've been in this house."

"Yes, it has." She'd come for a reason, and he didn't want to distract her by saying more.

"Sorry to intrude on your day like this. I wasn't sure you'd be home, but I ran into your assistant at the coffee shop. I didn't know Jesse Olsen worked for you."

"Yeah, she's a great assistant. I always forget that she went to school with us. She was always so quiet back then."

She swirled around to face him. "Anyway, she told me you left for the day. So here I am."

"Here you are," he repeated, allowing a small smile as he gazed into her eyes.

She broke their stare and drew her brows together. "But maybe I should have called first?"

"You always have an invitation here."

"Oh . . ." Her expression relaxed, and she briefly cast her eyes down. "It's been a long week." She looked toward the kitchen.

He followed her stare. "Want to have a seat? I don't have much, but I could make coffee?"

"A glass of water is all I want."

"I think I can manage that." He winked and stepped past her.

Willow chuckled. Hearing her laugh was music to his ears,

but he sensed her troubles beneath the surface. Humor always helped her in the past.

Monty followed them to the kitchen and when she sat at the table, the dog sat right by her feet, enjoying ear scratches from her. "Looks like I have a new friend."

"Monty is like Nova. When someone is down, he stays right by their side."

She was silent, her shoulders slumped forward as she continued to stroke the dog's upright ears.

Maybe he spoke too soon. He opened the cabinet to get a glass for her water.

"He's a beautiful shepherd." She leaned closer to Monty and smiled at him. "Thank you for sitting by me, buddy."

"I shouldn't have made that assumption. I'm sorry."

"It's okay. You assumed correctly."

"Bad week?" he asked, then filled the glass with water.

"I'm just juggling a lot with trying to cover things at the farm for my dad, and I spent all week moving my clients to virtual sessions starting next week. Since I'm still managing the farm along with the hired help, I'm only going to work part time for awhile on Tuesdays and Thursdays." She straightened up from Monty. "That'll have to do—until I figure out how to wrap things up in Connecticut. It's looking less likely that I'll return there anytime soon."

"Oh yeah?" He gripped the glass, trying not to appear too excited. This was about her, not him.

"Yeah . . . I've been thinking about it this week while sorting through all that. It'll take my dad quite a while, I think, to fully recover and be able to run things at the farm on his own again."

"How is he?" Grayson offered her the glass, then sat down across from her.

"Thanks. That's the good part of my week." She smiled and took a sip before continuing. "He's had a great start in physical therapy since he was moved to the rehabilitation center for inpatients a few days ago. I've been there most days, watching and visiting and pleased to see him walking, even if it's with a lot of assistance."

"That's such a relief. So do they think he will make a full recovery?"

"Right now, they are positive he will, but his lower back is still bothering him. They will continue to monitor that and work on it. But then this morning they actually began the discussion of outpatient treatment, which really perked him up."

"I bet he's itching to get out of there. He'll probably recover faster once he's home. My mom will be happy to learn how well he's doing, but I'm sure Daniel's been updating her —" He caught himself, but it was too late.

"That's nice that she and Mr. Parker talk."

Willow's unknowing expression made him want to shrink in his seat. Explaining about Daniel and his mother dating would be completely random to her and hard to do without telling her the rest of their story.

"Yeah, it's nice to see her more active with the community in general. She joined a cooking class and made some new friends there too." Hopefully that would keep her curiosity to a low roar for now.

"That's great." She picked up the glass and took another drink.

"Speaking of my mom, she felt bad for walking by you at the hospital without saying hello the night of the accident. I know she wants to talk to you about that but probably doesn't want to bother you while you're dealing with your dad's recovery."

"Yeah, I wondered about that at the time, but tell her it's no big deal. It was a rough day."

"I'll tell her. She was just worried about Liam. We all were."

"Tell her thank you for coming to the hospital. It meant a lot to see her there." She smiled and looked down at her water.

"I'm happy to hear that." He paused when she gave him a nervous glance.

"It meant a lot to see you there too," she said, tapping the glass. He could tell her mind was running, as was his.

"Did it? I really battled with the idea. I didn't want to make anything worse for you, but Liam is still important to me." When she looked back up at him, her eyes soft and exposed, he fought the temptation to wrap her in a protective embrace. "Your whole family is."

"Thank you. Your family is too," she said, barely above a whisper. "Speaking of, Abby and I have been talking ever since I saw her last week. Catching up has been really good."

"I was hoping you would. She's always looked up to you, even after you left for school. I'm sure she's excited to have you back in her life." He refrained from telling her how hurt Abby had been when they broke up and how tossed aside she felt when Willow stopped talking to her too—just as he'd done to Wesley. It was a relief to know she and Abby were able to put that behind them and start over—just like he had with Wesley.

Willow frowned. "I shouldn't have left her like that. There was no reason to cut ties with her, or any of our other friends here."

"You're here now. Don't stress too much about what happened back then." *I should tell myself the same.* He gave her an encouraging smile to keep the words from slipping out.

"You're right. I'm glad I have the chance to start again with Abby." She eyed him and he could see there was more.

"Me too," he added, bracing himself for what he guessed was coming next since they were on the topic of siblings.

"Just like you and Wesley," she said.

There it was. Grayson knew that eventually Willow would find out about the camping trip.

"I should have told you beforehand that I had invited him along to camp and kayak. I just wasn't thinking. I—"

"Grayson . . ." she stopped him. "It's okay. It really is. Wesley told me all about it and how much fun he had. I'm so happy he got to get out there again on the water, go camping, and enjoy all the things he once loved to do. I guess he just hasn't been able to face it since you two last went."

"Wait, what? The last time we went together before this past weekend was *years* ago," he said in surprise. "I mean, he told me it had been a while, but I didn't realize how long."

"It's been a rough go for Wes. He dated a girl for a few years and thought things were progressing toward an engagement, but it turned out she wasn't committed or faithful to him like he'd thought. He was so busy working as a bartender after high school and saving to go to flight school that he didn't notice her cheating and lies." She raised the glass to her lips again. "So kayaking and camping got lost in the mess of all that, I guess. Or . . . it was hard to go without you. Tyler was never into camping much, but you two spent so many nights together out on that pond back in high school."

"Yeah, we did." Grayson nodded, feeling bad he hadn't been there for his friend during such a hard breakup or for the opening night of Vineyard Helicopter Tours. "I'm sorry to hear he went through that."

"Well, that's all in the past," she said, waving her hand. "But I want you to know that you don't have to stop your friendship with my brother because of me. That's silly."

"And the same goes for Abby."

"Glad we established that." She gave him a cheeky grin. "Only took us eight years. But we all know that's mostly your fault."

"Hey, now!" he fired back. "Is that why you came? Cause we can go at it." He put his fists up as she laughed.

"You just can't handle it when I'm right." She beamed up at him, and he felt the essence of their relationship that once was. It was amazing that no matter how long it had been or how awkward things had become, there was still a part of them that had remained intact. It was just their dynamic, and it made him ache with missing her.

He watched her, unsure at first, but figured he could at least start their much-needed conversation, despite whatever she had or had not discussed with Tyler by this point.

"Can I share something with you?"

"Depends on if it's good or bad."

"It's . . . neither. But hear me out." He leaned forward. "Willow, I need you to know that when I didn't show up for prom night, it was because Jack had showed up in one of his worst drunken stupors I'd ever seen."

"I know. Tyler told me." She narrowed her eyes. "But I'm beginning to get a hunch that he never told me *everything*."

He didn't and neither did I. "There's a lot I need to share, but like I said during our trail ride the other day, I want you to have a chance to talk to Tyler first."

Willow nodded, looking down at her hands.

"I'm guessing you haven't yet. Are you avoiding him?"

She looked down at the table. "Kind of. But I don't even know why at this point. For the first two weeks after he called off the wedding, I was ready to talk. Every time the phone made a noise, I checked to see if it was him. I waited and waited."

Disappointment fired through him. "Were you hoping he'd change his mind?"

She glanced back up. "See that's the thing . . . No, I wasn't. In fact, the opposite. I had quickly realized during all that waiting that I didn't want him to change his mind and come back for me."

"I see . . ." He tried to keep his face even.

"When I acknowledged that truth, that I never really wanted to marry him at all, it threw me. I mean, we were together a *long* time."

"I can see how confusing that would be." Grayson wanted to say more but refrained. He didn't want to make this about him while she was sharing her heart.

"Very. My entire life got thrown upside down, but I'm not . . . heartbroken. And while I'm angry at how Tyler ended it—through a *text* message on our wedding day—I'm not actually upset that it did end."

"Which is why, I really think you two should still talk and soon." He sat back, trying not to let the idea of that suddenly worry him. What if Tyler somehow convinced her to be with him again?

"I know . . . But I don't know . . . Ever since I got that call about my dad's accident and came back home, I guess I've just been processing everything all at once and started pushing him away. But you're right. I do, and I will." Willow waved her hand. "Enough about that. I didn't come to bore you with my relationship woes."

"You're not boring me. I'm here anytime you need to talk." He wanted to ask her why she stayed with Tyler for so long or why she even fell for him to begin with, but she'd just opened up to him, and it was too soon to go there. Besides, did it really even matter anymore?

"I appreciate that." Her stare lingered on him a moment, and he put his hands on his lap to keep from touching hers as they rested on the table. "But I came by for two reasons. First, to tell you that I know about Wes and that it's all okay by me —not that either of you need my permission." She grinned. "I just wanted to tell you personally that it made me happy to hear about the camping trip. And second, I wanted to visit Nova. I'll never forget the look in her eyes when she first saw me last week, and I want to assure her that I won't leave her like that again."

Did she notice the same look in his eyes? "You are special to her, Willow." *And to me.* He clenched his jaw to stop the words.

"So, what time are you transporting Max and Nova to the fairgrounds? I can help you get them there if you'd like. I'm excited for them to show off their skills."

"I take it that you're going to come to the festival then?"

"Hmm . . . while that may be true, I did decide to come" —she teasingly arched her brow—"but it's really for Nova."

"Ah! Okay, the truth is out." He laughed. "Maybe we need to write up a parenting plan with a visitation schedule."

"Now we're talking!" She giggled.

"What did your parents decide to do this year?"

"Their booth is on as usual. One of the helping hands is getting the horses to the fairgrounds as we speak. I'm happy they decided not to cancel the pony rides with our horses."

"Me too. The kids always love that booth." He pulled out his phone and began typing a message. "Just letting Wesley know I'm all set for help with my horses. He had asked earlier."

"Oh, don't let me stand in your way. I can go say hi to Nova and then meet her at the festival later."

They locked eyes.

"You're never in my way, Willow. Besides, I just sent the message."

She glanced out the window, and he wondered if there was more on her mind than just coming to see Nova. But just like he knew when to joke around with her, he also knew when not to.

"Let's go get them ready."

Chapter Thirteen

The filtered radiance of the setting sun over the ocean had faded against the hazy backdrop of the horizon, encircling an array of pink and orange in the sky above. Willow stood under it, spellbound under its magnificence as she enjoyed a short reprieve from the festival's noise as the crowd grew.

Helping Grayson move the horses and set them up at his station, along with visiting her parents' booth, had kept her distracted the rest of the afternoon. It was wonderful to be there again witnessing the familiar sights and sounds of the festival she'd grown up attending. She was sad that her first year back at the festival wouldn't include her dad, but there was always next year.

At one point her mom walked by Grayson's booth while they prepped the horses for the first equine contest, and slowed, quietly observing them, but Willow didn't blame her —she'd have been curious too. After running into her and Whitney in the parking lot the first day she'd seen Nova, she and her mom didn't talk too much about Grayson. Perhaps her mom was giving her a little space to sort through things, but Willow hadn't been sure what she'd even tell her mom anyway. Things with Grayson were interesting, to say the least, but she was still trying to figure out if their spending time together meant anything significant. Although, her heart would disagree every time his green eyes held her in place.

Whitney had showed up with the kids just as she and Grayson finished saddling Nova and Max who both would be showing off in the first equine demonstrations that evening. Whitney allowed Grayson to take Maya on Nova for a private ride, and watching him interact with her niece was a beautiful sight. Grayson was a natural with Maya.

"Are you all set over here?" Willow had jogged over to her mom's booth and found her double checking the straps after their new hires saddled the horses.

"Oh yes, we're fine," Mom said. "One of our other farm workers just showed up to help too."

"Great. I'll sort of be all around the place. It's been so long since I've been to this festival, so there's a lot I want to see."

"I know. Go enjoy yourself." Willow started to leave as her mom turned back to the saddle. "Hey, Willow?" She stopped and faced her. "I love seeing you laugh again."

Willow stayed silent, a little thrown off by the statement. Mom winked and gave the straps one last tug before walking away.

Seeing me laugh . . . again?

Her phone buzzed in her back pocket, and she blinked out of her frozen stance and reached for it.

"Hey! Just checking in," Ivy said when Willow answered.

"I'm glad you did. I miss you!" She walked away from the booth and crowd toward the far side of the festival where it would be quieter. "I wish you were with me now. I'm at a festival I know you'd love."

"Well, say the word and I'll quit the store. I'd love to be on Martha's Vineyard . . . like, forever."

Willow smiled. Ivy was most likely not kidding. Ever since she'd met Willow in college and found out she was from Martha's Vineyard, Ivy jokingly hinted that she wanted to drag her back and live there with her on the island. Looking around at the place she had always loved so dearly, she knew it was time she told Ivy her *whole* story.

"Believe me, life here isn't all it's cracked up to be."

Silence on the other end meant her friend could sense her frustration beyond the situation with Tyler. "What is it, Willow? Tell me."

With a sigh, she glanced over her shoulder to make sure no one was near her, then walked a little farther to hide behind the old post-and-beam barn which was the center point of the festival.

"Tyler isn't the only man I am facing since being home. And I haven't even talked things out with Tyler yet. He keeps asking and I'm avoiding—"

"Wait. 'The only man'? Start there."

"I can't get into the whole story since I'm standing in the middle of a fairground at this festival, but my past here includes another man I grew up with and dated all through high school."

"Oh, we all have those. My high school boyfriend stalks me on social media every now and then. Remember I showed you—"

"This is different," Willow cut in. She needed Ivy to hear the bulk of everything as quickly as possible.

"Different how?" Ivy asked. "Do you still care about this man? What's his name?"

"Grayson. He—" Willow bit her lip in thought. "It's more than my feelings, which, I've realized since I saw him at the hospital the first day I got here, haven't exactly changed. And that has really bothered me since he, too, broke my heart. It's why I'm in limbo and partly why I'm pushing Tyler away, because I've been so confused."

"The plot thickens!" Ivy teased. "Plus, you're dealing with your father. That's a lot all at once!"

"Yes, there's that too. I'm trying to take this day by day, be present with how I feel, and let all the emotions come so I can make clear conscious choices." Willow winced. "Gosh, I hope all that sounds better to my clients when I tell them the same thing."

Ivy chuckled. "You're trying to play therapist to yourself. Don't do that. Take a breath and stop overthinking what the right thing to do is."

"But didn't you just hear me? The man I loved and dated the entire four years of high school, who also left me high and dry *on* prom night might I add—right before the fire happened—is back in my life as though he never left."

"What's with the men in your life ending things during important occasions?"

"I've asked myself the same thing." Willow looked up when she heard screams from one of the twisting carnival rides nearby. "But as you said, it's a lot to handle."

"Well, since Grayson is still in Terra Cove, you were bound to run into him at some point. Wait . . ." Ivy grew silent for a moment. "Did you say you ran into him at the hospital the night of the accident? Does he work there or something?"

"No, he came to offer me support."

"Really? After eight years?"

"Ivy . . ." Willow sighed and racked her brain to figure out how to say so much in so little time. "Grayson, Tyler, and I were best friends growing up. My dad was an important part of both of their lives."

"Okay, I understand now."

"But seeing him show up at the hospital wasn't what threw

me. It was how I felt when I first laid eyes on him. Why was I so taken with Grayson the *second* I saw him? I should want to slap him for what he did to me on prom night, leaving me high and dry after four years together with no explanation. I've since had some answers about what happened that night, but still . . . eight years and it's like my heart picked right back up where it left off without a hitch. As if Tyler never happened. There's more to share, but I wanted to at least start there."

"Okay, well, there's still time for a good slap." That made Willow laugh. Her friend's humor reminded her of Grayson's, only making her fuse of irritation intensify. "Just breathe, Willow. I know you're laughing, but I can still feel your anxiety through the phone. It sounds like unfinished business is why—"

"'Unfinished business'? Do you not remember that I was about to say 'I do' to Tyler only weeks ago?"

"Of course I do. And clearly marrying Tyler wasn't the right thing for you."

"Tyler ended it, not me!" Willow's nerves fired up and she wanted to leave and go hide in her parents' house. Every time this confusion overtook her, she got stuck. Just like how she'd been in Connecticut whenever she thought about Terra Cove —halted in place.

"Willow, we both know you and Tyler were done a long time before that. Perhaps you two never were what you thought, even from the beginning, especially now that I'm hearing about this Grayson guy."

"How exactly could you come to that conclusion when you just learned about Grayson?" Willow looked around again, relieved that no one had spotted her yet.

"Because Tyler has never taken hold of your heart like he should have. I've been your best friend for nearly a decade and hearing how you talk about Grayson . . . there's passion in your voice. Look how he is exciting you and confusing you all at the same time. Besides, if you ever loved Tyler Parker like you thought, you would have talked to him by now. Who knows, maybe even tried again. But now I'm beginning to understand what Tyler must have seen, which is why it's over."

"And what's that?"

"That he never had a chance."

Ivy's words struck her, but instead of getting mad at her friend, she stayed quiet to listen.

"Look, I didn't want to remind you of this when you were staying with me right after you two split up, but don't you remember the engagement party?"

"Yes, I do." Willow's eyes snapped shut against the memory of that night, recalling how her siblings and Ivy confronted her before the party began, asking her the same question: Was she happy with Tyler? She knew she hadn't been for a long time, but Tyler had felt safe, especially after that night. And now, being back home, surrounded by the people and places she'd avoided for so long, she realized being safe hadn't served her at all—nor had it been true love.

"Are you still in love with Grayson and want him back?" Ivy asked, cutting right to the chase.

"No . . . Maybe . . . Gosh, I don't know. I don't even know how to explain what I'm thinking right now. There's so much history with Grayson. And Tyler. Those two men are my entire childhood. I know our recent conversations have mostly been about my dad's recovery, so I haven't shared this yet, but I also found out that Grayson has been working at the brewery this whole time and Tyler never told me."

"What? That's terrible. So, what are you trying to say here?"

Willow couldn't put her finger on what she was getting at. It was about more than old feelings. Ever since she learned that Grayson had been working with Tyler all this time, something else felt off about it. Her earlier hunch that there was more to this mess with Tyler and Grayson had been growing stronger since her trail ride with Grayson. He'd needed to say more that day, but she couldn't exactly force it out of him. He'd made it clear that Tyler needed to talk to her first, so she'd already connected the dots that whatever it was, it included both of them. And Grayson was pushing Tyler to be the one to tell her whatever it was.

"I'm not sure," she finally said to Ivy. Voices nearby had Willow lowering her voice. "But Tyler knew how badly things ended between Grayson and me, so to keep that from me makes zero sense. Which means there's more to this that I don't know. I don't know, Ivy . . . It's just confusing chaos over here. And now Grayson is back in my life."

"Okay, so this sounds to me like a love triangle gone wild."

"Again, it's more than that. I guess what I'm trying to say is that I think they're keeping something else from me. I feel it."

"Then confront them."

She loved how cut and dry Ivy was, how she always got right to the point. It wasn't that easy for Willow, especially when it came to Grayson and Tyler and their life here in Terra Cove. Leaving after high school had been a much easier way to handle everything, and a part of her wished she could just go back to Connecticut—avoiding this tangled web. But that hadn't solved anything before and wouldn't now.

She knew Ivy was right. She needed to talk to both men, especially Tyler, which was the exact suggestion she'd give her clients in this situation. Her dad was more stable now, the farm had the help it needed, her clients were sorted out with virtual appointments . . . So, what was stopping her? Why was she so hesitant to get to the bottom of this?

The commotion of the nearby rides as people cheered with every twist and turn caught her attention once again. The sweet smell of her childhood festival favorite, homemade fried

Twinkie, saturated the air and evoked a sense of solace. She relished a time of such simplicity.

"Willow!" a familiar male voice called out from behind her.

"I have to go, Ivy. I'll call you later."

Willow hung up and when she turned around, she watched Grayson walk toward her. Everything in her life felt like it had spun out of control, yet somehow tossed her right back to where she'd started: in front of Grayson Turner.

The dark pools of his eyes grew sharper as he got closer, the same eyes she fought so hard to forget, drawing her right back in like a verdant oasis when she should be demanding an answer from him. What happened on prom night—beyond Jack's drunken appearance? What else did she need to know? When his face lit up as he approached her, a sense of clarity washed over her, and she knew in her heart that everything Tyler had told her that night so long ago just didn't add up anymore.

"The festival hasn't changed one bit," she told him once he was by her side. "Those Twinkies are calling my name."

"We definitely need to get one and wash it down with a root beer float," he said, flashing her a smile. She thought of all the summers they'd shared a float during this festival. The first summer they were together, they took the sweet drink closer to the sand to enjoy under one of the big beech-trees. That was where they'd been when he told her how he had loved her since they were kids. Was he lying then? *No way.* Feelings like that don't just stop out of nowhere because of a belligerent drunk who had made other multiple random appearances during the four years they were together. If only she'd concluded this back then . . .

"And we can sit with our stomachaches on the Ferris wheel." She glanced up at him.

"I'm about to bring Nova out for her first show. I know

you wanted to watch but I noticed your parents' booth is building quite a line."

"I better go see if my mom needs more help." She started to back away, still locked in his gaze. "Save me a ride later?"

"You know it." He flashed her a grin, leaving her almost rooted in place.

Looking past him at the crowd around her mom's booth, she finally managed to tear herself away and made her way over to help, but stopped short when she saw Tyler coming toward her. His stance was hesitant as he approached her, and she hated how things had become. While there were still so many questions to be answered, for a moment she hoped they would somehow find peace from their past and each other. Staying angry with him, despite all the lies, wouldn't mend anything.

"I didn't know you would be here," Tyler said, standing awkwardly in front of her. It was still strange not to greet each other with a hug or kiss, even though she knew for certain now it was something she didn't want from him anymore.

Willow shrugged. "Well, I'm here."

"I saw your mom at your parents' booth, and she told me you were walking around here somewhere . . . with Grayson."

"My mom did?" She ignored the part about Grayson and glanced toward her parents' booth to see her mom watching them.

"Yes, she did. How was your week? Your clients must be itching for you to return."

"It was a long week of visiting my dad, helping with the farm, and calling all my clients to switch them to telehealth sessions starting Tuesday."

"That's great that you have that option." Tyler gestured toward the food trucks as familiar faces passed them. Many were staring. Small island gossip would be impossible to avoid, but since their fiasco in the parking lot at Maggie's Market, Willow had already become used to it again since being home.

"Would you like to get some food? I hear the fried vegetable tempura truck is back this year."

"No, thanks. I'm going to help my mom with the pony rides." She looked at him and saw his face fall.

"Okay . . ." Tyler looked past her.

"We'll talk soon, Ty. Okay?" For the first time in weeks, she truly felt ready to talk things out and hear whatever he needed to say. But once again, not a good place with an audience around them.

"I just . . ." He took a breath. "I wanted to know how you're doing?"

Grayson's face flashed across her mind. "You know, I'm doing better. Really, I am."

"Good." Tyler stared at her for a second before glancing down at the ground. "I'm glad to hear that."

"How are you?"

Tyler's eyes widened in surprise. That was the first time she'd asked him since their relationship ended. "I'm . . ." He let out a sigh and crossed his arms. "I'm frustrated."

She rolled her eyes. "If you're frustrated, how do you think I feel?"

"I know. Willow . . ." He stepped closer to her and was practically next to her ear so the crowd couldn't hear. "I've been working out my own issues in my head these last few weeks, but a lot of them have nothing to do with you. I've made so many mistakes, and it's overwhelming me is all."

Pulling back, she saw Grayson in the distance, walking Nova to the entrance of the pen for the show and observing the entire conversation. Here she was, standing with the man she was set to marry only a few weeks prior and all she wanted to do was push past him and go to Grayson. How could her feelings shift so fast? But as she looked back at Tyler, it occurred to her that perhaps they'd never changed in the first place. Ivy had been right: Tyler never stood a chance.

"There's no better way to sort it out than to start," she said, closing her eyes for a moment to gather herself. "How about we meet tomorrow on the beach? Around noon?"

"I'd like that." He moved toward her again, but she leaned back, shaking her head.

"Please don't." Tyler had been all over the place since he'd ended things, but she didn't falter as she stood firmly with her hand up.

Glancing between both men, emotions surging, she needed a breather. She walked past Tyler and toward her mom who had resumed tackling all the pony rides alongside her helpers. Watching her interact with the kids and bringing them joy, despite all the stress from her dad's accident, made her admire her mom more than she ever had before.

No one from Terra Cove had expected her to show up tonight and continue their family's tradition of giving these children pony rides after what had happened, but she did it anyway. Dad may have been the one running the horse farm all these years, but her mom's loyalty to the town and taking on this night without her husband made Willow stop short. Tears suddenly blurred her vision, and this time not because of any man but because she hadn't shown that same level of support to her own family. Hiding from them after that terrible night did nothing but make it all worse.

When she reached the booth, her mom must have noticed her red eyes because she told her helpers she'd be right back. Mom hurried over to her and extended her arms and Willow fell right into them.

"Willow, what is it?" she asked, holding her tight.

"Just . . . everything." Willow let the tears keep falling, releasing years of tension she'd let build up. "I'm so sorry, Mom. I never should have done that to you and Dad and stayed away like I did. What if we had lost Dad that day and I wasn't here?"

"Well, we didn't lose him. That's all in the past now. And you're here now and everything is alright. Your dad will be okay, so don't put your mind there." Her mom stroked her curls.

"Yeah, I am here now, and I have to deal with not just Tyler, but Grayson too."

"I see that. You and Grayson looked rather . . . friendly with each other. But this all needed to happen. You have a lot to discuss with both of those men."

"I don't get it, Mom." Willow straightened. "For the first two weeks, all I wanted was to talk to Tyler and get an explanation for why he left me. Now, since I'm home, where he is too, I've sort of stopped waiting. It's just that . . . I feel like there's something he's been hiding from me. They both are. Maybe it's all in my head, but either way, I've been struggling to face that. Not to mention all the memories with Grayson, and old feelings."

Her mom stayed quiet for a few moments, running her honey strands that had loosened from her ponytail behind her ear.

"My sweet Willow. Like I said, everything will be okay again. If you think there's something they aren't telling you, you can't hide from knowing. You know that doesn't work. Face them. Your heart is trying to sort it all out, and it's a lot, so I don't blame you for having so much confusion around Grayson. And talking to Tyler will be hard, but you can do it. You have to put that behind you."

"I know." Willow slowly drew in some air. She heard her mom and knew her emotions were trying to take control of the situation, but she couldn't help but question: *What* was her heart trying to figure out? Both relationships were behind her. "And I'll be meeting with Tyler tomorrow to talk."

"Good. You two need to somehow find a way to let it all rest now. It's over. And even though both men are here, coming back was what you needed. Home is where memories are made and scars are healed."

"Thanks, Mom." Willow hugged her again, her words flooding her like a soothing balm on her wounded heart.

Grayson's smile from earlier seared into her mind as she and her mom walked over to help with the booth. The way he laughed echoed in her thoughts and kept her in a trance while she helped walk each child around the tiny pen. She tried to shake off the sensations buzzing through her body as memories of them played through her head like a movie. And the time she'd spent with Grayson so far since she'd returned had introduced her to a whole new man—a man she had been growing more curious to get to know.

A tap on her shoulder snapped her out of her daze, and her mother nodded behind her. In the near distance, Grayson was waiting for her with his hands tucked in his jeans—the same way he used to stand in the hallway waiting for her outside of every class in high school. But he wasn't that boy anymore. His gaze showed no emotion as she approached him.

"How'd Nova do?"

"She's a pro. But it was Max who won first place in the jumps for accuracy."

"Wow! Sorry I missed it."

"It's okay. I told her you will see her show off next time." He gestured behind him. "The line at the Ferris wheel is shorter now." He dropped his hand and tugged at the belt loop on her jean skirt, pulling her toward him. *Nope . . . he certainly wasn't that boy anymore.* The Grayson back then had never been so bold.

"Grayson . . ." She put her hand over the top of his, still attached to her belt loop. "*Everyone* is here and can see us."

"So?" But he let go anyway and put his hand back in his pocket. "Come on, let's go for a ride. Unless you're still afraid of that thing?"

"I know it's your favorite, so I can handle it."

A couple minutes later, the car on the Ferris wheel swayed a bit as it lifted them up, making Willow's stomach lurch. Grayson put his arm around the back of their seat, subtly moving closer.

"Still able to handle it?" He shifted, making them swing when the wheel stopped to let on more people.

"Oh please. Of course I—"

The car swung faster as he moved his body back and forth. "How about now?" He smiled at her.

"Stop!" She couldn't help but laugh at his playfulness.

"Okay, okay. Nice and still." Grayson patted her leg and stopped moving, allowing the car to slow before the wheel started turning again. They reached the top and Willow shut her eyes, then felt a slight nudge. "Come on, take a look. The festival is always so cool from up here, especially at night."

The sun had long since dropped below the horizon, and the festival was lit up with lights below them. She could see all the people enjoying themselves, walking through the vendors, carnival games, and barns. The car began to descend before going right back up for another round as she held her breath. The wheel stopped halfway up, and she saw Tyler looking up at them. They caught eyes before he walked away. His expression was one she knew well. It was the same one he always gave her and Grayson after they started dating: a look of curiosity that extended deeper into a longing to be the one next to her. Only now, his expression had changed just before he turned away, to one of pure bitterness.

"He's talking to me tomorrow. We're meeting at noon."

When she didn't hear a response, she glanced at Grayson and saw he had been watching Tyler too. She recognized the irritated glint in his eyes. If it wasn't Tyler staring at her with Grayson, it was the other way around—a trio she had been in since she was a kid, going around and around, just like the Ferris wheel.

"Good luck." That was all he said before the wheel stopped to let them off. When she turned to Grayson again before she stepped off, she thought about her conversation tomorrow with Tyler. She'd needed to put that relationship to rest but what about them? Grayson had been and still was the only man her heart truly revolved around. So now what?

Chapter Fourteen

After launching off the rock, Grayson dove into the water. The Saturday midday sun was hot, and the air was dense with humidity. The cool splash enveloped him like a warm hug, reminding him of a bygone era of his childhood that had been carefree . . . before Jack's abuse. Sure, he'd swum in the ocean plenty of times since high school, but not once had he jumped off the rock since he'd been without Willow. But the silence when he'd woken was almost oppressive, a stark contrast to the day before with her at the noisy festival, and the urge to dive off the rock had come on strong.

He floated to the surface, engulfed in the rush that leaping into the waves still retained—the perfect antidote to his racing thoughts.

Now cooled off and much calmer, he tried not to think about the way she'd looked at him on the Ferris wheel the night before, but no amount of rock jumping could shake it. Maybe he'd been dreaming it up in his mind, but no, he hadn't. He'd recognized that face, but it wasn't the same one he used to know. The transformation from girl to woman had struck him hard, like he'd just fallen in love all over again, leaving him breathless. The same fiery passion shone through her mature features, unmistakable and unchanged.

The impulse to call her had been overwhelming him all morning, but today was the day Tyler would finally tell her the truth, and he wanted to give them both space. Moving his body through the water, his mind shifted to how innocent she'd also appeared, so unaware of what had been kept from her—and he was partly to blame. She'd been so shocked finding out he'd been working with Tyler, so how would she react to the news of Tyler and him being brothers?

Once closer to the shore, Grayson stood and trudged through the shallow waves until he reached the warm sand. He toweled off, put his t-shirt on, and sat down facing the sun. Salty, humid air clung to his skin, but it felt good after a peaceful cool swim with no one else at the beach. Just him and the calming influence of the ocean against his frazzled nerves as his mind spun with thoughts of Willow.

For years he'd longed for this to happen and to have her back, but after all she'd endured, he was hesitant. Both relationships had put her through so much and he couldn't help but feel that maybe she deserved a lot more. He'd struggled with this thought many times since seeing her again, that perhaps she should be free from both of them—but his heart wrestled with the notion every time she smiled at him. It was like this inner war to stop himself from letting her go again, and after last night, the grip she had on his heart was too strong to fight anymore.

Voices nearby caught his attention and when he looked over, he saw Tyler and Willow step out from behind one of the boulders. *They planned to have their discussion here at the beach?* He wished he'd known, then he wouldn't have come.

He jumped up to try to leave before they spotted him, and he noticed that Willow's body language seemed stiff.

Maybe he already told her?

Before he could escape, she cast her eyes away from Tyler and when they met his, he couldn't tell if it was his imagination, but her face lit up at seeing him.

The answer to that would be no, he hadn't told her.

"Grayson?" she called out, walking a few steps ahead of Tyler. "I didn't know you'd be here."

"I didn't know we had to tell him," Tyler said, the irritation in his voice evident.

Willow turned back to Tyler. "Oh, I didn't mean it like that. I'm just surprised."

"It's a good day for a swim." Grayson glanced at her outfit: jean shorts and a blue tank, but she didn't appear to be wearing a bathing suit top under it. "Taking a beach walk?"

Tyler shrugged off a backpack and pulled out a blanket and some food. He then paused next to Grayson, eyeing him like a lion in a stare down over prey. "What's it to you what we're doing?"

"Well, this looks cozy. A nice little picnic." Grayson tried to keep calm, but to him, it didn't appear to be the type of discussion he'd expected. Tyler seemed to be setting up something romantic. Was he even planning on telling her anything, or was this just an attempt to get her back? Anger simmered, and Grayson clenched his jaw to keep from blurting everything. This was exactly what he'd been worried about.

"I told you yesterday, Tyler and I are going to talk." Willow offered him a smile, but he couldn't take his attention off Tyler. His attitude had set Grayson off before he even set up the picnic, and as he was about to fire back, he felt Willow's hand on his arm. "Grayson?"

When he looked at her, a breeze caught her soft waves, sending a strand blowing across her face. On instinct, he brushed it away, and to his surprise she didn't step away.

"It's nice to see that you two have gotten reacquainted." Tyler's voice was growing more aggravated.

"Give it a rest, will you?" Grayson nearly shouted. "What's with the attitude?"

"No attitude. I just don't like how nosy you're being. I asked Willow to come here so she and I can talk through things."

"Or from the looks of it, to reel her back in?" Grayson stepped closer, now only inches from his face.

"It's none of your business." Tyler seethed and Grayson balled his fists so hard they started to ache.

"Tyler!" Willow put her hands out as if the two men were about to pounce at each other. "He wasn't being nosy. He was sitting here by himself enjoying the beach, and we were probably the last two people he expected to come here."

"All of a sudden it feels like we're kids again, and you, always defending him," Tyler snapped at Willow before he glared at Grayson. "I came here to talk to Willow, so—"

"So talk." Grayson narrowed his eyes at Tyler. "Because there is quite a lot you need to tell her, isn't there?"

The intensity of their exchange must have alarmed Willow because she was now standing between them. "I feel like I'm missing something here."

"Leave us be." Tyler met his stance, giving him a warning look and while everything in Grayson wanted to spill the truth right then and there, he looked down at Willow's puzzled and anxious face and stepped back.

"Fine." Grayson put his hands up and decided to give Tyler *one* more chance to tell her what she needed to know.

He turned to leave, and he could sense her eyes on him as he walked away. When he started to make his way back up the trail that led to the road, he glanced down at them. They were sitting on the blanket, and he could faintly hear Tyler talking, but then Willow peeked at him. So much for taking a swim to clear his thoughts.

He got in his truck to leave and turned it on but didn't move. The way she'd gazed up at him made him nearly run back down to the beach and scoop her up. What if that was what Tyler had planned to do too? Convince her that they should try again.

When he finally put the truck in drive, he didn't go home. Instead, he headed straight to the rehabilitation center to see Liam Anderson.

———

"Grayson," Liam said from the chair in his room, raising his brows as Grayson walked through the door.

The nurse at the front station said he'd arrived just after Liam's physical therapy session and when he was about to have lunch, which made it perfect timing for a conversation. After walking into the room, Grayson immediately halted in his tracks when he saw Daniel.

"Come on in. I didn't expect to see you. Daniel here was just about to wheel me to lunch."

"I'm so sorry. I should have called first. You have company. I'll come back another time," Grayson said. He hadn't even thought about the fact that other people could have been there, but Daniel was the last person he'd expected to see, considering all that happened with the failed wedding.

"Nonsense," Daniel said. "I was just stopping by to see how Liam was and have some lunch with him. Why don't you join us?"

"Yes, please. The more company the better, besides"—Liam squinted up at him—"you look upset and obviously came here for a reason."

"If you need me to go, I'll leave you two to talk," Daniel

said, and helped Liam from the chair and into his wheelchair. He was still moving very slowly.

Once he was safely in his chair, Liam sighed. "I hate this thing."

"I bet," Grayson said. "I don't mind you being here, Daniel. In fact, I could use your advice too." Daniel unlocked the wheels and got behind the chair to push. "How are you feeling, Liam?"

"To be honest, just frustrated. The head injury seems to be healing faster than the rest of me. It's my back that is the most troublesome. A lumbar sprain is what they tell me happened. They have me doing all kinds of weird things in physical therapy for it."

"You'll get there. Just be patient with yourself and don't rush it," Grayson said, and followed Daniel as he pushed the wheelchair to the cafeteria and chose a table. "Need me to check out what they have today?"

"No need. I want a roast beef sub," Liam said. "Tell them it's for me. They know how to fix it."

Daniel locked the wheels and followed Grayson to get in line to order. He was glad the center was small enough that they remembered how Liam liked his sandwich. He couldn't imagine dealing with an accident like that and having to be away from his own bed for so long in a larger recovery center. The smaller options on the island must have made it feel a little more comfortable with more attention on him.

Both Daniel and Grayson chose a chicken salad sandwich and chips for themselves and took the food back to the table. They ate in silence for a few minutes before Liam put his sandwich down.

"I know it's not just the delicious subs that brought you here." Grayson smiled at the hint of sarcasm in Liam's voice. "Why the visit on such a gorgeous day?"

"Because you told me not to be a stranger, so here I am,"

Grayson teased, making Liam laugh. "And now that I know the food here actually isn't half bad, I might just come back."

"Do you remember Rachel's chicken salad sandwiches?" Liam pointed to Grayson's plate. "They are the best."

"How could I forget? Her cooking is amazing." Grayson wiped his mouth with a napkin and put the half-eaten sandwich down. "In all seriousness, I came because I know you'll talk me out of making a mistake."

"And what mistake is that, son?" Daniel asked.

Grayson sat back. Daniel referring to him as his son still threw him a bit, but in a good way. The image of Tyler and Willow on the blanket before he left the beach and why he'd come here made him refocus.

"I want to blurt it all out to Willow. I've had it with Tyler. Sorry, Daniel." He gave Daniel an apologetic look. "I know he's your son."

Daniel cleared his throat. "But so are you. Please continue."

"This morning . . ." Grayson paused, noticing Daniel lean to the side of his chair, hand under his chin. A position he had come to learn. It was Daniel's "preparation" stance for whatever he was about to hear.

Grayson turned to Liam. "I came to tell you that I ran into Tyler and Willow at the beach just now." He drew in a long breath, hoping he wasn't going to sound petty, especially with Daniel listening too.

"Go on." Liam picked up his water and took a sip, giving Grayson a chance to gather his thoughts. He wanted to get the right words out, and his frustration had been hindering his ability to think straight since he left the beach.

"They went there to talk, and I happened to already be there," Grayson explained.

"Well, it's about time," Daniel said. "I hope it's a good

conversation and he tells her everything. So why are you mad at Tyler?"

"I agree," Liam said. "Remember what I told you. Don't be mad at him for doing what I asked."

"I do remember, but something didn't feel right. Tyler doesn't seem to be in his right state of mind. It could just be me overthinking it, but I don't think it'll be the conversation we're all hoping for. I think he's trying to fix their relationship, and I don't think that's right considering what he told Mr. Anderson recently."

Daniel looked at Liam. "What did he tell you?"

"That he ended it because he knew Willow didn't love him and she was unhappy," Liam answered. "Are you sure that's what he's doing, Grayson?"

"He had a picnic."

"I see . . ." Liam blew out some air. "All he seems to think about is himself. This will confuse my daughter even more."

But will it? Grayson sure hoped not, but all he could do was let *her* decide what she wanted.

Daniel nodded. "I have to agree with both of you. He's giving her mixed messages and that's worrisome. Look," he sighed, "Tyler is my son, and I love him, but he has caused a lot of pain. The way he ended things on their wedding day was just downright cruel and embarrassing. I'll never forget the looks from our guests when we told them the wedding was off."

"It was a nightmare. Rachel is still angry, but she's getting better," Liam said.

Daniel nodded. "I don't blame her. First off, he should have pulled Willow aside and told her to her face what he felt—and much earlier than waiting until their wedding day. And secondly, he cannot go back and forth like this."

"I agree. I can't believe it's taken him over a month to talk to her, although I heard she wasn't making it easy for him," Liam said.

"No, she hasn't. But she's angry and confused and rightfully so," Daniel said. "Tyler is often quick to react when emotions get the best of him, and he makes poor decisions that make situations worse."

Grayson listened quietly and couldn't help but wonder again, was Willow still *that* mad? Her laugh while he cracked jokes at the festival as they brought Max and Nova to his booth flew into his mind.

"Look, don't get me wrong," Grayson cut in. "I'm glad they are talking finally, but all I'm saying is seeing the setup on the beach and how defensive he got toward me, it just left me with a bad feeling that he's not going to tell her what he's been hiding, and I know that's important to you, Liam."

"Because it needs to be said," Liam said. "I don't want my daughter to be lied to anymore. Who knows? Maybe he'll spill the truth after all."

"I understand your position on this, Liam," Daniel said. "Especially after the way Tyler treated her on their wedding day."

"When I saw them, I didn't handle the situation well," Grayson said, switching tracks.

"What happened?" Liam asked.

"Nothing major, but I wasn't expecting them to walk onto the beach with a full picnic and when they did, I was very clear in my annoyance."

"I would have been too. Willow doesn't deserve to be led in circles." Daniel shook his head. "What a mess."

"An ongoing mess," Grayson said. *If only I didn't let Jack's drunken confrontation that night all those years ago get the best of me.* He clenched his jaw to keep from letting his anger get the best of him now. Beating himself up once again over something he had no power to change was useless, but it was so hard to control. In all the other times the fool showed up and started intoxicated arguments, Grayson never cowered to it. Yet he let the same man who abandoned him and his sister, long before Jack even *knew* about his mother's affair, take something so special away from him—Willow. His weakness that night and allowing Jack's words to influence him led him to make a bad choice and push her away, but he wouldn't give up so easily now.

"Let's just wait and see what happens," Daniel said.

"May I say something else?" Grayson asked, glancing at Daniel.

"Of course, go ahead." Daniel nodded at him.

"You sure?" Grayson shook his foot under the table in an attempt to steady his nerves.

"Grayson . . ." Daniel leaned forward. "Say what you need to get out."

"That means a lot to me. It really does." His eyes stung with emotion as he stilled his feet. "I never should have left Willow on prom night. Four years with her, and I didn't show up on one of the most important nights of our teenage years. All because of drunken lies from Jack. Yes, he broke the news about the affair, and that was painful, but I let him confuse me with everything else he spewed out."

"You were just a kid," Daniel said, reminding Grayson of Wesley's words. But hearing the same from Daniel impacted him on a deeper level.

"I know, and I've finally come to that understanding after holding on to all this shame about how I acted. That mistake has gripped me for so long."

Daniel's eyes seemed to glaze over. Had he said too much? The last thing Grayson intended was to make Daniel feel like he was stuck in the middle between him and Tyler.

"No . . ." Daniel finally began, keeping his focus steady on him. "You shouldn't have left her on prom night the way you did. Even I know that. Heck, everyone on Martha's Vineyard knows that. But like I said, you were young. You weren't in your right mind to go after her, but I wish you had."

"I do too," Liam said.

"If you both think that," Grayson slowly said, hoping he wasn't about to make them mad, "then why did you support Tyler marrying her?"

"Because I thought that was what she wanted. I love Willow. She's always been the daughter I never had," Daniel said.

"That is my exact answer too," Liam said. "Look, it broke my heart watching her cry that night in her beautiful dress. I remember thinking I would do anything to see her smile again, especially after the fire, and I thought Tyler was able to accomplish that, so I gave them my blessing when he asked for her hand."

Grayson nodded. "I can understand that. That's part of why I refrained from trying to get her back. I thought she was happy too."

"She wasn't. I know I haven't shared this with either of you, but I spoke to Tyler for a long time the morning after the wedding. It had become clear to him what he had fought against for years, that he was her second choice, even after eight years together," Daniel said. "I hope he remembers that today as he talks to her and doesn't try to make something more out of their relationship when it just isn't there."

"Maybe if he had been honest about how he felt, they could have worked on their relationship," Grayson said.

"No." Daniel shook his head. "There was no fixing what they struggled with, and believe me, they tried for a long time after they got engaged to make their connection deepen, without success. I just wish one of them had come to this realization long before she put that wedding dress on."

"I wish I knew what she wants now." Grayson's eyes fell to his hands.

"Grayson, her heart had its number one spot filled long before Tyler." Daniel's unwavering stare when Grayson looked up told him exactly who he meant. "And since she's been home, it's clear to many of us that the love you two shared wasn't just a passing teenage fling."

"You think so?"

"We all know so," Liam said. "Even someone stuck in the hospital can sense that."

"Okay . . . but besides their relationship troubles, why does Tyler struggle with telling her what happened with you and my mom?" Grayson asked Daniel.

"That's the burning question that nobody can answer." Daniel shrugged, but Grayson still held hope that he'd find out the answer. He didn't want to stay mad at Tyler. Harboring anger, like he'd learned with Jack, only served to perpetuate more harm and resentment.

"It should have started with me. I needed to be the one to tell Willow the night of prom," Grayson said. "If Tyler doesn't tell her today, I'm taking over."

"Good." Daniel patted his shoulder and gave him an apologetic look. "I'm sorry this has been so hard. I've watched you over the years and knew you weren't happy either. I knew you still loved her."

"How?"

"I love your mother, Grayson. I always have. Like you love Willow."

"I don't mean to pry, but if you've always loved her, why did you and my mom marry other people?"

"Your mother . . ." Daniel looked away. "Keeps to herself a lot and is a very easy-going woman most of the time, but sometimes she tends to get a bit—"

"Stubborn?" Grayson smiled at Daniel when he sat back

laughing. While his mom had always stayed out of a lot of social events growing up and people always labeled her as "quiet," he'd come to learn as an adult that it was because she got in her head too much. It was always easier for her to be alone in her thoughts. Something he could sure relate to.

"That's exactly right," Daniel continued. "We were together on and off for years as teenagers and for a long time after that, but a couple of silly misunderstandings led to our split, and she put a wall up that I couldn't get through. She met Jack . . ."

I wish she never met him. "I see," Grayson said instead. He quickly realized if she hadn't, then Abby wouldn't be here.

"When things get tough." Daniel shifted forward again, looking directly at him. "Your mom withdraws a lot and freezes in her own stubbornness, pushing everyone away."

Hearing Daniel explain what he'd always known about his mom suddenly hit hard—he was, in fact, just like her.

"I did the same thing with Willow." When Grayson looked at both men, he saw them nodding in agreement. "I got in my own head too much after that night and listening to Jack . . . I pushed her away. I withdrew . . . I . . ."

"Have the same love for Willow, that I always had for your mom." Daniel gently filled in. "That is clear to me."

"And me," Liam said. "I can see it right now."

"I'm starting to think it's apparent to everyone," Grayson said, eyeing Daniel again. "I'm really glad that you two are working it out now . . . finally. I'm surprised it's taken this long for you two to get together with that kind of history, especially after both of you split from your spouses."

"Your mom didn't want to be in the spotlight over the demise of my marriage to Tyler's mom, so she figured it was best to keep to herself," Daniel explained. "Don't keep doing the same with Willow."

"I don't know, Daniel." Grayson looked up at the ceiling.

"Seeing Willow again shook something in me. I haven't been able to think straight at all."

"That's what love does," Liam said.

Grayson glanced at Liam. "Yeah . . ."

"And that's the kind of love I want for my daughter."

"I don't even know how she feels about me." The energy between him and Willow had been building, but did she really want him again?

"Time will tell," Liam said. "At least don't let her leave Terra Cove again without telling her what you have to say too."

———

THE CONVERSATION WITH LIAM AND DANIEL HAD taken some of the weight off his chest by the time Grayson returned to his truck. It felt good to release his frustrations to the older men and hear their counsel, but it didn't solve the fact that at any moment he might hear from an angry Willow. He checked his phone before turning on the ignition and saw a missed call and a voicemail from her. *Here we go.* He clicked to listen.

"Hey, Grayson. It's me, Willow. I'm sorry for how Tyler acted out there on the beach. We spent an hour talking, but he only went around in circles. I ended up telling him I needed to go because all he kept saying was that he missed me. And I don't know why I'm rambling all this to you on a voicemail, except for the fact that all I could think about when you left us at the beach was that . . . I miss you, Grayson. Can I come by this week and see Nova . . . and you? Tuesday afternoon would work for me. Please call me."

Grayson's hands were shaking by the end of the voicemail. He replayed it to make sure he'd heard her right. She missed him. Her words sent his heart racing, nearly causing him to get out of his truck and jump with exhilaration.

Hesitation took over just as fast as the happiness had. Her voicemail also meant Tyler had once again dropped the ball. He leaned his head back on the headrest. Her voice played through his mind, and how sweet it sounded. Then his own words from moments ago. *"If Tyler doesn't tell her today, I'm taking over."*

He meant what he'd told Liam and Daniel, and he hit call on her number but got her voicemail.

"Willow," he began, the words burning to come out. He wanted nothing more than to tell her he missed her too and still loved her, but he kept control. Not on a voicemail. "Of course you can come see us. Nova is always here for you, and so am I. Tuesday afternoon is good for me too? Four work? Let me know."

The air-conditioning blasted against his sweaty face when he turned the truck on and drove off. A few minutes later, a text message notification crossed his dashboard. It was from Willow. He tapped the screen.

> Sorry I missed your call. Bad reception at my sister's house. See you Tuesday, Turner.

Grayson turned up a familiar song and tapped his thumb on the steering wheel, his excitement momentarily masking the tension. But at that moment, none of it mattered. She missed him and was coming to see Nova again. Perhaps the special essence that mare possessed could work its magic with them once again. It was time to lay out the truth and get his girl back.

Chapter Fifteen

State Beach was packed for a Tuesday, which was normal for Martha's Vineyard in July. The calmer waves on this side of the island were better for Willow's niece and nephew, and Whitney had managed to find a spot to plant their stuff closer to the water's edge. Maya was happily digging a hole right where the water touched her toes and laughing at a seagull that kept inching closer to her.

"Good thing she doesn't have something to feed the bird, or we would have fifty of them swooping around us. She loves to give them half our snacks," Whitney said, reaching to give Brandon another toy to chew on as he sat inside his beach tent.

They'd decided to take the kids to the beach after lunch at a local diner since Willow was finished seeing patients for the day. Even though she was only working two days a week for now, she'd wanted to pace herself instead of filling both days completely.

"The weather couldn't have turned out better—not a cloud in the sky. All that rain we got yesterday pushed out the humidity too." Willow was sitting near Maya and helping her dig so she could fill the hole up with water. "Mind if I take Maya for a walk?"

"Sure, go for it. I'm going to see if this little guy will have his bottle and a quick nap before we leave." Her sister crawled into the tent, and Willow stood up and extended her hand to her niece.

"How about we go find some seashells?"

"Okay, Aunty Willow!" Maya jumped up. "I'll bring my bucket." The girl picked up her little pink sand bucket and hurried over.

Willow took her hand, and they started walking alongside the water, letting the small waves roll over their feet.

"You're getting so big, Maya. Remember last summer when you came to visit me and we went swimming in my pool?" The condo she and Tyler had shared had a community pool that they had spent many summer days lounging by.

"Yes! I had a purple swim vest then, and now I have just arm ones!" Maya grinned at her, squeezing her little eyes shut when the sun hit her face. Despite the matching honey-blonde curls they shared, Maya looked identical to her mother. Whitney had let her daughter's hair grow longer, which made her look even older than the last time she'd seen her right after Christmas.

"That means you're getting to be a better swimmer then, right?"

"Right, Aunty Willow! Didn't you see how good I swimmed at Mimi and Pappa's pool?"

Her precious niece's pronunciation error made Willow's heart melt. "Of course I did. I even saw how you jumped in toward your daddy. So brave! Last summer, that was hard for you."

"Not anymore! Mommy says I faced my fears. Now I'm not afraid of nothing!"

"Good!" Willow agreed, enjoying the innocence of a four-year-old mind.

The little girl's bravery inspired her to have some too. She was seeing Grayson later that afternoon, and while she didn't exactly have a script ready, she wanted to be honest and let him know how she felt. Listening to Tyler tell her how much he'd missed her on Saturday made her wish it had been Grayson talking to her instead. A shiver ran down her spine as she remembered the way he'd tugged her belt loop and gazed into her eyes at the festival.

Maya pulled her to the sand and began looking for shells. "Got one!" She plopped a white clam shell into her bucket. "Mommy says to make sure they aren't broken. We don't want Brandon to cut his fingers, now do we?"

Willow laughed. She could almost hear her sister repeating those exact words. "Of course we don't."

"Aunty Willow?" Maya squinted up at her.

"Yes?"

"Are you leaving again and going back to Con-Conni—I can't remember how to say the rest."

"Connecticut. Don't feel bad, it's a tricky name." She smiled adoringly at her niece. "And that's a really good question. I don't have a final answer, but I'm thinking I'm not. I don't want to leave, and too many people want me to stay." *Let's just hope Grayson feels the same way when I talk to him later.*

"Really?" Maya gazed up at her with wide eyes. "So we can do this all the time then! Collect shells, go swimming—"

"And eat pizza!"

"Yes!" The girl jumped in the sand.

"Let's see what else we can find."

For the next half hour, she and Maya collected as many shells as they could. Willow helped her niece tirelessly fill her bucket and thought about Maya's question. Looking around the familiar beach, she watched her sweet niece and knew the rest of her family was nearby, and it felt like this was where she was supposed to be. Terra Cove was home. She'd told Tyler during their talk on the beach about their condo and needing to sell it. When he realized that their conversation wasn't leading them back together, he finally relented and said he would take care of contacting the Realtor.

"So you're staying here?" Tyler had asked, and she'd nodded. *"Is there someone you're staying here for?"* He'd known the answer but asked anyway, and when she nodded again, his face had fallen. He seemed to finally understand there was no chance for them anymore—there never had been.

When Maya yawned and placed her nearly full bucket by her feet, Willow scooped her and the bucket up and began to carry her back. A breeze blew by them, and she smelled her fruity sunblock and a whiff of coconut in Maya's soft hair from her shampoo. She always caught Whitney inhaling their wonderful scents, especially after their baths. Watching her older sister as a mother excited her for what her future could be like when she had kids. A tingle ran through her against the weight of her niece as Grayson's face flashed in her mind at the thought of being a mother someday.

When they got back to the tent, Whitney was sitting in her beach chair holding Brandon, who was sound asleep. Willow handed Maya her shovel again and the girl luckily got absorbed in her hole, leaving Brandon to sleep awhile more.

"How long as he been out?" Willow whispered as she sat down on her towel close to the tent.

"He drank half his bottle and was asleep within a minute. I'm so thankful. When he skips his naps while we're out, he's a bear by the time dinner hits," she said, keeping her voice low.

"I talked to Tyler over the weekend," Willow said, and her sister's eyes immediately widened. "I know, I know: Why did I wait until now to tell you?"

"Uh . . . yeah. Why did you? What happened?"

Willow shifted a little closer so Whitney could hear her easier, while keeping her voice as quiet as possible. "Nothing. Absolutely nothing."

"Where did you two talk?" Whitney shifted Brandon to her other arm.

"The beach at the preserve."

"Look, Mommy!" Maya had filled her other bucket with water, and when they both turned toward the girl, she poured it into the hole. "It's a lake!"

Whitney gave her a thumbs up and a big smile, and Willow went over and drew a line with the shovel around the hole. "Think you can dig up a road around your lake?"

"Sure can!" Maya went at it, and Willow sat back down.

"So you met him at the beach to talk, and . . . he said nothing?" Whitney asked, reaching down for her water bottle while Brandon continued to snooze.

"Oh, he said a lot and we talked, but what I mean is, we talked about nothing. He started off pretty good. Apologizing for how he handled the wedding, for humiliating me and our family, and recognizing that he should have spoken to me in person, not end an eight-year relationship in a phone call with one weak follow-up text."

"That sounds like a lot more than 'nothing,'" Whitney said, reaching for a few chips from their snack bag.

"Yeah, that part was fine. But after he apologized, it all went downhill. He went round and round telling me he's regretted it ever since."

"Do you wish he hadn't?"

"Initially, yes." Grayson's green eyes jumped into her thoughts. "But here we are, only a month later, and I'm okay with the fact that we didn't get married . . . I'm more than okay."

Her sister raised a brow. "Does Grayson have anything to do with that conclusion?"

Willow almost said no but stopped herself. Lying to her sister was useless. "I can't lie to you, Whit . . . I've truly enjoyed spending time with him. It's like we—"

"Picked right back up where you left off?"

Brandon opened his eyes and smiled at Willow with his precious baby grin. Whitney gave him the rest of his bottle, and Maya called out for them to see her road.

"Good job, Maya!" Whitney said. "Maybe you can now make it like a stream around the lake. Try pouring water into the road and see what it does."

"Okay!" Maya jumped up and picked up one of her other buckets to fill with water.

"That's exactly how it's been. I've . . . ." Willow paused, debating if she should finish that thought. She watched Brandon suck down the remainder of his bottle before he sat up, energized and ready to play. She handed him some toys that were near her and thought about the beginnings of her relationship with Tyler, suddenly feeling compelled to share.

"I've never really talked much about the early days with Tyler, but when Grayson left me that night and Tyler showed up instead . . . I saw a side of Tyler I'd never seen before."

"What do you mean?"

"He told me how much Grayson didn't care and hadn't for a long time. That he had been trying to figure out how to break up with me for months. I know we were just teenagers and at the time I initially didn't believe him. I thought he was just trying to be 'the better man.'" She held up her fingers to make air quotes. "Tyler and Grayson always had a competitive streak between them, but then the fire happened."

"The fire that was never your fault, Willow." Whitney handed Brandon a small shovel he was reaching for.

"I know that now. I didn't realize until I came back home

that I needed to face everything here to truly get over what happened. Ironically, I think being a therapist to others only helped me ignore my own issues all these years, and in a way, enabled me to justify not coming home. I've been guilt of hypocrisy, having told them to always tackle their problems head-on while I was avoiding my own."

"Yeah. You were tucked away over there in Connecticut focusing on clients and never yourself."

Her sister was right, but the words still stung. "I know, and I wish I could take it all back. But I'm here now, and something I did accomplish in that conversation with Tyler was to get things rolling with selling our condo because I'm staying."

"Oh, Willow!" Her sister reached over and hugged her tight. "I'm so happy. What about your clients?"

"I haven't figured that part out yet, but I will."

"So, what *did* make you believe Tyler all those years ago?"

"My own stubbornness over seeing Grayson walk right by me without a word after the fire department got the fire out."

"Well, you two were only teenagers, and communication takes many mistakes to learn how to do right. Even Jason and I aren't the best at it sometimes."

"Yes, but I was also stunned. It only seemed to validate what Tyler had told me. But I knew deep in my heart that Tyler had lied and it wasn't the Grayson I fell in love with. The Grayson I see today . . ."

"I knew it." Whitney grinned. "You do still love him."

"I sure do." Her cheeks warmed against the thought of seeing him soon. "Which is why I shouldn't have let that one terrible night influence me to listen to Tyler. And I definitely should have listened to you and Wesley back then, warning me about—"

"The look," they said together, chuckling.

"You know," Whitney said after a minute, "you didn't

listen to me back then, but I hope you do now. Tyler has loved you just as long as Grayson has. You were like their shining star right between them. Everything was fine with you three until you chose Grayson. I'm not surprised Tyler took the opportunity and dove in when it presented itself, even though that was wrong. And putting Tyler aside, *why* Grayson left you may be an unsolved mystery, but I know it's not because he didn't love you anymore or whatever Tyler told you."

"I know that now. Being home confirmed that the first time Grayson saw me. He looked at me just like he always had." Willow closed her eyes against the memory of seeing him that first time at the hospital. "Which is why I've concluded that there's more to this, and I want to get to the bottom of it."

"Then it's not Tyler you need to talk to . . . It's Grayson."

Whitney was right. Tyler was only backpedaling, wanting to return to how things were before their wedding day, but she was past that. It wasn't what she wanted anymore. Everything was coming to a head as it should have a *long* time ago.

"Yep. I'm heading to Grayson's when we get back."

———

WILLOW CAREFULLY DROVE HER FATHER'S TRUCK down Grayson's long driveway a couple hours later. This time she listened to Grayson's initial warning about all the bumps and dirt because when she surprised him the day before the festival and came to see Nova again, her car had been covered in dirt afterward.

Grayson was standing in the driveway waiting on her. He was wearing his bathing suit and no shirt, with a towel tossed over his shoulder. After she parked, he opened her door and she took his offered hand as she hopped out of the truck.

"Went for a swim?" His hair was still wet and she found

herself staring at him more than she should as they walked to the barn.

"Yup. Just got back from the beach," he said, finally dropping her hand. She hadn't even realized he'd held on to it. It almost felt . . . normal. "Our air-conditioning broke at the office today, and I left a little early to go cool off in the ocean." They reached the barn and he opened the door.

"How's work going? I'm sorry I've never asked you about it. It took me a couple weeks to come down from the shock of learning you worked with Tyler."

Nova's head immediately popped out from her stall.

Grayson stopped and started to say something but then shook his head. "Never mind."

"No, tell me. What is it?" She touched his arm, and he looked down at her hand before he raised his chin back up and silently stared into her eyes. Then he turned his body toward her, lifted his hands, and brushed them through her hair, drawing her closer and sending a flutter through her stomach. She didn't want him to stop, but Nova's loud whinny startled them, and Willow took a small step away.

"Looks like she's hurt I didn't say hi to her first." Her heart thudded as she moved closer to the stall.

"Yes, I'm aware. But seeing you . . ." He followed her every step and closed the gap again, and she tried to avoid him, but those eyes that she'd loved almost her entire life hooked her. "It's just that there's so much I need to say, but apparently Nova does too."

Willow looked at the mare, moved away from him again, and ran her hand down the horse's neck. "I know, girl. I came to see you, and Grayson is interrupting us," she teased, casting him a cheeky grin. "Let's get you saddled up, Nova."

"I'm going to go get changed and let you two do your thing."

"Sounds good. I'm just going to warm her up and a few

jumps," she said and looked up at Nova. "No big trail ride today, girl."

A huff from Max's stall made Grayson laugh. "Don't worry, boy. I'll take you out soon." He looked at her again. "I'm sure you could guess from his win at the festival that jumps are his favorite exercise."

———

AN HOUR LATER, WILLOW ROUNDED THE PEN AND saw Grayson standing at the fence with Monty sniffing around his feet, all showered and wearing his usual jeans and a t-shirt.

"How's it going?" he asked when she trotted up to him.

"She seems a bit tired, so I think I'll call it quits for the day."

Grayson opened the fence and she dismounted, then walked Nova out.

"Sometimes she gets like that, but she also might be faking it," he told her.

"Oh yeah? Why's that?"

"Because she wants us to spend time together."

"Normally I'd argue against a horse's ability to be that perceptive, but this is Nova we're talking about."

They unsaddled the horse and led her back to her stall, then Willow leaned close to her. "Thank you for the ride. I'll see you soon."

"Are you in a hurry to get home?"

Willow shook her head. "Not at all."

"How about some crab legs? I picked some up on my way home."

"Sounds perfect."

A while later, as the late-summer sun peeked the last of its orange rays through the trees, Willow sat back in her chair on the deck and picked up her glass of white wine. They'd stuffed themselves on crab legs, baked potatoes, and salad. Monty was sleeping by her feet, enjoying the occasional head rub.

"You're his new favorite," Grayson said as he tipped his beer bottle toward the dog.

"He really is a great dog." She looked out at the view again. "It's so peaceful out here."

"It's my favorite place to be. I just built this deck last year." Grayson took a long swig of his beer. "Being out here is my nightly routine now."

"I may have to come back and join you. This is lovely."

Grayson didn't respond as he watched her.

Willow glanced at him. "Or . . . not?"

"That's not what I was thinking," he said, his expression even, which reminded her of trying to read him through their relationship in high school. His ability to joke around and grow serious all within one sentence had always baffled her.

"What were you thinking?" She swallowed her wine a little too quickly, anticipating his answer.

"Willow, are you happy?"

Monty shifted his position and stared up at her, clearly sensing the tone in his owner's voice.

"In a general sense . . . yes, I'm happy. I love what I do, helping people in therapy, although I wish I could bring Nova into my sessions with them. Even though I've only gone a couple times, getting back on and riding this past month, not to mention helping my parents with the horse farm, has helped me cope with everything. Horses are so therapeutic. I might need to look into suggesting this for my clients."

"Just like it helped me after Jack left. You were by my side the entire time, showing me how to ride and . . . just being there." He put his beer on the table and scooted his chair closer to her. "But that's not what I mean. I know you like your job. I meant these last eight years. The thought of you being heartbroken again has really torn me up."

Willow looked up toward the sky, catching some birds flying over. She watched them soar together through the air. She thought about what she told Whitney earlier on the beach about marrying Tyler, and when she looked back over at Grayson, what she'd said to her sister rang true.

"No, I wasn't happy."

"Do you love him?"

Willow nodded. "I do. He's been one of my closest friends since we were kids, so of course I care for him and therefore, I love him."

Grayson's eyes clouded over as he straightened up and his foot started bobbing up and down. She knew what it meant and placed her hand on his knee and looked him in the eyes.

"But not the way a woman should love a man to marry him."

His foot went still. "When did you know that?"

Placing her glass down, she leaned onto the table. He did the same, and their hands touched with his fingers brushing through hers, giving her something to look at while considering her answer. She didn't want to stir up more drama between the three of them. At the same time, she was tired of holding this in, especially when it involved Grayson, and besides . . . it was what she came here to do. Be brave and share her heart, just like her niece reminded her earlier about her swimming success.

"Almost right away with Tyler," she said, keeping her attention on their hands. "But I was so hurt by what happened with us, the fire, and watching my dad lose so many horses, that I shoved it all away, and Tyler became this safety spot for me." Her eyes moved up to his. "But that wasn't the right thing to do."

"I should have come for you. I've wrestled with that mistake for a long time."

"Are you still upset that you didn't?" she nearly whispered, the intensity of his gaze telling her there was more to his upset than just him not chasing after her.

"Of course I am. Willow, I have never stopped loving you. And believe me, I tried. I spent the last eight years dating, traveling, and doing just about anything to move on." His voice rose in frustration. Monty stood up and put his head on Grayson's leg, breaking them apart. "Everything's cool, boy." He stroked the dog's head until he settled back down.

"I wish I'd known that. Tyler said . . ." She knew this would anger him, but she wanted answers. "That you asked him to take me to prom and that you were done with me. Of course, it's been so long I can't remember the exact wording."

"That's not exactly how I phrased it to him that night before he showed up at your house. I only asked him to *escort* you to prom, so you could go have fun with our friends while I calmed down. I wasn't done with you, Willow . . . I'm still not done."

Tears stung her eyes. She longed to be able to turn back time and erase the last eight years with Tyler. "I should have never been with Tyler."

"We can't change what has happened. I don't want you to dwell on what could have been. It doesn't get us anywhere, believe me, I've done enough wishing." Grayson sighed, running his hands through his hair. "But I want you to know, I did come for you initially. I came to my senses and went to your house to explain what had happened with Jack, before I heard everything Tyler said to you outside the barn. Then you rode away on Finn, just before the fire broke out."

"I'm sorry you had to hear that." Tears began to fall down her cheeks and he quickly wiped them away. "Why did you walk away from me after the fire?"

He stood up and took his beer to the side of the deck. The sun was nearly down, the only lights behind them coming from the house. "I blamed myself for that fire . . ." he began as she stood up and met him by the railing. "And starting that fight with Tyler and distracting your dad from that faulty tractor. And worse yet, letting all the nonsense that Jack said to me that night get to my head. It's been a long eight years healing from that man's abuse."

"That was something you needed to do then," she said, realizing now how much Grayson had been dealing with at the time. She was so absorbed by her own trauma of the fire that she didn't stop to see that Grayson was dealing with his own. "And I blamed myself for the fire too. But truth is, it was no one's fault."

Grayson kept his face turned toward the sunset. "I know . . ."

"And what happened to us wasn't all your fault. I shouldn't have run away like I did with Tyler and stayed away. There was no reason for that. But we were young, and—"

Grayson put his bottle on the railing, reached for her hips, and kissed the top of her forehead. "I don't want to hear you tell me how sorry you are," he whispered in her ear. "You have *nothing* to apologize for."

Her pulse sped up and Willow breathed in his comforting scent. She wanted him close, for his lips to find hers . . .

But, of course, that was the moment her phone buzzed on the table. She started toward it, but his hands remained around her waist, holding her in place.

"Wait, before you answer . . . There's something else I need to tell you."

"Okay . . ."

His expression had turned serious, only justifying all her earlier suspicions that there was something he and Tyler were keeping from her.

"Should I be worried?" She studied his worried face.

"Let's sit down." He gestured to the table and just as she

pulled her chair out, her phone buzzed again. This time she could see it was her mom calling.

"Wait. Mom has called me twice now. My dad . . ."

"Call her back," Grayson said, staying by her side as she tapped her mom's number.

"Willow, there you are." Mom sounded breathless.

"What is it? Is everything okay with Dad?"

"That's why I'm calling. I'm rushing out the door to get to the hospital."

"What? The hospital? Why?"

"He got up too fast from his chair and with his back still in bad shape, he fell. They aren't sure if he hit his head, but the staff at the rehab center called an ambulance to have him checked out, just in case."

"I'm coming. I'll be there in fifteen minutes." She hung up and looked at Grayson. "My dad fell. I—"

"Go. Don't apologize. We can talk another time." Willow gathered up her purse and hurried to the truck with Grayson at her heels. "Please call me when you find out more."

"Yes. I will." She hopped in the driver's side and sped off. *Please be okay*, she thought on repeat. She'd been so ready to know what Grayson wanted to tell her, but right now, all she could think about was her dad.

Chapter Sixteen

"So we meet at the table again," Daniel said to Grayson as he entered the kitchen the following morning behind his mom. They had texted to ask if they could stop by before Grayson left for work because his mom had the prize Max had won him from the festival that he forgot to claim. When they got to the table, his mom put down a grooming tote with a nameplate that read: Terra Cove Agricultural Fair 2025. Inside the tote was filled with various grooming equipment and certificates to restaurants on the island.

Grayson had poured everyone some coffee and filled them in on all he knew about Liam. An hour after Willow left last night, she called to tell him that so far everything was checking out just fine, but they wanted to keep her dad overnight for observation anyway.

"Yup, here we are." Grayson pulled up a chair next to his mom, who glanced between them.

"Am I missing something?" she asked. "What about a table?"

"Grayson and I had lunch on Saturday at the rehab center with Liam," Daniel said. "I meant to tell you that last night."

"Oh, really?" Mom looked at him.

"Yeah, I needed some guy talk," Grayson said, and she beamed. "Which seems to make you happy to hear.

"Yes, it does. Guy talk is good," she said. "So you haven't heard any more updates from Willow since last night?"

"No. She only updated me that one time. I think based off the little she told me that everything will be fine, but still, it was quite a scare."

"Yes, it was. I'm relieved he'll be okay." Mom glanced at Daniel with a smile.

"You're extra smiley today," Grayson said to her before he smirked at Daniel. "Any idea why?"

"She's just happy I'm taking her to try that new Italian restaurant that opened over in Vineyard Haven," Daniel said. "For a date tonight."

"A date, huh?" Grayson asked.

"Yeah, I guess." Daniel playfully shrugged.

His mother laughed when Daniel reached over and pulled her close. "You promised!"

Their flirty exchange was something Grayson hadn't witnessed before. Seeing his mother so happy was long overdue.

"I'm glad to hear this," Grayson said.

"I hope you mean that?" Daniel gave him a questioning stare.

"Why wouldn't I? I see two people excited to spend time together. What's there not to be pleased about?"

"Then it's just Tyler who can't come to grips with my relationship with your mom," Daniel said, sitting back in his chair.

"We're grown men." Grayson rolled his eyes. "I'm sorry he's never shown interest in you two together."

"Well, he's allowed to be a little hesitant with this. He's always been that way, but I don't blame him. When his mother and I split, don't you remember how mad he was? All those outbursts?"

Grayson thought for a moment, but outside of a few discussions about his parents divorcing right before they finished their senior year, he didn't remember much else.

"Honestly, no. Of course he didn't want the divorce, but I don't remember him being particularly upset like you describe."

"I guess it was just at home then." Daniel looked out the window.

"Listen, Daniel. It was all such a long time ago, and it's not like you and my mom are a secret anymore. Well, to anyone but Willow."

"I know when you called me last night about Liam that you'd tried to talk to her before she left for the hospital. You're going to try again, right?" His mom looked nervously at Daniel. "And maybe you and Tyler can find a way to be at peace too."

"Not maybe. You will fix this, Grayson." Daniel's sharp tone was serious. "I can't see my two sons like this anymore."

"Yes, sir. I most certainly will talk to Willow again." He turned to his mom. "And I've been thinking the same thing. I don't want to stay mad at Tyler or have this ongoing tension between us. I know a lot has happened, but he's my brother—whether he wants to admit that or not."

"How about I take you to breakfast before I make my way to the office?" Daniel asked her.

"I'd like that," his mom said before she reached over and picked up his hand. "Everything will be alright."

After they left, Grayson finished getting ready for work. He was running late, but he'd already texted Tyler to let him know. They had a meeting soon with the new marketing manager. Running a brewery business had him wishing they could include some cold brews with what he was about to tell Tyler after their meeting.

———

"So let's break down the next steps," Tyler said as he clicked to show the next slide. Grayson slid into the meeting, which appeared to be halfway over, and quietly watched. Tyler acknowledged him with a quick glance.

"This is a brief timeline of everything we went over today, and I'll make sure it's emailed to you as well," he said to Grayson before looking back at the screen.

The new marketing manager lifted his hand and turned to Grayson. "Real quick since you're here, I'll need a list of the new staff at the Boston location so I can get going with those department heads for the grand opening in a few weeks."

"I'll email it to you right now," Grayson said and pulled his laptop out of his bag while Tyler continued.

For the next hour, the meeting went through the next steps for last quarter's projected growth and loss stats for the upcoming holiday season, events in all locations, media outreach for Boston, and then the men tied up a few other loose ends while the administrative assistant who'd also been in the meeting typed follow-up notes.

When everyone else left the room, Grayson stayed in his seat while Tyler packed up, avoiding his stare.

"We can sit in silence if you like." Grayson's sarcasm made Tyler pause. "Or we can cut to the chase."

"I'm not in the mood, Grayson. Can we just stick to the work we both need to do, like we've always done?"

"That right there is the problem," Grayson said as Tyler organized the paperwork in front of him. "It's why things between us are like this. We've spent eight years avoiding what we really needed to talk about, and that's Willow."

"No need." Tyler put his laptop and paperwork in his briefcase. "She made it clear when I talked to her at the beach that she's done with me. She's all yours, just like she's always been." He picked up his briefcase and tried to leave, but Grayson stood and blocked the door.

"Whoa, hold on. Would you just please take a seat and talk to me?"

The air grew thick with tension as Tyler glared at him before he sank into the chair behind him. "So talk."

"First of all, calm down. You're good at this, Tyler." Grayson took his seat again.

"Excuse me?"

"You're good at pretending like nothing has happened, making up something in your head to get what you want or to avoid. We can't do that anymore. Whether you like it or not, Willow is here, and it's time she knows."

"She doesn't need to know."

"Is that why you didn't tell her at the beach?" Grayson threw his hands up. "Are you *serious*? Do you even hear yourself?"

"Yes. I mean it, Grayson. She never needed to know about your mother and my dad," Tyler's voice grew louder, and Grayson realized this was the first time he heard how angry it made him. "It was wrong of them to begin with and still is. The fact that your mother is even visiting him in front of Willow and for everyone else in town to see is—"

"The right thing to do," a female voice said from the doorway. Both men shot around.

"Mom?" Tyler said, immediately standing up again. "I didn't know you were coming to the island."

"Because I didn't tell you," she said and looked at Grayson. "Sorry to interrupt your conversation. The assistant pointed to this room when I asked where you were. May I come in?"

"Yes, please, come have a seat." Grayson gestured to another empty chair, and she closed the door behind her before stepping into the room. "How are you Mrs. Par—not Parker anymore."

"Grayson, you're an adult now, please call me Morgan. And it's Whittler now." She settled in a chair after Tyler gave her a quick kiss on the cheek. "And I'm doing quite well."

"I heard you were in Florida when you got the call about Liam. Vacation?" Grayson asked.

"Yes, my husband, Tom, inherited his parents' condo on the beach near Tampa, so we're often traveling down there. How are you, Grayson? It's been so long since I've seen you."

"Been good. Busy with work here, and I moved into my mother's old house. I've been slowly fixing it up."

Morgan smiled. "That's great."

"So, what brought you back, Mom?" Tyler asked.

"I came to check on you." Morgan exhaled as she glanced at Tyler. "Your dad filled me in on Willow returning to Terra Cove shortly after you stopped the wedding."

"Check on me?" Tyler repeated, clearly confused by the look on his face.

"Yes, to see what is going on with you."

"Did he ask you to do that?" Tyler asked.

"Yes, he did. He's worried, Tyler. I am, too—for both of you. You two have created quite a . . ."

"Mess?" Grayson filled in for her.

"Yes, a mess. A big one." Morgan glanced between them. "Look, Tyler, I know how mad you were when your dad and I divorced—"

"Hold on. You didn't take time out of your busy schedule to come mend some old wounds of mine. Mom, it's alright about you and Dad. I'm well past that."

"Let me finish," she said, then faced Grayson. "This involves you too, so I'm glad I caught you together."

"I am too. I was just telling him we need to resolve this."

"Resolve what?" Tyler crossed his arms in defense.

"Tyler, your father and I didn't split up because of his affair with Nicole all those years ago."

"But you said—"

"I know what I said, and it's not true." Morgan looked directly at Grayson again. "When his father and I were divorcing during his senior year, I had just gotten confirmation of what I'd suspected for a long time about your mother. I had an intuitive feeling that Daniel was your biological father." She turned her attention back to Tyler. "But I let my anger after years of an unhappy marriage take over, and when you found out about it, I told you the affair was the reason I was leaving your father. But it wasn't."

Grayson suddenly remembered the moment he told Tyler about the affair the day of prom—and how badly Tyler had initially responded. *"Of course! You get to have my dad too!"* Tyler had yelled in response. But just as fast as he got mad, he did what Tyler was known to do and covered it up with a lie. Now, after knowing how much Tyler had loved Willow, too, all those years, and how Morgan blamed the divorce on his mother's affair with Daniel . . . Grayson understood that Tyler must have felt like everything was being taken from him. Why didn't he see that before?

"I think I'm beginning to understand everything a little more clearly," Grayson said.

"Well, I don't!" Tyler shouted and put his hands on his forehead, then leaned back in his chair before straightening up again. "I don't even know where to start with what you just told me, Mom."

"Let's just start with the facts," Morgan said. "The first fact is, I exploded that day I told you that, Tyler. I shouldn't have involved you at all, but you had just come home from school after your dad and I had our day in court, not to mention I was already so drained from years of a declining marriage. What I didn't tell you—and I can see now how important it was for you to know—was that after your father had his affair with Nicole, I had one too . . . with Tom. When you were about two years old. So clearly, our marriage was over years before the divorce."

"What? Then why did you two stay together at all?" Tyler asked.

"For you." Morgan blinked slowly, drawing in a deep breath. "But not without bitterness, which only grew stronger as the years went by. Once your father and I finally did what we should have done years prior and split, we were both happier."

Grayson hadn't seen that part coming about Tyler's mom lying to him out of spite, and he waited for Tyler's reaction, which seemed to be a mixture of shock and understanding. Tyler got up and quietly went to the window while Grayson and Morgan patiently waited.

Eventually, Tyler turned around and looked directly at him. "I have a lot of apologizing to do to you and Willow."

Grayson studied him, trying to understand. "Apologizing for what, exactly?"

"For taking out my own hurt with my parents and my jealousy over you and Willow and lying to her. You needed a friend that night, and I was anything but that. I'm sorry, Grayson."

"Look, I can't speak for Willow"—Grayson stood and placed both hands on the table and look Tyler in the eyes—"but you and I can work through this. I held on to a lot of old wounds from childhood for years, so I get it."

"This conversation needed to happen years ago. But better late than never, I guess," Morgan said. "Tyler . . . I am so sorry for how I acted. Your dad and I both made a lot of mistakes in our marriage, including affairs. His just produced a baby, who is your brother, which I am so thankful for."

"You are?" Tyler asked.

"Of course I am. You never had any siblings—well, that you knew of." She smiled at Grayson. "And you not only had a best friend growing up, but he's also your brother, and no years were ever wasted between you two. And you both have Willow, who needs to know all of this."

"Yes, she does," Grayson agreed. "Let me handle that. It should have come from me in the first place."

"Are you sure?" Tyler asked.

"Yes." Grayson looked at Tyler. "You're my brother, and we have a lot of messy history, and all these hurts take time to heal, but they can heal." For a moment all he saw was the kid he once called his best friend, who was now a man trying to rise above his childhood wounds—just like Grayson had to do with Jack.

Morgan glanced at Tyler, who appeared deep in thought, which Grayson understood—it was a lot to take in. "I want you to know, your father and I do not regret or feel shame anymore over what happened in our marriage. After all, we got you out of it—and you, Grayson. I have long since forgiven him and vice versa. There's no hostility on my part about him and Nicole. She's a wonderful woman who makes him happy. That's why I came here, to tell you this in person."

"Thank you, Mom," Tyler said, and she got up to hug him, giving Grayson a faint smile over her shoulder. Things weren't completely resolved between the two men, but it was a start.

———

When Grayson left work later that day, he felt lighter. He and Tyler had made a huge step forward, leaving him with profound relief. After Morgan left, they went to lunch and talked a little longer, which was long overdue.

Now, as the late-afternoon sun cast over him on his way to his truck, he knew the next conversation may not go as smoothly, and he needed to unload to a friend. He got his phone out and found Wes's name.

"Hey, Grayson," Wes answered, the background noise loud. "Sorry for the noise. I'm just leaving the hangar. What's up?"

"Can you meet me at the brewery for a beer?"

"Be there in ten."

————

As soon as Grayson stepped inside the brewery, the relaxed vibes soothed him. He admired all the artwork from local artists lining the exposed brick walls alongside the brewing equipment. It was the perfect laid-back feel he needed to talk with Wesley. When he walked up to the bar, a mixture of tourists and residents were seated around it, some familiar faces turning to greet him.

"What'll it be, boss?" one of the bartenders called over to him.

Grayson glanced at the specials on the stand-up menu on the bar. "Hmm . . . I'll try the Beach Road Ale." He pulled out a stool and sat down to wait for Wesley.

The bartender delivered his beer, and the roasted, smooth ale went down easy. "Well done," he said, holding up the beer mug to the bartender.

"That looks like the Beach Road. It's my new favorite." Wesley appeared next to him. "Make that another one."

The bartender gave him a quick nod and pulled out another glass mug.

"It's delicious. I'll need to come back before the summer is over and it's off the menu. Although, our fall lineup is always amazing too." Grayson held up his mug next to Wesley's when the bartender placed the second one down. "Thanks for meeting me. How was the day of tours?"

"Went well, but I wasn't the pilot today. I was mostly in the office doing the boring stuff." Wesley took a sip of his beer and looked around the bar. "It's packed for a Wednesday afternoon."

"It's happy hour in the middle of July on Martha's Vineyard. This isn't anything different from how it normally is."

"True." Wesley shrugged. "So tell me. How is everything?"

"Before we get to me, I wanted to start with you. How's your dad?"

Wesley put his hands around his mug and stared straight ahead. "It was a nerve-racking night for the girls and me, particularly my mom. But he was released from the hospital a couple hours ago and went back to the rehab center. He has a bruise on his hip from the fall. Thank goodness nothing worse occurred."

"That's a relief. I haven't heard from Willow all day. She updated me about an hour after she left my place to tell me your dad was okay so far."

"I had a nice long chat with her last night while we waited in the hospital for the doctors to tell us it was safe to go home." Wesley eyed him, tapping the sides of his mug.

"Did you?"

"Oh yeah . . . And let me tell you, does she have her heart set on you, my man."

"Does she?" Grayson took a long sip of his beer, trying not to grin too wide.

"I see that smile!" Wesley chuckled. "But she still has no clue about Tyler and you. What's going on with that?"

"I asked her to come over last night so I could lay it all out. Honest!" Grayson held his hands up.

"I'm just messing with you. I know my dad's fall kind of cut into that." Wesley scrunched his brows together. "You're still going to talk to her though, right?"

"Of course."

"Good. Because Tyler . . ." Wesley shook his head. "I don't know. That guy really upsets me. Did she tell you he tried to fix everything when she met him at the beach last weekend?"

"Yeah, I knew about that." Grayson took another swig of his beer. "But don't be so mad at Tyler. I actually had a good conversation with him earlier today. His mom was here. There were some things we didn't know. He's not a bad guy."

"Okay, I'll take your word on that." Wesley glanced at him. "Willow really shared her heart last night, and I probably shouldn't tell you everything she confided in me, but she really hopes you feel the same way."

"And how's that?" Grayson watched him hold up his mug to grab the bartender's attention.

"Want another?" the bartender asked Wesley, who nodded.

"Yes, please."

"Coming up," the man said, pulling a new mug out.

"She hopes that you want to get to know her too," Wesley said.

"What do you mean, 'get to know her?'" Grayson asked. Hadn't he known her his whole life?

"Yes, 'get to know her,'" Wesley repeated. "Look, you two still love each other, that's clear. But that was then, eight whole years ago, when you were just teenagers. Now you have the opportunity to learn about who each of you have become. It'll be like falling in love all over again."

Grayson's eyes widened. "Wow . . . Yeah, you're absolutely right. The attraction hasn't ceased at all, and when I look at her, I see the same eyes I've known forever, but the woman standing in front of me has so much more to share. It'll be tricky with the distance if she decides to go back to Connecticut, but I'm not going anywhere."

"Which means?"

"I feel the same way." Grayson held up his mug when the bartender handed Wesley his. "To a second chance." They clanged their beers and Wesley grew quiet again.

"She's not going back to Connecticut."

"She's not?"

"Nope. She told me that she and our parents have been discussing some possibilities with her next steps. She said she's really been thinking this through. She'll have to move her practice entirely online or rebuild a new one here, but one thing was clear in that conversation: She's starting over right here in Terra Cove."

"Wow . . . This is great news and will make things a lot easier for us."

"Now you just need to get past all the secrets so you can begin again." Wesley held up his beer again. "To a clean slate!"

When Grayson clinked his mug again, his nerves fired up as he remembered what his mom had told him—that everything would be alright.

Maybe it really would be and Willow would take the news just fine. He'd probably been overthinking it. The important thing was she still loved him, and he loved her. That'd be a strong enough starting point for any hard conversation. Right?

Chapter Seventeen

"I'm sorry, Mom. I didn't know you were out here or I would have come out to help earlier." Willow lifted one of the horse's hooves and began to clean it. The sun broke through the Saturday morning clouds after overnight thunderstorms, and the air was comfortable, a perfect start to the weekend.

"Don't apologize. One of our weekend hires called out sick today, so I'm trying to pick up some of the work that needs to be done. I didn't ask for your help because you've been working so hard juggling everything between your clients and the farm, so I wanted you to rest this morning."

"It was definitely a busy week, but it's too nice of a day to waste it sleeping."

Her mom smiled. "Thank you. Your dad and I are so grateful you're here." She closed the gate to a stall and then came to stand by her. "I've been meaning to ask you how things went at Grayson's Tuesday night. Dad's fall that night kind of distracted me."

"Understandable." She glanced up at her mom who was

clearly eager to hear her response. "I had a nice ride with Nova." She picked up the next hoof.

"I love knowing Nova is back in your life. You two have a connection like nothing I've ever seen, and believe me, I've witnessed a lot of riders with horses. But that's not really what I meant."

Willow knew her mom was fishing for information, but the last thing she wanted to do was let her parents down with anything she told them. They'd been pretty open about her spending time with Grayson again, but they also just wanted her to be happy and she didn't want to get their hopes up. The truth was, she wasn't sure how things with him would turn out.

"Well, Grayson cooked me some dinner, which was nice," she said, keeping her eyes on the task at hand. "Something he certainly couldn't do when we were teenagers. He could barely make toast back then." They both laughed. "And Nova has been the perfect comfort since all this happened with both Tyler and Dad's accident."

"I bet. Nova is a special horse, but horses have always done that for you. Ever since you were a little girl, it's like you could understand them on a level no one else could. You don't even know the relief it is to know you're back riding again."

Her mom was right. Willow could recall countless times she'd sneaked off into her parents' barn and talked to the horses. She'd tell them secrets and brush them—it was her escape. It still was.

She put the hoof down and stood up to face her mom. "It's a relief to me too."

"Have you ever thought about incorporating horse therapy into your work?" Mom asked.

Willow considered the question and remembered when she told Grayson something similar. "I just told Grayson about how I wished I could bring horses into my sessions with my clients somehow. Nova has really helped me focus on my own emotions and what I've ignored for so long. Riding is so grounding and I think it could really help others process their own struggles much easier."

"That's what I mean. I didn't know about horse therapy until your dad and I went out to dinner right before his accident, and we ran into an old friend who told us how it really helped her niece. And we both thought of you."

"I'm going to have to look into that. Since staying in Terra Cove seems to be on the table for me, at least I have horses here to try it out on."

"Nova would be the best choice for that. Our horses in training probably wouldn't work for therapy yet. There's special training involved with that, but Nova is so gentle."

"That's true. Not much therapy would get done with a colt bucking around." Willow's thoughts started to go wild with curiosity over the suggestion of horse therapy. "Thanks for bringing the idea up. I'm going to see what I can find out."

"You're welcome. It really is something I can see you doing."

Finished with the hooves, she hugged her mom and headed back inside to figure out the rest of her Saturday. Sweat beaded at her forehead from the work in the stables, so a shower would be the first thing. She had forgotten how tiring the work was, even after a month of doing it, and found herself yawning. Maybe a nap by the pool would be next.

Checking her phone, she saw a missed call from Grayson and hit call.

"Hey, stranger!" he said.

"Long time no talk!" she joked back. It had only been four days since she saw him last, but it felt like a lot longer. "I saw you called. How are you?" She turned on the shower and went to find some clean clothes to lay out.

"I sure did. Do you have any plans today?"

She opened her dresser drawer. "No, I don't."

"Good. Can I steal you for the day?"

The tingle down her spine instantly gave her energy again. "Depends. Where to?" She stared at her clothes, waiting to hear the answer before picking an outfit.

"Somewhere I never took you before, but it's the perfect temperature to do today."

"I see. So you're going to keep me in the dark?"

"Wear some comfortable clothing and sneakers. I'll pick you up in half an hour."

"Sounds good. I'll make sure the gate is open."

After they hung up, Willow chose her black yoga pants and one of her dark green workout tops. He said sneakers, so she assumed that meant they'd be outside walking somewhere.

After a quick shower, she decided to get her hair off her face but checked the time on her phone first. He hadn't given her much time to get herself ready, but she managed to get her curls pulled back in a French braid. With a little lip gloss and mascara, she felt alive again. The fatigue had washed away with the shower—and the excitement of seeing Grayson.

Downstairs, she found her mom in the kitchen.

"You look much more refreshed! I made you some scrambled eggs and avocado toast."

"Thanks, Mom." She sat down at the table with minutes to spare before Grayson was supposed to be there and picked up her toast.

"The weather is gorgeous. Anything planned?"

"Actually, I just made some plans," she said, chewing and swallowing as fast as she could. "Grayson is picking me up any minute and taking me somewhere, but it's a surprise."

"Oh really?" Her mom turned from the counter. "Well, don't choke. He can always come in and wait for you to finish breakfast."

She studied her mom. "Or . . . you just want to see him."

"Or that." The corners of her mom's mouth twitched. "I just haven't really talked to him in so long."

Wheels crunched to a stop outside. "Then I'll tell him to come on in." Willow put her toast down and stood up to wave at him from the doorway.

When he got to the door, she leaned close so her mom wouldn't overhear from the kitchen. "My mom's wanting you to come in."

"Should I be worried?"

"Hmm . . . maybe," she teased and gave him a nudge. "She just wants to say hello."

They walked back to the kitchen and her mom was sitting at the table with a cup of coffee but instantly stood when she saw Grayson.

"Why, hello there!" Willow watched in amazement as her mom came over and hugged him. "So good to see you."

"It's great to see you too, Rachel."

"I mean, I've seen you around town here and there, but you know what I mean." She sat back down.

"Coffee?" Willow quickly asked, realizing how awkward this must be for them.

"Sure, thank you," he said and took the empty seat next to Willow's. "How has everything been, outside of what happened with Liam?"

"Busy, but that's a good thing."

"Have the stables been keeping full?"

"Very. We've had a one-year wait list for training for a long time now."

Willow handed him his mug and when he peeked up at her, she saw her mom watching their glances over her own mug.

"Wow, that's really good. I'm happy the horses are still keeping you and Liam going."

"My dad will be out there training those horses until he

can barely stand anymore," Willow said, and they all laughed, loosening the conversation some more. "That is, once he recovers."

Grayson filled her mom in on the plans for the brewery over the next six months, mentioning that they have their eyes on another new location in Connecticut, while Willow finished her breakfast. By the time she was done, they were easily chatting, and she got up to put her plate in the sink.

"I'm sure you two could catch up all day, but I'm still wondering where you plan on taking me?" Willow said, coming back to the table.

"Let's get in the truck and I'll show you." Grayson looked at her mom. "It was good to chat, Rachel."

"Same. I'm happy to hear how well things are going for you at the brewery," Mom said and got up to walk them to the door. "I hope you have a wonderful day!" she said, holding the screen door open as she waved them off.

The joy on her mom's face as she watched them get in the truck was heartwarming. So much for not getting their hopes up.

———

THE RIDE DIDN'T TAKE LONG BEFORE WILLOW recognized where he was taking her. She could see the lighthouse ahead and the calming view of the Atlantic to her left. Driving through Aquinnah and going to the top was one of her favorite things she and Whitney used to do when they wanted to get out of Terra Cove. Afterward, they'd stroll through the shops on the main road. Visiting Aquinnah was something Grayson had never been interested in doing. It was fun to see how much he'd changed.

The drive was barely fifteen minutes, but when she looked out over the clay cliffs the town was known for, with the ocean in the background, it always felt like she was somewhere far away—at the edge of the world.

"I think the surprise is over," he said.

Willow glanced at him. Grayson reached over and put his hand on top of hers, giving it a squeeze.

"I'm glad you're finally bringing me here." Willow closed her eyes, feeling the warmth of his touch as he held her hand, and everything began to replay in her mind. Starting high school together hand in hand, all the dances and school events, their date nights, watching thunderstorms under the summer sky, teaching him to ride Nova and all the trail rides after that, spending time at the cove, and their entire childhood. Without realizing she was upset, a tear fell down her cheek.

Grayson turned into the parking area and found a spot for the truck, then leaned over to face her and wipe away the tear.

"What is it?"

"How did we get here, Grayson?"

"We drove," he joked with a small smile as she brushed back some loose baby curls at her temple.

"Grayson . . ."

He put his finger to his lips, then said, "Hang on. Before we go there, I think a little lighthouse therapy is needed."

They got out of his truck and hiked the short distance toward one of the island's famous lighthouses, Gay Head Lighthouse. After a ten-minute trek along a well-maintained trail, they reached the redbricked structure. The pitted, worn brick walls on the exterior were marked by over a century of salty breezes and winter storms. Going up the narrow, winding staircase, Willow was overcome by the familiar space —climbing to the top was like going back in time. Grayson was on her heels as she steadied herself with the rough handrail along the creaky iron stairwell as they made their way up the dizzying ascent.

They reached the top and the whole island spread out

before them in a stunning view from inside the small glass enclosure. Willow looked out over the sparking blue ocean, almost wishing she could jump off and dive into the freeing water. As they enjoyed the view in silence, she began to truly understand how much she'd missed the Vineyard—this was home. Grayson moved closer to her—and *he* was her home.

"This view is incredible," he said, keeping his attention straight ahead. "I can't believe I always said no to coming here with you."

"It blows me away every time. It's so beautiful."

"Me too . . ." he said, and she could feel his eyes on her. Voices from other visitors climbing the stairs distracted them. "Let's go outside and look."

They made their way back down and walked over to the edge of the cliff, as far as they could go. Memories of standing in that exact spot many times before flooded her mind. The iconic red-and-gray Aquinnah Cliffs carved out by glaciers millions of years prior kept her steady against the memories as she watched people on the beach below them. The magnificent scenery was always so ethereal and she was suddenly glad he was the one bringing her to see it after all the years away.

"Thank you for taking me here. I had almost forgotten how amazing this is."

"Willow," he said and gestured toward the beach, "I need to talk to you about something, which was another reason I brought you here. Can we go sit by the water?"

Willow turned her attention from the cliffs to him. "Are you finally going to tell me what you and Tyler have been keeping from me?"

He nodded. "Let's just go down there and we can talk by the water."

Everything in his demeanor changed while they walked down to Moshup Beach. She didn't understand how they went from the light-hearted banter when he'd called earlier to the drawn-out expression on his face while they moved down the trail.

When they found a spot far enough away from others, they sat down.

"I just realized I didn't bring a blanket to sit on," he said, holding her hand as she sank into the sand next to him.

"I'm not thinking about a blanket. I'm wondering what is going on."

Grayson pulled his legs up and leaned over his knees as he gazed out toward the waves. "I honestly don't even know where to begin."

"How about just anywhere? What is it, Grayson?"

"Before I tell you, I want you to know something. Both me and Tyler were put in a really strange position with this information when we first found out, and it's been tough to navigate. I was hoping that by bringing you out here, away from town, it would make this conversation easier, but it's not."

"Now I'm feeling anxious. Just tell me."

"Okay," he said and turned to face her. "Tyler and I . . . are brothers."

Willow's eyes widened as far as they could go as she tried to repeat what he'd just said until she understood it, but she didn't.

"Did you just say, you two are . . . *brothers?*"

"Half brothers," he said, breaking eye contact and looking down at the sand. "But yes, that is what I said."

"Half . . . brothers?" She knew what that meant, but she was rapidly trying to piece together *how*.

"My mother and Tyler's father had me. They had an affair—"

"I got it." Willow put her hand up. She couldn't believe it. And it suddenly made sense why his mom and Daniel were friends, which still seemed out of the blue since they never talked to each other while she was growing up. "Now I get why they talk so much now."

"Yes, but that only started recently. They . . ." He paused, looking at her again. "Are sort of seeing each other now."

"So wait just a second." Willow shook her head, her emotions so jumbled with this news that she couldn't pinpoint exactly how she felt. "You said it was hard for both you and Tyler when you found out. When was that exactly?"

Grayson's eyes glossed over and his lip trembled. "Since . . ."

"Tell me right now, how long?" Her voice grew louder, but she couldn't help it. She had a bad feeling about what he was about to tell her.

"Since prom night," he whispered.

"*Prom* night!" she shouted and rose to her feet. "You *both* knew this for the last eight years and—" She was at a loss for words, mainly for why Tyler just spent eight years with her and never told her.

Grayson stood up. "Willow, please, let's talk this out. I know this is surprising."

"Yeah, it's surprising alright! Finding out you two are related is big news, but finding out my two closest friends of my entire life kept this news from me for *eight* years is something I can't even begin to understand!"

"I know, and I am so sorry it has come to this. I should have told you the minute I found out. I . . ." He reached out to her, but she pulled back.

"Is this why you left me? Why you suddenly disappeared on me on our prom night, leaving me crying in my gown and ending four years together with no explanation? Over . . . that?"

"That is exactly what I did. I pushed everyone away, literally, when I found out. And that was wrong. I should have come straight to you."

"You think!" Willow saw people down the beach watching them and lowered her voice. "How can I trust you now that I know you kept something like that from me? *Both* of you did!" She put her hand up when he tried to speak and kept going. "So Tyler is your brother. Okay, fine. You should have just told me! But instead, you pushed me away . . . What did I have to do with all that?"

"Nothing. Absolutely nothing, Willow. I was wrong, and I'm sorry. It's just that . . . it was Jack. He showed up right before I was supposed to go pick you up. He was drunk as ever like I told you the other night, and said—"

Willow shook her head and held up a hand to silence him as she backed away. "I've heard enough for today. Don't you dare follow me."

Without another word, she turned and walked away, leaving him standing on the beach. She knew he was watching her leave, but she didn't care what else he needed to say. This was too much for her to process and what was worse, Tyler had kept it from her too. Eight years and not a word! Both men abandoning her in a wasted gown. How could she trust Grayson now? What else had he kept from her?

When Whitney pulled up a short while later, Willow didn't even notice. She had found a bench to wait near the Aquinnah shops and kept her face down so the people passing by didn't see her tears that wouldn't stop falling.

"Willow," her sister called through the window. She stood and got in the car, but they stayed parked. "I'm not going to force you to talk, but just know that I called Wesley on the way here, and he filled me in on why you were most likely upset. Did Grayson tell you?"

"That he and Tyler are brothers? Yes, he did. Wesley knew?"

"Apparently so. Grayson told him when they went camping over the Fourth."

Great. Another man in my life keeping things from me. "And he didn't think to tell me?"

"Don't be mad at Wes. It's not his news to share," Whitney said, and the two women sat quietly for a couple minutes before her sister broke the silence. "I can't even believe it."

"You and me both," she said, looking over at her older sister whose face fell when she saw Willow's swollen eyes.

"Oh, Willow. I don't even know what to say. Why did they keep this a secret?"

"I don't know. I kind of left Grayson in the middle of the conversation down at the beach. I was just so shocked."

"I don't blame you."

"I've had this strange feeling since I found out about Grayson working with Tyler—that there was something more I didn't know. Well, I was right. I know this doesn't impact me directly, but it's just the fact that these two men kept something so important about their lives from me for so long."

"Yeah. I know you're disappointed with Grayson, but I'm mad at both of them."

"I am too. Tyler will be hearing from me alright, but he and I are over." Fresh tears spilled down her cheeks. "I wanted to start over with Grayson. Now I don't know if I can trust him."

"Let's just get home and we can talk some more." Whitney put the car in drive and the entire way home they fell into much-needed silence again. She needed to clear her head so she could confront Tyler.

Chapter Eighteen

The first light of dawn crept over the horizon as the kayak glided effortlessly across the calm surface. A shimmer of silver reflected Sunday's early morning light across the pond, and the world began to awaken around Grayson as his paddle smoothly stroked the water. Taking a break, he scanned the horizon, drinking in the serenity and trying to ignore the pounding in his head.

A night of hardly any sleep had him up before the sun to work out his stress on the water. The look Willow had on her face before she backed away from him at the beach the day before rattled him all night. He knew that expression. It indicated something he swore he'd never cause her to experience again—heartbreak.

Anger simmered under the throbbing emotional pain as he paddled faster. The sun continued its climb, but nothing was brightening his spirits. He wasn't sure how to fix this and thoughts of losing her all over again were more than he could bear. When he was finally spent, he made his way to the edge, pulled the kayak out of the water, then lay on the sand in pure fatigue. Between the conversation with Willow, spending the rest of the day yesterday clearing out the soap shack to keep himself busy, being up most of the night, and working out for an hour on the water, he finally felt like he could sleep for hours.

When he got home, he fed Monty and didn't even bother going upstairs. He lay on the couch and immediately fell into a deep rest.

———

The sound of a doorbell seemed miles away, but when Grayson opened his eyes, the ringing grew clearer. The knock that followed prompted him to get up and answer the door, and he found Wesley standing on his porch.

"There you are. I was ringing the doorbell for nearly five minutes," Wesley said, coming in when Grayson moved aside. "I saw your truck, so I knew you must be somewhere around here."

"What time is it?" Grayson rubbed the grogginess out of his eyes.

"Noon. Were you still in bed?" He looked down at Grayson's bathing suit. "Or on your way to the beach?"

"No, I was asleep on the couch. I went out kayaking earlier. I need some coffee." They headed for the kitchen, and Wesley sat at the table, rubbing Monty who was excitedly greeting him while Grayson got the coffee going.

"I hope it's alright that I'm here, but I needed to see how you were. I already know what happened from Willow."

Grayson leaned against the counter while the coffee dripped into the pot. "I bet you do, and I can imagine how that must have gone. She was so mad when she left me yesterday. I barely got a chance to explain anything after I told her."

"She's angry alright. She even let me have it when I

stopped by my parents' house yesterday afternoon because she found out I knew before her and didn't tell her."

"Sorry you got caught in that crossfire . . ."

Wesley shrugged. "It's alright. It's you who needs to hide though," he teased. "Look, she's just mad, but that was to be expected. I think she just needs to go process learning the first part. She will calm down, you know Willow."

"I do, but I don't know, Wes . . . There's only so much one woman can take with all that Tyler and I have put her through over the years. There was no reason to keep this from her."

"No, there wasn't. I know when we went camping you said you always assumed Tyler had told her, but did you really believe that or were you just avoiding the topic too?"

"Yes, I . . ." Grayson sighed, surrendering to Wesley's truthful statement. "It was something I just convinced myself of. You're right . . . I avoided the topic too."

Wesley grew quiet as Grayson poured coffee into a mug.

"Want some?" Grayson asked him.

"No, thanks." Wesley shook his head. "It looks like you'll need the whole pot."

"Sure feels like I will. I'm so exhausted, and it's not just from all the yardwork and kayaking, I'm emotionally drained."

"Imagine how Willow feels."

"Yeah, that's why I'm at such a loss for what to do. I can't stand the thought of her hurting again." Grayson stayed at the counter, nearly chugging the coffee. "How did the conversation end after she told you?"

"There were a lot of tears. She said she doesn't know how to trust you again, and then she told me she needed to go lie down. Whitney went with her. I had a sunset flight scheduled for newlyweds, so I had to leave. And I haven't seen her yet today. I stopped by the house, but she left early to go somewhere." Wesley looked at him with sorry eyes. "But I did manage to tell her at least once that no matter how mad she is, she can't ignore this with either you or Tyler."

Grayson nodded, his tired mind trying to figure out how to approach her again. "I'm at such a loss. I don't want to burden her—"

"Do you love her?" Wesley stood up and crossed his arms over his chest.

"I've never stopped."

"Then you go after her. You didn't before. Don't make that mistake again. Don't hide." He came over and placed a hand on Grayson's shoulder. "It'll be okay." He lowered his hand and stepped back. "I have to get going. I'm waiting to see if my dad will be discharged today. He's finally cleared for outpatient rehab. And I have a new pilot starting this week, and I'm taking him up for a test flight soon."

"I bet your dad can't wait to get home. I hope they do discharge him," Grayson said. "That's earlier than they expected right?"

"Yes. They originally were thinking it would be at least another week or so, but he's made such great progress, and they agree home is best for him. Anyway, I'm off. Call me if you need anything."

"Will do. Thanks for coming by."

A few minutes after Wesley left, Grayson was sitting on the couch deep in thought when his phone lit up and he saw a text from Tyler:

Hey. I had lunch with Dad and wanted to check on you. He just heard from Liam that you finally told her. And that it was rough. We knew it would be. Hang in there.

Grayson typed his reply.

Thanks for checking in. It was very rough.
Talk soon.

He re-read the text from Tyler. His eyes reddened seeing "Dad" without "my" before it—a first after so long.

Willow was hurt and he understood that, so it was hard not to feel guilty about this moment of happiness. Despite how hard it was to know Tyler had been with her and how that happened, for the last eight years, he'd been without one of his best friends. He hoped they could find a way to come together again ... as brothers.

His phone notified him again, this time with a text from Liam.

Hi Grayson. I'm being discharged today
and will continue my recovery as an
outpatient. Can you come to the rehab
center in an hour?

Before he responded, Grayson wondered why Willow's dad wanted him there for the discharge, but he wasn't going to say no, so he replied, *yes*, and then took a shower and waited until it was time to leave.

———

AFTER MAKING THE LAST TRIP TO RACHEL'S CAR with Liam's things, Grayson headed back inside the rehab center. Rachel was at the front desk signing some paperwork.

"I think that was the last of it," Grayson said, coming up behind them at the desk.

"We will do a thorough check of the room when we clean it, Mrs. Anderson, and let you know if you left anything behind," the lady behind the desk said.

"Thank you. You all have been excellent," Rachel said.

Grayson leaned toward Willow's mom. "To put up with his moods, they sure have been," he joked.

"I wasn't that bad!" Liam chuckled.

The receptionist smiled and a nurse came over to wheel Liam outside. "It was our pleasure to take care of you, Mr. Anderson. I'm so pleased with your progress," the nurse said, and they all walked out. "I will leave you here." The nurse locked his wheelchair. "Just leave the chair on the other side of the double doors. Mrs. Anderson, we will see you Tuesday for outpatient?"

"Bright and early," Liam said, and the nurse went back inside. "I cannot begin to tell you how excited I am to sleep in my own bed tonight."

"I'll go get the car," Rachel said and headed to the parking lot.

"I bet you are." Grayson looked down at Liam. "It'll be a good night's sleep."

"Speaking of." Liam shaded his eyes against the sun as he glanced up at him. "Maybe you need one too? No offense, but you look terrible."

"Is it that obvious?" Grayson rubbed his face in an attempt to wake up more.

"Very," Liam said.

"Well, I've been better." Grayson tried to give him a reassuring smile.

Liam nodded and drew in a long breath. "It's been quite a morning, which is why I asked you to meet me here before I called my own kids about the green light the doctor gave me for discharge. I knew that here would be the only place I'd be able to talk to you alone before I left because Willow is home and I couldn't ask you to meet me there. Besides, I needed you to lift all my stuff for Rachel."

Grayson smiled. "Don't even have to ask, *sir*." They both

laughed before Grayson grew serious again. "I take it you wanting to check on me meant she told you."

"Yes. She called me last night, crying. I could hardly understand her at first, but I managed to calm her down so she could get it out." Liam looked straight ahead and they saw Rachel driving the car toward them. "I filled her mom in on everything now that Willow knows. If I had told my wife sooner, the news would have come from her and not you or Tyler. There's no way she'd have kept that quiet."

Grayson watched the car stop at a stop sign. "Was she mad?"

"No, she wasn't. Shocked. Yes, very surprised to hear about the affair and a little upset it was a secret for so long, but glad it wasn't anymore."

"I don't know what to do to fix this with Willow," Grayson said as the car slowly pulled up.

"Well, that's also why I wanted you here, so you can see my face as I tell you this: Do not give up," Liam said, and Grayson looked down at him. "I'm serious. If you pull back and let her go like you did back then, there won't be any chance left with my daughter."

"Does she even want to give me a chance now?"

"Yes." Liam smiled at his wife as she joined them on the sidewalk. Grayson helped Rachel put him into the car and put the wheelchair back.

When Grayson got back to the car, Liam had the window down waiting on him. "Sure about that, sir?"

"All she kept saying over and over through her tears to me, Grayson, was how much she loves you."

When they all left, Grayson's thoughts spiraled in every direction. He loved her, too, but all he could do was hope that would be enough.

———

Maggie's Market was quiet, which he'd expected since most tourists in the area were likely at the beach before the round of rain that was due over the next couple days. He'd decided to make a quick stop to keep himself moving as he thought about how to approach Willow.

After filling up his basket with a few grocery items, he was standing in line to pay when he saw her out of the corner of his eye. Willow walked in, but she wasn't alone. A woman was with her that he didn't recognize, taller with long brown hair. They didn't see him and continued into the store, disappearing in an aisle, but not before he saw her face. Her tired eyes and sunken expression were impossible not to notice, even from where he stood.

It was his turn to pay, and he quickly put his groceries on the belt.

"Grayson?" a woman's voice asked, and he turned around and saw his mom behind him in line.

"Hi, Mom," he said, and she watched how fast he kept loading the belt.

"In a hurry?"

He paused and stepped close to her. "Willow just walked in. I told her about me and Tyler yesterday, and she was pretty mad. I don't want her to see me and feel uncomfortable and get even more sad than she already looks."

His mom turned to look behind her. "Don't feel like you have to hide. You're getting groceries. You're allowed."

He put the last of his things on the belt. "I know, but I'm just trying to give her some space to breathe. She was terribly upset yesterday."

After he finished paying, he waited for his mom and they walked out to the parking lot. Luckily Willow didn't see him, and once he'd put all his bags in the back seat of his truck, his mom came over and held the door open as he got in the driver's seat.

"Grayson, you already know I stayed away from Daniel for years after you and Tyler found out," she started with a concerned expression. "And that made both of us worse . . ."

"And now you are together. I'm okay, Mom. I promise."

She picked up his hand and kissed the top. "I know you are okay. You always are."

"What do you mean?"

"What I mean is that's what you always say—when you really aren't. How could you be? This situation between you and Willow and Tyler has been confusing and hard to endure. And you are not alone."

"I don't want you to worry about me. Just focus on what is budding between you and Daniel."

"The three of you affect Daniel and me. Grayson, you're not listening." She drew in a long breath and began again. "Tyler isn't the only one who pretends like nothing happened when tough situations arise. I know you told him that was what he does when his mother came to your workplace."

"So you heard about that."

"Yes, I did. Morgan came over last night and talked to me and Daniel before she headed back home to New Jersey. What I'm trying to say is that we all concluded that you *both* do a fine job of ignoring everything and acting as if all is well." She let go of his hand and shrugged. "Must have learned that from someone, but I can't think of who . . ."

"Don't be so hard on yourself, Mom," Grayson said.

"Just make sure you don't give Willow too much of a breather." She patted his hand. "I'll see you later."

"Okay. Thanks, Mom," he said and shut the door after she walked away.

When he turned on the ignition, he couldn't escape the truth of her words—or those of Wesley and Liam. Gripping the wheel, he stared ahead at the people walking through the parking lot as something else Wesley said earlier suddenly popped into his head. *"I'm taking him up for a test flight."* An idea suddenly occurred to him.

He pulled out his phone and found Wesley's name and hit call.

"Well, that was fast!" Wesley joked when he answered. "You caught me at a good time. I just got back from the first test flight with the new guy."

"Willow's never flown with you, correct?" Grayson asked.

"Nope. Why do you—" Wesley paused. "Wait, I think I know what you're getting at."

"If you're thinking what I am, when is a good time?"

"I have time Wednesday morning. Early though. I'll block it off so no one books that time."

He remembered Willow telling him that her virtual sessions would only be on Tuesdays and Thursdays. "Perfect. Keep it blocked off. I think doing something big like this will catch her attention. If I can get her up there, that is."

"Grayson, now you're thinking. And I know you can get her here."

When they hung up, his body reignited with energy as he worked through the plan in his mind.

Chapter Nineteen

"I know the rain is halting any beach plans for the day, but we can still have some fun," Willow said, pushing around the eggs on her plate Monday morning. As soon as Whitney brought her home on Saturday after she'd left Grayson on the beach, she called Ivy, who immediately booked herself a ticket on a ferry the following morning.

"Rain won't stop me from exploring this place. I've been waiting years to come here," Ivy said, and Willow laughed.

"I know. I'm so happy you're finally here."

They had spent Sunday afternoon around the farm with Willow showing her the horses, swimming with her sister, Jason, and niece and nephew, and grilling steaks for dinner to celebrate her dad's homecoming. Despite the circumstances of why Ivy finally made it to Martha's Vineyard, they had a good day.

When Whitney and Jason took the kids home after dinner, Willow and Ivy sat on her parents' patio and watched the sunset while sipping white peach sangria, and Willow filled Ivy in on everything. She shared more about Grayson and her childhood with both him and Tyler—the good and bad memories—all of it. And their conversation replayed through her head long after she went to bed.

———

"Why didn't you ever tell me about Grayson?" Ivy had asked, picking up her wineglass.

"I really don't have an answer," Willow said. It was all she could say because the more she thought back to meeting Ivy in college and them becoming best friends, there was no excuse to have kept this from her. After all, Ivy told her all about her childhood and her relationships up until that point. "I guess I just wanted to pretend Grayson had never happened. I was so heartbroken."

"I can see that." Ivy stared at her as the setting sun peeked through the trees, lighting up her friend's hair. "Is that what we're going to do now? Pretend he doesn't exist again?"

"It's different now."

"Is it? Because what I see in front of me is my best friend completely heartbroken all over again." Ivy eyed her and brought the glass to her lips for a sip. "But this time, it's because she truly loves him."

"Ivy, it doesn't matter. I'm hurt."

"So?" Ivy said.

"What are you saying to me? That you want me to call him after he's hurt me now twice? How could I trust anything now with him?"

"What I'm saying is, I understand he messed up. And so did Tyler. Keeping something that important from you was wrong. I'd be upset too, and when you called me yesterday, I heard the tears, and I am not disregarding them, but I also heard a woman who is still madly in love and never got a chance to explore that beyond a high school romance."

"I don't know," Willow said, still feeling defensive.

"I do. Willow, when you talk to me about Tyler, it's clearly over. When you talk about Grayson . . . It's clearly not."

"But Grayson kept secrets from me. Important ones. They both did."

"People make mistakes. The three of you are not perfect, and the intimate relationships that have formed have been challenging, but I don't blame either one of them for loving you like they have. I just think the lack of communication was the core to all of this and some other personal hurts that have nothing to do with you. Those two men should have discussed this long before Grayson had to stand on the beach yesterday and tell you that Tyler was his brother. But there has to be a reason why they stayed silent. Maybe you need to let Grayson finish explaining."

Willow nodded. She heard Ivy, but so many years had passed, and so much emotion was involved, not to mention three stubborn people. And she was just so tired.

———

Ivy's words sat with Willow for hours until she finally drifted off to sleep. And now all she wanted to do was curl up on the couch for the rest of the day.

"I read on the ferry ride over about the trolley tours in town. They even operate in the rain." Ivy smiled with pleading eyes. "I know that would be beyond boring for you since you know everything about this place, but . . ."

"Sure, let's do it."

"Great! And then, you know me and my love for history . . . Maybe we can we hit up one of the museums I read about?"

"Anything for my best friend." Willow chuckled and went upstairs to get ready.

"We need to go inside one of those gingerbread cottages before I leave. Oak Bluffs was fascinating to learn about with that revival campground and those colorful cottages." Ivy's face was practically glued to the window of the trolley as she took in all the sites and listened to the tour guide.

"West Tisbury is next, everyone, otherwise known as the 'west side' of the island. Also known for its bustling agriculture and famous summer market, it's a popular place to stroll through. Just a couple weekends ago, the towns of Terra Cove and West Tisbury joined together for their big summer festival filled with local food vendors, rides, horse shows, and more," the tour guide said.

"I wish you were here for that," Willow told Ivy. "My parents always participate and do pony rides for the kids."

"If only I was invited sooner . . ." Ivy teased and used her phone to take pictures of the passing scenery. "But really, remind me again how some man was the reason you left all this?"

"I know, I know. It really is stunning each time I see everything around me. I'm blessed to have grown up here."

The trolley went through West Tisbury's town center, and the tour guide explained its history, including the famous reconstructed century-old post-and-beam barn that was the focal point of the big festival. Willow remembered how she and Grayson went inside after Nova and Max were settled at the fairgrounds. There were hundreds of people around them, and every time she stole a glance at him as they walked through together, his unblinking green eyes were glued to her.

Willow looked away from the barn while the trolley slowly passed it. "When we get to Edgartown next, the guide mentioned that we will stop for a while, and we can eat some lunch. Stella's has some of the best seafood. It's outside, but there is covered seating."

When they arrived in Edgartown, the rain had slowed to light drizzle, which was perfect timing to stroll through the tiny downtown.

"Wow, look at those homes." Ivy pointed ahead once they stepped off the trolley.

"Those are the wealthy captains' houses from the past," Willow explained of the impressive clapboard-styled historical homes lined up next to each other.

"I could roam the streets here for hours, but I'm starving," Ivy said, scrolling through the photos she had taken so far.

"Same. Let's head to Stella's."

The restaurant was busy despite the weather and after they ordered, the drizzle had stopped completely. They took their food to an umbrellaed table out on the deck that one of the staff had just dried with a towel.

"Your salmon burger looks delicious," Ivy said, picking up one of her shrimp tacos.

"It's my favorite. I've yet to find anywhere else that can make it like Stella's, and I've tried everywhere in Connecticut with no luck."

Willow checked her phone and saw two missed calls from Tyler.

"By the look on your face, you must have a message from either Tyler or Grayson," Ivy said.

"It's Tyler calling me back." Willow sent him a quick text explaining that she had a friend in town and would call him back later. "He's been trying since Saturday night, but once you got here, I haven't been able to answer." She put some salt on her side of fries.

"What did you tell him again in that voicemail?" Ivy slowly chewed, trying to conceal the smile that was forming. "I'm sorry, I'm not amused by the situation. I just know that when you get angry, sometimes you spill out the most random things."

"Oh, I did, times a hundred. I started yelling about things I was mad at him about from a year ago." Both women laughed. It sure felt nice to let loose with her best friend. "I'm so thankful you came. Only you know how to make a situation like this seem entertaining."

"And I'll be right here when you talk to him. If you want. When we get back to your house, I think you need to set up a time to get that conversation over with."

"I know. It'll help having you ready to debrief after," Willow said, looking out past Ivy toward the water. "Eight years . . ." She shook her head. "Eight whole years he had to tell me this."

"And Grayson should have told you right away. Both of them are in the wrong."

"I know. I guess I'm still shocked that they are related."

"Yeah, that's something isn't it?" Ivy picked up her water.

"But now that I really think about it, when I was about thirteen, I remember seeing Grayson's mom walk out of the general store in town once, but Tyler's dad was just going in. They both looked startled when they saw each other, and I couldn't hear what they were saying, but I remember Nicole was nearly red in the face while smiling at him. I clearly recall thinking in that moment that they looked like they were flirting. Nicole is a beautiful woman though, so I figured why wouldn't Tyler's dad flirt? I just ignored it after that."

"I bet there were other times, you just didn't notice."

"Probably. But Nicole hardly went anywhere when we were growing up. She was sort of a recluse, so I think that's why I remember the general store. It was one of the few times I actually ran into her in town."

"Well, it's their business what they did back then and still is today, whatever they are doing together. We're all adults now, and while, again, I'm not saying it was okay to keep all this from you this whole time, what *I am* saying is that the news is out and it's not something any of you need to fight over. What's done is done. You also need to remember that this impacts *them* . . . not you. Think about it. How do you think *they* feel with knowing they are related?" Ivy shrugged. "That's just my opinion."

Ivy had the ability to be direct in a way that made it hard to be offended. Fact was, she was right. Willow should temper her anger and instead focus on moving past what had happened, rather than wishing there had been a different outcome.

"I hear what you're saying, and I know you're not wrong, but . . ." Willow looked down at her half-eaten sandwich.

"But?" Ivy pressed her.

Willow knew what she was about to say would send a ripple of worry through her family because the last time she'd left town it took an accident to bring her back.

"But I think I need to focus on the life I've created in Connecticut. Yes, Tyler and I are selling the condo, but I can find somewhere new to live that I can afford. My practice is already there, and I wouldn't need to start over. I can just resume in-person sessions. I was going to stay here, but now, I don't know . . ."

"What about the farm?"

"My parents hired help, so they'll be fine until my dad fully recovers. I'll call Tyler and make peace, and then I think it's just time to go back to Connecticut."

Ivy didn't respond, and she wasn't sure if that was a good or bad thing. Her friend always had something to say.

"I'm glad you'll at least call Tyler," Ivy said after a minute.

"I will when we get back to my parents' house."

Once they finished lunch, they got back on the trolley to finish the tour, and then Willow took Ivy to see a couple museums. As Ivy walked through everything, reading the descriptions and looking at all the artifacts, Willow followed her in a daze as she battled the uncontrollable déjà vu that had overcome her.

Leaving the island felt like the most logical thing to do now, and the easiest—but was it right?

———

WILLOW KEPT HER EYES CLOSED WHEN SHE HEARD Tyler's car stop in her driveway late the following afternoon. She had been dozing by the pool while waiting on him and Ivy was inside chatting with her mom. After she and Ivy got back from touring the island, Willow had called him and asked him to meet her there after work today. It was time to get this conversation over with.

"Willow? Are you sleeping?" Tyler opened the gate by the pool and came to sit by her.

"I'm awake. I've just been resting." She peeked an eye open and saw him looking up.

"Under overcast skies?"

"It's not raining anymore, and the temperature is comfortable out here. Besides, it matches my mood." Willow straightened up on her lounge chair and lifted the back so she could sit upright.

Tyler folded his hands together on his lap, his expression solemn. "Thank you for allowing me here to talk."

"It needed to happen and well before today."

"I know, I—"

She held up her hand. "I don't want excuses."

"It's just been a lot to handle."

"Before you got here, I've been trying to figure out where to start. So I'll just say it. Grayson is your brother. The only thing that's sat in my mind for nearly three days now is how? *How* could you have kept that from me?"

He immediately leaned forward on his chair as if he'd been waiting for the question. "I've asked myself the same question for years."

"If that's true, then why didn't you just come out with it? Not to mention you two worked together. There's no reason that should have been a secret either, especially because *everyone* knew that, except me."

"It wasn't a secret, I just . . ." He let out a sigh. "I just got caught up in my own frustrations with my parents' divorce at the time and jealousy that I let the secrets build once I found out about the affair, and before I knew it, eight years went by."

"I just can't believe both of you kept this from me, but mostly you because we spent so many years together. We were about to get *married*, Tyler."

"Yes . . . I was wrong not to tell you," he said, glancing down at his hands. "Look, while I can't speak for Grayson, what I'm trying to say is, we both had our own struggles with the reality that, after over a decade of friendship and all the time we spent together growing up . . . suddenly we were brothers. It was a shock."

"I bet it was. It was for me, too, learning about it well after the fact," she said, then looked out toward the pool. What he'd just said made her remember what Ivy had said at lunch at Stella's, that she hadn't paused for one minute to think about how the news had impacted them.

As a therapist, that should have been instant, but as herself, the person who'd been hurt, she'd let her emotions override all critical thinking. In the end, none of this had anything to do with her. Their parents had the affair, not hers.

"I haven't even thought about you two with this. I've just been so hurt that it was kept from me. I was your best friend too. I was there growing up alongside both of you. Whatever happened with either one of you affected me too." Tears welled in her eyes, and she clasped her hands together as she tried to stay calm. "Like watching Jack abuse Grayson. Remember how upset we'd get over that?"

"Yeah . . . And, Willow, there were so many times I sat with this and wanted to blurt it out. But I was so afraid of upsetting you, and honestly . . . I was angry at myself about it. In my mind, I think I just wanted it all to go away."

"That's not something you can make go away, Tyler." She turned to him but paused. He'd been hiding from that truth—just like she hid from the fire. "Believe me, I've tried to do the same."

"You mean prom night?"

"Exactly. The fire was shocking and devastating all at once, not to mention losing Grayson. For eight years, especially once I became a therapist, I didn't want to own up to the fact that I still hadn't processed the trauma of that fire. It was like I somehow pretended it never happened."

"Every time I saw Grayson at the office or in passing while I was in Terra Cove, I did the same."

"Well, neither one of us can pretend anymore and Grayson is your brother, whether you like it or not."

"I know that now . . ." He sat back in his chair and paused. "My mother was here the other day."

"She was? Why?" Willow knew that just like her, it had been years since Morgan had been in Terra Cove.

"Because of this situation. She needed to come tell me the truth about her split with my dad. See, when I found out from Grayson about the affair the night of prom, my parents were in the middle of their divorce. My mom told me then that she was leaving because of Dad's affair. That's why she came—to finally tell me that finding out about the affair wasn't what split them. They were long over by that point. I needed to hear that."

"Wow . . . I wish I'd known." She stared straight ahead again, lost in thought, trying to absorb that new information.

"I wish you did too. I hated keeping this from you. But again, I was so mad and I took it out on Grayson, letting the jealousy I'd always had over your relationship with him affect my decisions. Because he had you, at the time it felt like he was going to take my dad away from me too. Now looking back, I know that I was just being immature."

"We were just teenagers, Tyler, don't beat yourself up over that," she said, looking back at him.

"Yeah, but I'm ashamed of how I acted anyway. I let my own jealous rage control me on prom night . . . and steal you away."

"So you decided it was best to lie and tell me that Grayson didn't show up for prom because he was done with me?"

"That's right. I was young, angry, and reeling from the divorce. I let jealousy get the best of me and started things with you so I could hurt him in order to feel better myself. I was so bitter."

For the first time, the fuzziness she'd always felt while she was with Tyler, the longing for what she'd had with Grayson that never left her, became clear as she pieced together the details.

"So everything you told me on prom night about Grayson . . . was not true?" She knew the answer to that as Grayson had already shared his side from that night, but she needed to now hear Tyler's.

He broke their gaze, hanging his head. "No. It wasn't. Grayson's father—well, Jack—stumbled into the house, drunk, like I told you then—but what I left out was that he told Grayson about his mother's affair in the nasty way Jack talked to him. Along with some other very hurtful comments. Grayson was so upset that he couldn't handle going to prom, and he simply asked me to escort you instead. That was all.

He needed time to think through what he'd just found out. To be honest, I did too. But I wouldn't admit it. And I betrayed my best friend. I came in like a bulldog with you and started our relationship based on a lie . . . and it's been a lie ever since."

"Tyler, don't say that. We care about each other. We just . . ."

"Were never in love," he finished for her, and she could see the beginnings of a smile. "Willow, you love him, and I love that *for* you. I want you to be happy. And despite how we ended, this entire thing helped me see clearly what happened back then, so I can finally start to heal."

The tears she'd been holding back finally slid down her face. "Do you mean that? Because, Tyler, I don't want you out of my life. At all. We have way too much history to just throw it all away."

"I mean every word. Your friendship is one of the most important things in my life. But, Willow, our worlds have changed over the last eight years as the three of us have matured and grown. But what hasn't changed is what you and Grayson have. True love found as early as yours has left an indelible stamp on your hearts that cannot be replicated."

She choked back a sob hearing him say that. They both stood up and quietly hugged for a long while.

"Thank you, Tyler," she finally said and pulled back. "I'm so glad we talked."

"Me too. I feel so much better getting all that out."

Willow walked him to his car and saw her mother and Ivy peeking out the window, probably bursting at the seams with curiosity over how this conversation went. She waved as he pulled down the driveway, then stood there long after he left with his words lingering. *"An indelible stamp on your hearts that cannot be replicated."* That may be true, but was it worth risking her heart again? Three days ago, she'd been sure that

Grayson was what she had wanted, but now . . . she couldn't shake the fear.

Her mom came up behind her and put her arm around her.

"I think . . ." Willow turned to face her. "I think it's time I go back to Connecticut."

Nothing was spoken for a few minutes as they both looked down the driveway again, now empty.

"Running won't resolve anything," her mom finally said.

"Staying may not either."

Chapter Twenty

The last of the soap shack was finally cleaned out and in its place was a dusty, empty old hut. Grayson stood inside it late Tuesday afternoon, just before the sun fully set. Holding the light from his phone up, he moved it around the space to see better now that the light outside had faded. While the structure held great potential to be remodeled into anything, he suddenly had no idea why he'd even bothered.

As he stepped back outside, Monty came up to him and sniffed his jeans. "Yeah, I must smell bad. That was quite a project. Come on, boy. Let's head back so I can shower. The sun is nearly down." Grayson started walking back. "At least it looks better now that all the shrubs and weeds are gone." Monty jogged next to him, nose to ground.

Grayson had spent the last few hours after work finishing up the project, trying his best to keep himself distracted. He was excited for what he'd planned with Wesley the following day for Willow. They'd be taking her up for a surprise private helicopter tour of the island. He hoped it would soften the blow of seeing him again and he could talk to her. If she agreed to go, he'd also get to be a part of the special experience of her first flight with her brother.

He and Wesley had worked out the details of how it would go down, particularly with getting Willow to the hangar, which her brother said he'd take care of. Only the love Grayson had for her could take care of the rest.

After his shower, he heard a car coming down his driveway and when he glanced out the window, he saw Daniel getting out.

"Hi, Daniel," Grayson said when he opened the front door and stepped aside to let him in.

"Sorry to intrude without calling. But what I have to say will only take just a couple of minutes," Daniel said as he came inside, then bent to pet Monty who came to greet him. "I love this dog."

"He's my buddy for sure. A wonderful pet."

Grayson commanded Monty to go sit on his bed so they could talk.

"And so well trained."

"Well, with him being such a big dog, you have to keep them in order. Besides, he's all I have, so he better behave." Monty's head cocked to one side as he listened to his owner, and Daniel laughed when the dog barked in response.

"I think Monty disagrees with you," Daniel said, taking a seat on the couch in the living room next to Grayson. "Because he's not all you have."

"It sometimes feels that way."

"He's not." Daniel shifted toward him. "You have me. I came by to check on you, son, and to see you alone without anybody else to distract us."

"You don't have to worry about me." Grayson stared down at his feet. "I assume you heard about how the conversation with Willow went. I'm so mad at myself."

"Look at me." Daniel paused, waiting for Grayson to

comply. "Anger has been the driving force for years for all of us. I was angry at myself for all the mistakes I made in my marriage to Morgan, Tyler was mad with me and his mom, and you've had to deal with the aftermath of Jack's abuse all while being mad at yourself, too, over Willow. The secrets and lies and ignoring the truth prevented us from moving forward in life."

"Well, Willow is pretty upset because of the truth." Grayson thought about the following morning and all he could hope was she wouldn't be too mad to let him carry through with his plan. "I deserve it though. I was really a jerk."

"Grayson, listen to me. I know time has helped the wounds of your childhood with Jack's abuse, and you've come a long way, but once you accept what he did to you while you were growing up, your heart will start to open up in ways you didn't see coming."

"What are you getting at?"

"I'm asking you, have you accepted what Jack did, how he treated you, what your mother and I did? Have you accepted who you are outside of all that's happened? The man you want Willow to meet?"

"Yes . . . but does this matter when it comes to her?"

"Of course it matters. I did the same thing with Nicole and kept her at a distance over my self-pity."

"You two seem to have it figured out."

Daniel laughed. "No, we haven't. Not at all. But we aren't giving up. And I don't want you to give up either." He stood up and patted him on the shoulder. "Don't let her slip away again."

After he left, Grayson sat thinking about what Daniel had said for a long time. He'd heard every word, and the conversation gave him more motivation for his next move.

———

Grayson heard his phone, but since he'd been woken up out of a dead sleep, he'd questioned if it was real. When it rang again, he finally sat up. It was still dark. *What time is it?* His phone stopped and when he looked at the time on his screen, it was before 6:00 a.m.—and he had five missed calls from Wesley.

Grayson called him back and Wesley's loud voice woke him right up. "Grayson, finally."

"Hey, aren't I meeting you and Willow at the hangar later this morning? Were you not able to convince her?"

"Willow left last night with her friend Ivy who came to visit," Wesley said. "They went back to Connecticut."

A twist of unease shot through his stomach. "Left?"

"She went back to Connecticut."

Grayson pulled his eyebrows together. "What?"

"Yeah. She's gone."

Grayson swung his legs over the bed. "Give me her friend's number."

"Okay . . . There. Sent."

"Thanks." Grayson pulled his phone back and saw Wesley's text with the number. "And can you by any chance land close to Mystic, Connecticut?"

"I think so. Give me at least two hours to try and coordinate that. But what are you planning?"

"To go get my girl. Just like we planned."

———

The low rumble of a helicopter idling under the hangar echoed as Grayson walked up to Wesley's office door a couple hours later. Inside, Wesley was leaning over the receptionist's desk signing something and looked up when Grayson entered.

"Well, here we are. I don't know what you have planned,

but the weather is good to get up there and make the trip, so there's positive news." Wesley came around the desk.

"Are we set to go and land in Connecticut?"

"Yep. I have a connection at the private heliport right in Mystic. The management cleared us to land around 9:30 a.m. You get a hold of Ivy?"

"Yes, she said to let her know what time we would be there, gave me her address, and said she would handle everything else."

"Alright, are you ready to do this?" Wesley asked.

"More than ever."

"My sister's first flight with me and it's going to be an exciting one!"

Grayson grinned at her brother's elation as they walked to the landing pad where the helicopter was parked.

They passed the other helicopter Grayson heard while walking into the office, and Wesley jogged over to the pilot who opened the door.

"Audio good now?" Wesley hollered. The pilot gave him a thumbs up, and Wesley re-joined Grayson. "That's my new pilot. He's been great."

"I'm so proud of you, Wes." Grayson pointed around him. "You've built a reputable company offering helicopter tours. I hear people around the island talk about them all the time."

"Thank you. That means a lot. I'm excited to take you up!"

"My first time and it won't be my last." Grayson sent a text to Ivy to let her know they were about to take off and their approximate ETA.

"Normally, I'd take you up in the Robinson if we were just island hopping today, but since we're going to zip over to Connecticut, we'll take something a bit faster. Then we'll tour the islands when we get back. This helicopter we're taking is called the Bell 407, and we use it for private charted flights."

Wesley opened the door to the passenger side. "You'll be next to me on the ride over."

Grayson got in and looked at all the controls. He knew what none of them meant, but it didn't matter. Wesley handed him a headset and the engine roared to life, the blades above spinning faster by the second. When they began to lift off, Grayson braced himself against the disorienting vibrations as they climbed higher.

"Let's go get Willow," Wesley said through the headset, sending a rush of exhilaration through Grayson as they began the journey.

CHAPTER TWENTY-ONE

"Willow?" Ivy's voice was above her.

Am I dreaming? Willow peeked one of her swollen eyes open and quickly realized she wasn't dreaming. Ivy was standing over her bed. "What's wrong?"

"Nothing. I just want you to get up."

When Willow opened both eyes, she wiped at the mascara she hadn't bothered to wash off the night before. After getting back to Ivy's apartment yesterday evening, followed by staying up talking well into the night, Willow had not planned on waking up until at least lunch time since it was Wednesday, and she had no sessions with clients.

Now that she was back in Connecticut, she could switch to her regular full-time schedule. Guilt rippled through her stomach just as soon as she thought to do that. Even though her parents had help, she still had been doing a lot for them and suddenly second guessed being here. Maybe she let her emotions get the best of her with such a hasty decision.

"What time is it?"

Ivy waved at her, "Come on. Rise and shine."

"Have you lost it? We didn't go to bed until at least three

in the morning." Willow picked up her phone and saw it was only 7:36 a.m. "Ivy, it's seven thirty in the morning. Go back to bed. Even your store doesn't open for hours." She lay back on her pillow, but Ivy ripped her covers off.

"I have something planned, and trust me, it'll perk you right up. But I need you to get up and take a shower. You look like you got in a street fight with all that eye makeup smudged everywhere. And make the shower fast! We have somewhere to be."

"If you weren't my best friend and I wasn't so tired, I would yell . . . loudly." Willow sighed and got up, went to the bathroom, and turned on the shower, then stood in it for at least twenty minutes, until she heard Ivy knock on the door.

"Hurry up! And wear something comfortable and cute."

A half hour later, dressed in jean shorts and a blue halter top, Willow found Ivy in the kitchen putting her empty coffee mug in the sink.

"Okay, let's go," Ivy said.

"Wait, I want coffee too."

"And you'll get some at Rise Up Diner." Ivy picked up her keys and purse.

"You flung me out of bed after hardly four hours of sleep to go to the *diner*?"

"They have the best make-your-own omelets. And they are always quick to serve there. Sounded like a good start to the day. Stop complaining, we don't have a lot of time."

"For what?" Willow said as Ivy pulled her arm.

A short drive later, they were seated in a booth, scanning menus.

"See? Isn't this nice? We got a corner booth too." Ivy smiled as the waitress came over and filled their waters and offered coffee.

"That's because it's a Wednesday," Willow said after the waitress left. "No one is here. Everyone is working or maybe some people are still in bed. Which is where I am going as soon as I eat a sausage-and-tomato omelet."

"No, you're not." Ivy smiled over her water glass.

"You're killing me," Willow groaned. "I know I was a mess last night, but I cried it out. I'll be fine today. I just need sleep. So you don't need to drag me around half of Connecticut to cheer me up."

"I'm not going to."

The waitress came back over and took their orders, then Ivy quickly changed subjects, talking about the boutique. Willow was amazed at the amount of energy her friend had with how little sleep they'd gotten. When their food came, Ivy was just smiling at her as they ate.

"You're really creeping me out now." Willow picked up her coffee. "You're never this perky. You have something to tell me, don't you?"

"Not exactly." Ivy pointed to her plate. "Are you nice and full?"

Willow pushed her plate away. "Yes. I forgot how good their omelets are here."

"Good." Ivy pulled out her phone and looked at the screen. "Because it's nearly ten now and I need to take you to your next destination, but I wanted to make sure you weren't starving. I don't know how long this trip will take."

"Ivy, cut it out. Tell me where you're taking me."

"Back to my apartment."

Willow nearly tripped as she followed Ivy out of the diner after they paid. "Good, that's where I wanted to go anyway. I'm exhausted. Thanks for breakfast though, that was nice." She could tell by the look on Ivy's face that going back to her place did not mean her plan was complete. "I'm not going to be able to go back to bed, am I?"

Ivy shook her head as they got in the car, then giggled as

Willow glared at her. "No, you're not. I'm sorry, I'm just so excited."

"For what?"

Ivy held up her hand to wait and drove the few minutes back to her place in silence. When she pulled into the parking lot of her apartment, Willow looked at her for an explanation.

"For you to see him."

"Who am I—" Willow turned and saw him. Grayson was leaning against another car, arms folded, his gaze glued on her. "What is he doing here?"

"He's not alone," Ivy said, and then Willow saw her brother get out of the car's driver's side.

"Wesley?"

"Now you know why I made you shower." Ivy nudged her and opened her door, but Willow was frozen as she watched Grayson walk toward her.

He opened her door and offered his hand to help her out.

"Grayson? What are you doing here? With Wesley too?"

"Oh, him? He's just my pilot." Grayson smiled back at Wesley, who waved.

"I don't understand. Why are you two here?" Willow asked as he shut the door behind her and pulled her close.

"To come get you," Grayson said, grazing her cheek with his fingers, his gaze lingering on her lips. He bridged the gap between them and cradled her face with both hands, his lips brushing against hers with a soft, hesitant caress. Willow pulled back and their eyes locked as her heart raced through a lifetime of memories before their lips met again—urgently. She lost herself in the sheer force of rekindled passion before they breathlessly broke apart.

"You came for me this time," she said, still holding his arms and trying to reorient herself against the passion of that kiss that left her dizzy, dissolving any previous worry she'd had.

Giving her heart to the one who held it first was a risk always worth taking.

"As I should have eight years ago," he said, putting his arms around her. "I love you, Willow. Let's go home."

———

Ivy helped her repack the little she'd taken out of her suitcase since they only arrived the night before. Willow stood in the guest room of her friend's apartment and hugged her tight.

"I know you'll come back to pack up your condo and get your car, but you're leaving for good this time," Ivy said, then stepped back and wiped her wet eyes.

"If you ever want to open up your second boutique, I have just the location." Willow smiled. "Martha's Vineyard would love your stuff."

"You know, that doesn't sound like a bad idea." Ivy turned her head in thought. "I really loved it there, and I don't know what I'll do without you here." They walked out of the bedroom and met the guys in the living room.

"Then you'll just have to come hang out with me on the beach. I know just the man to come get you," Willow said and looked at her brother. "This may not be your last private charter."

"Oh really?" Wesley said and glanced toward Ivy. "Just let me know when, and I'll be at your service."

"Uh-oh," Grayson whispered before picking up Willow's suitcase and leaning closer to her ear. "I see what you're trying to do there."

"Can you blame me?" she whispered back. "Look at them staring at each other. Maybe they always have, and I never noticed before."

"Okay, you two lovebirds, let's get going. I was lucky to

borrow a pilot friend's car, but we can't take it all day," Wesley said.

They all followed Wesley out, and as they drove away, Willow rolled the window down and waved at Ivy.

"Don't worry," Wesley said, glancing at her in the rearview mirror. "I'll come back and get her anytime you want."

When they arrived at the heliport, Wesley handed them each a headset, and this time Grayson sat in the back next to Willow.

As the engine came back to life, Willow's eyes widened and Grayson laughed. "Nervous?" he asked, putting his arm around her.

"A little. Maybe I should just drive my car back and I'll meet you in Terra Cove."

"No way," Wesley said through the speakers. "You've never flown with me before and that ends right now."

Willow glanced at Grayson. "I know Wesley is experienced, but this is my first time in a helicopter in general."

"It was mine too, but Wesley is right. You can't have a brother as a pilot and not get in the air with him," Grayson said as the blades spun wildly before they lifted off.

As Willow watched the ground get farther away the higher they climbed, she thought about what Grayson said and knew he was right. She had missed so much with her family and would have missed so much more if he hadn't come for her.

She was going home at last . . . with Grayson by her side.

———

"WE'RE PASSING OVER BUZZARD'S BAY," WESLEY informed them. "I'll cross over the Cape and start at Province-town, then head down toward the islands from there."

Willow got her phone out, suddenly feeling like Ivy on the trolley tour. "Look, Grayson! Cape Cod is like a canvas of different colors down there!" She snapped a few shots, soaking in the view. "It's simply breathtaking!" She excitedly turned to him, but he wasn't looking out the window.

"I know," he said, then took her chin and leaned in for a kiss. "And now I get to stare at this view all the time."

Willow's love for him reached new heights, and while they soared over the coastline, she was excited to finally start their future—getting to know each other in a whole new way. They enjoyed Wesley's tour for the next hour as he pointed out as many landmarks as he could.

"Okay, you two, look down," Wesley said a short while later.

Willow shifted in her seat and looked out the window. "I see the rock," she said as her brother slowed the helicopter a bit, turning so they could see their beach with a better view.

Grayson shared her window and kissed her cheek. "Where it all began."

They both took in the site where their journey started with a kiss that finally sealed their hearts together. The gentle waves drifting in and out of the cove whispered secrets of their past and reminded her that their love had always been her rock guiding her toward a destiny she could no longer deny.

Epilogue
Two Years Later

As the sun slowly crept over the horizon, Willow sat tall in the saddle on top of Nova with her golden curls that now fell down her back again blowing gently in the morning breeze. A cascade of soft pink and orange painted the sky above her, ushering in a gorgeous day. Drawing in the crisp air of the early season, she squinted slightly as she gazed out at the pastures. The sweet scent of saltwater and blooming flowers greeted her senses, signaling the start of summer on the island. It was a perfect early June day—and the most important day of her life.

Leaning down, she stroked Nova. "Ready, girl?" She leaned into the saddle and tapped her heels as Nova started to walk then quickly trot around the pen. After a few warm-up rounds, they gained speed as she guided the mare over the first jump.

"Willow!" Whitney called from the fence. "We have a long day of pampering you and getting you ready. Would you get off that horse!"

Willow led Nova to the fence. "Hey, Whit! I didn't hear you pull in."

"That's 'cause you're lost going around that pen. Ivy should be here soon with bagels and coffee."

"Okay, but can I do a few more rounds?"

"Just one. We have a lot to do!" Whitney instructed.

Willow rolled her eyes and took off with Nova again just as Grayson came outside with a coffee mug in hand. "I heard bagels are on their way. You didn't have to go to all that trouble for me," he teased his soon-to-be sister-in-law.

"You can have one and then off with you!"

"Getting kicked out of my own house." Grayson chuckled.

"You mean our house," Willow said once she trotted over to the fence.

"Our house. Music to my ears." Willow had moved in with him about a year prior, but it still felt new. Grayson leaned over the fence. "I can't believe today is the day," he said to her.

Another car pulled into the driveway, and Ivy got out, followed by Abby from the passenger's side holding a tray of coffees. Ivy opened the back and got out bags of food, then held them up toward them. "We're ready!"

Grayson shook his head. "I'll never know what you women need hours for when getting ready."

"You don't need to," Abby said once she got to the fence. "Your job is just to be waiting for your bride when she walks down that aisle. Now get lost. You can't see her." Abby handed Whitney the tray of coffees, then opened her purse, pulled out keys, and handed them to Grayson. "The groom's suite awaits you at my place."

"Mind if I have a look at the bagel selection in there?" Grayson bent over to open the bag just as Abby swatted his hand away.

"Hands off, groom! Those are for the bridal party. Wesley said he was meeting you for breakfast. Correct?"

"Yup. With Liam, Daniel, and Tyler." Grayson straightened and glanced at Willow one more time. She rounded the corner and came right over.

"Isn't it bad luck to see me before the wedding?" Willow asked and dismounted Nova, then walked her to the gate.

"I don't think it counts until you're in the dress." Grayson met her at the gate and wrapped his arms around her waist. "I can't wait to make you my wife today." He leaned down and kissed her neck as Nova huffed.

"See, even Nova wants you out of here," Ivy said. "And would you two knock it off? There's plenty of time for that later."

"How's the new apartment treating you and Wes?" Grayson asked Ivy.

"Well, since I spent the entire last two weeks opening the new store, I haven't had much time in it. And it's now summer, which means Wesley is in the air all day, every day giving tours. We haven't unpacked many boxes." Ivy looked at Willow. "And this one with the wedding prep took over the rest of my time."

Willow smiled at her friend. "I'm just thrilled you and Wesley moved in together and that you're finally here in Terra Cove! Your boutique will be a hit, I know it. And you got it open just in time for tourist season."

"I'm so glad I was able to do that. It's already slammed with customers."

Willow leaned closer to her friend, giving her a slight nudge. "Everything has worked out because the right man 'swooped down out of nowhere and captured you.'"

A grin broke across Ivy's face. "I told you that would happen and it did, quite literally. Our first date, with Wesley flying into Connecticut to pick me up in his helicopter, will be a story for our grandkids one day, for sure."

"Grandkid talk already?" Grayson teased, making Ivy blush.

"Would you put that horse in her stall already, and let's go eat and have coffee before the salon ladies arrive to do our hair and makeup?" Whitney said, motioning for everyone to go inside.

"I'm going to grab my tuxedo and I'll be out of your way," Grayson said and followed the women inside.

Willow guided Nova out the gate and into the barn. When she got the saddle off and put Nova in her stall, the mare stuck her head out.

"Today's the day, Nova." The horse huffed in response. "I know you've been waiting a long time for this." She leaned closer. "Thank you. I couldn't have done any of this without you," she whispered to her special friend. Max leaned his head out of his stall. "You, too, buddy."

When Willow turned around, she checked on the other three horses before she closed the barn doors. Grayson had done a lot of work to his five-stall barn to get it ready to house more therapy horses. Six months ago, she opened Terra Cove Equine Therapy Center, and she still couldn't believe all the progress. Shortly after her grand opening, newspapers from all over the Cape and the islands called her for an interview, and her client list grew fast. People ages four years old to adult came for sessions, and she'd just hired another new therapist to join her. The old soap shack that Grayson had remodeled into three private therapy rooms made for a perfect office. Their lives had blended together in almost perfect harmony, but it was still a long two years of healing and moving forward with Tyler.

Grayson was putting his tuxedo in his truck and shutting the door when she walked over to him.

"Well, I'm off. The bridal suite, a.k.a. Turner Oasis, is all yours, *Mrs. Turner.*"

"*Soon-to-be* Mrs. Turner. I haven't said 'I do' yet," she joked as he scooped her up, making her giggle as he twirled her.

"Then I better hang on to you tight so you don't run off on me. . . again!" He kissed her cheek before putting her back down.

"Hmm . . . never know. I may come to my senses before I walk down that aisle."

"Oh! I see how you want to play!" Grayson cradled her again and tickled her, and she erupted into laughter.

"I'm just excited a dress won't go wasted today—finally," Willow said, catching her breath.

"Nope. It most certainly won't."

Willow eyed him for a moment, unsure at first if she should bring it up, but he mentioned Tyler's name on the list for breakfast. "I'm really glad Tyler is joining you guys this morning."

"Me too." Grayson nodded. "It hasn't been the easiest couple of years, but he and I have made some great strides together. He's not standing as a groomsman, but at least he's coming to the wedding."

"That's more than we could have expected. He's your brother after all, so I'm glad things keep improving between you two. I know this hasn't been easy for him or for us, but your dad is really happy about it and that he decided to come to the wedding."

"Yes, he is, and so am I. But you better get in there before your sister comes back out," he said, taking a few steps back. "And yells at me!" He turned and jogged around his truck to the driver's side.

Willow grinned and waved before she walked into the house. The women were excitedly chatting away about the day ahead, and Willow closed her eyes to take it all in. She'd been dreaming of this day and marrying Grayson Turner since she was fifteen years old.

———

THE WEDDING WAS SEAMLESS, AND THE JOY WAS felt by all. Friends and family gathered around Willow and Grayson as they said their vows on her parents' property. The Andersons rented a large outdoor tent for the event, transforming the backyard wedding into a gorgeous reception. There had been no other place where Willow wanted to marry him, and to her surprise, another guest was transported for the big day.

Nova was striding around the pen behind the beautiful wedding arbor that Ivy decorated with flowers and white draping. Having Nova there meant everything to Willow, and when she saw her mare being guided out by one of her parents' helping hands just as her dad started to walk her down the aisle, it took everything in her not to cry.

"Don't ruin that makeup," her dad whispered as he gently led her down the aisle.

"I can't promise I won't, but this time, it's happy tears."

At the end of the reception, Grayson led her in one last dance under the glow of the lights the tent had all around them.

He twirled her for the guests before pulling her back in. "Ready to start our lives now, Mrs. Turner?"

"I'm ten years ready, Mr. Turner."

Their guests stood and encircled them as they swayed to the music. Their lips met in a tender kiss, and the room rippled in low cheers, marking the culmination of their shared history and the beginning of their future together—a union that was always meant to be.

Acknowledgments

To all my readers, as always, a heartfelt thank you to each and every one of you. Your enthusiasm and support mean everything to me. From all of your reviews and messages, you keep me going . . . writing well into the late-night hours. I am honored to be a part of your reading journey and have such a wonderful community behind me.

I am forever grateful to Jenny Hale and the team at Harpeth Road Press for their unwavering dedication and for continuing to pave the way for my career. Their expertise and tireless efforts have once again brought my work to life and out into the world for all my readers to enjoy.

To my editors—

Karli Jackson for taking another concept of mine and building the foundation this story needed to grow. To Elizabeth Mazer for bringing the characters together in this love-triangle storyline. To Jodi Hughes and Lauren Finger for their meticulous attention to details and finding the plot holes.

Once again, to Kristen Ingebretson for pulling it all together on another visual masterpiece!

A special thanks to the people "behind the scenes" from Martha's Vineyard: historians, restaurant owners, and residents of the island for answering all my questions and making sure I made this story stand out with its gorgeous setting and history.

A Letter from Lindsay

Hello!

Thank you so much for picking up my novel, *Where It All Began*. I hope this heartwarming story and the breathtaking beauty of Martha's Vineyard will leave you feeling more capable and courageous with whatever life may bring.

If you'd like to know when my next book is out, you can sign up for new Harpeth Road release alerts for my novels here:

www.harpethroad.com/lindsay-gibson-newsletter-signup

I won't share your information with anyone else, and I'll only email you a quick message whenever new books come out or go on sale.

If you did enjoy *Where It All Began*, I'd be so thankful if you'd write a review online. Getting feedback from readers helps to persuade others to pick up my book for the first time. It's one of the biggest gifts you could give me.

Until next time,
 Lindsay